White Coat, Black Heart

By: Sierra Maze

Content Warning

This book contains depictions of adult themes, including graphic medical imagery, violence, and death. Reader discretion is advised.

While *White Coat, Black Heart* is a work of fiction, it portrays medical and ethical dilemmas that may be distressing to some readers. The story includes realistic clinical scenarios that reflect the high-stakes environment of hospital medicine.

Copyright Page
White Coat, Black Heart

This is a work of fiction. Names, characters, places, and incidents are the product of the author's imagination or are used fictitiously. Any resemblance to actual persons, living or dead, events, or locales is entirely coincidental.

Published by Brainchild Publishing
www.brainchildpublishing.com

ISBN-13: 979-8-9996209-1-0
Cover design by Sierra Maze
Interior design and formatting by Sierra Maze
Printed in the United States of America

To every overworked, underappreciated clinician who still fights for what's right. You are seen.

Prologue

The Killer

* * *

She called it a "nothing case." Rolled her eyes. Dropped the chart like it was beneath her. *"Another train wreck. Just ride it out."*

That's what she said. Ride it out. As if medicine were a storm to weather, not a series of decisions that shape life or death.

They always think it's the chaos that kills. The crashing vitals—monitors shrieking, numbers flickering red. The alarms, shrill and relentless, echoing off the walls. The blood, warm and metallic, pooling faster than anyone could move.

But it's not. It's the quiet. The moment just before. The stillness when no one is watching closely enough.

One of the residents joked about "playing God" after placing a central line. The others laughed like they'd rewritten the textbooks.

I smiled with them. Of course I did.

He didn't notice the tremor in his hand. Didn't double-check the guide wire's position. Didn't see the way the patient's eyes fluttered, just for a second.

But I did.

She missed the rising lactate. Ignored the subtle drop in pressure. Dismissed the early signs of organ failure like they were background noise. To her, the patient was already gone— A body to practice on.

The arrogance is always louder than the alarms. They think no one notices. They think mistakes vanish in the chaos. They don't.

They think they're in control. That the badge, the coat, the title makes them untouchable. But it doesn't take much. Just a nudge—if you know where to push.

And I do.

A moment. A twitch. A silence too long. And then—spiraling pressure, blank eyes, alarms too late.

This wasn't an accident. Not hers. Not mine.

I gave her a choice. I always do. Do it right. Pay attention. Prove you deserve that coat.

She failed. Just like the ones who failed us.

And tonight, I made sure her name goes on the death certificate. Not just the chart.

Chapter 1

Vital

Dr. Elise Navarro – ICU Medical Director

* * *

"CODE BLUE, MEDICAL ICU, ROOM SIX-FOURTEEN. CODE BLUE, MEDICAL ICU, ROOM SIX-FOURTEEN. CODE BLUE, MEDICAL ICU, ROOM SIX-FOURTEEN."

The call crackled overhead in an even, unfaltering cadence just as Elise Navarro pushed through the hospital's glass entrance. She paused for half a second after the first blue, waiting for the room number—then pivoted sharply when she heard Six Fourteen and broke into a jog toward the stairwell.

The ICUs were stacked on top of one another, the medical ICU on the sixth floor. She didn't trust the elevators during a code—not anymore. She took the stairs two at a time, her coat still on, bag slamming against her hip with each step.

By the time she reached the unit, the hallway outside Room 614 was already thick with motion. It was shift change, and the nurses had just started morning report, so there were twice as many people as usual, adding to the chaos.

As she crossed the threshold to the room, Elise caught a trace of mint under the chemical tang of alcohol and blood, cool and clean like a snap of winter air. She didn't know where it came from, but she always seemed to notice it when she ran to codes.

A nurse rushed past, scanning the counters. "Where's the pulse doppler?"

"Coming!" someone yelled from down the hall.

The code cart stood just outside the door, drawers flung open, syringes strewn across the top like a broken toolkit.

The pharmacist drew up a fresh round of epinephrine, a saline flush already prepped in the other hand. A housekeeper had gotten trapped in a corner when she quickly dragged her cart of oversized trash bins out of the way, wide-eyed but silent.

It looked like chaos, but it wasn't. It was choreography.

Inside the room, the scene snapped into focus.

Chest compressions were underway—nurses, interns, and residents rotating every two minutes. An intern, drenched in sweat, leaned over the body with his arms outstretched, his elbows locked and his hands layered on top of each other resting on the man's chest. He pushed hard, the sternum giving an audible pop under his palms.

"Harder!" Elise barked.

He flinched, then pressed deeper—the full two inches required to generate adequate blood flow. Elise heard the ribs crack again. The arterial line pulsation grew from a faint ripple to a clean swell, blood pressure with compressions rising from the 60s into the 90s.

A line of nurses and residents waited for their turn. The patient—early fifties, overweight—lay supine, his abdomen bouncing grotesquely with each compression.

The monitor showed:

Art line: 89/20 mmHg, with compressions

HR: 0- compression artifact only

SpO_2: 62%

Capnography: 8

A resident gripped the oxygen mask tightly over the patient's face, latex fingertips slipping slightly on sweat-dampened skin, chin thrust forward in a desperate jaw-thrust maneuver.

The respiratory therapist bagged rhythmically. Another resident hovered with a laryngoscope and ET tube in hand, waiting for a pause. A third stood at the foot of the bed, calling out meds.

"Three rounds of epi. No change."

"Fluids?" Elise asked, stepping in.

"LR wide open, almost a liter in. Norepi was at 0.04—we upped it to 0.5."

She frowned. This wasn't right. The patient had been improving. Lactate down. Pressors nearly off. Vitals stable all night.

Stable. Not great. But not dying. What changed?

"What was his pressure before the arrest?"

"106 over 62. MAP of 78."

She watched the art line pulse in time with compressions.

"Hold compressions."

The room froze.

On the monitor, the waveform gave one brief rise—then flattened.

A resident at the head of the bed jumped in with the laryngoscope. Seconds later: "I'm in."

"Resume compressions!" called the code leader. A new resident was already on the stool, hands locked and ready.

The ET tube slid in. The cuff inflated. The tube secured. The Ambu bag was disconnected from the mask, attached to the ET tube, and ventilation resumed—rhythmic, mechanical, relentless.

Another dose of epi.

Two more minutes.

Pink, frothy fluid bubbled in the tube—pulmonary edema, wet and gurgling. Blood oozed from old IV sites in slow, glistening ribbons, the sharp metallic scent rising around them.

Elise touched it—thin as water.

DIC.

A familiar weight settled in her chest. Not panic. Something colder.

"Hold compressions."

She scanned the monitor:

> Asystole. Completely flat.
> HR: 0.
>
> SpO_2: 0%.
>
> Art line: 0/0.

No waveform. No pressure.

"Resume compressions."

"I'm still looking for the pulse," said the nurse with the Doppler.

"Art line counts. Resume!" barked a resident.

At least someone had listened during rounds.

Elise ran the checklist in her head. Morning labs had been drawn just before the arrest—no electrolyte derangement. No acidosis. Vitals had been good. He'd asked the nurse about breakfast.

PE? Maybe. But after only one day in bed? That was too fast.

She yanked her handheld ultrasound from her bag and scanned the chest—lungs expanded—no pneumothorax. Moved to the heart—no pericardial fluid.

"Hold compressions."

The ultrasound screen was silent—no visible motion. The heart didn't even twitch.

She looked at the monitor. Still flat.

Nothing.

"Any last ideas?" Navarro asked the room. Only the hiss of oxygen and the distant hum of machines filled the silence. "Any objections to calling this one?" Those were the two questions she always ended a code with. She had already covered her bases, but it was a way of respecting the team and the trauma that these events brought upon them. Giving them back a measure of control helped ease the sting.

"Time of death: 06:11."

Gloves snapped. A monitor gave one last chirp before falling silent. The team stepped back, shoulders sagging, the hush stretching long and heavy. A nurse turned off the monitor. The room dimmed, just slightly.

Another nurse quietly closed the man's eyes.

The housekeeper from earlier moved quickly around the room, eyes averted from the body, gathering debris—discarded gloves, empty syringes—erasing the evidence of the trauma that had unfolded here before the family arrived. Elise turned to the bedside nurse, who stood frozen near the IV pole, hands still gloved, shoulders tight. Her eyes shimmered, barely holding back tears.

"You okay?" Elise asked, her voice low, steady.

Madison nodded, but her voice cracked. "He was talking just a few minutes ago. He said he felt better. He asked about breakfast."

Elise exhaled. "I know. It doesn't make sense. Don't forget—this is a coroner's case. He's been here less than 24 hours, so we need to leave everything as it is. No pulling lines, no removing the tube. Maybe the autopsy will give us some answers."

The nurse nodded again, slower this time.

"If the medical examiner releases the body, let me know right away. I want to be looped in."

She turned to go, then paused.

"Actually…" Elise glanced back at the nurse, her tone softening. "I'll make the call myself. Why don't you take a minute. Call me when the family gets here."

"Okay," the nurse whispered, slowly peeling off her gloves before letting them snap in the garbage can, a dejected look on her face.

Elise stepped into the hallway and leaned against the glass.

Through it, she saw two residents at the workstation. One was on his phone. The other laughed and joked. "No more labs, no CT orders," one said, smirking. "It's always an easier day when they don't survive."

She turned away.

Back at the terminal, Elise pulled up the chart. Lactate had been improving. Fluids were working. Vitals were stable.

Nothing in the chart had warned her. No sign of impending death.

She scrolled through the notes. Orders. Timelines. Medications.

Nothing glaring. But unmistakably... off.

It was too sudden. Too unexpected. Too irreversible.

This wasn't the first death that felt… awry. It was as if the body had simply shut down. Without reason or warning.

She closed the chart. Looked again at the monitor.

After rounds, she'd start pulling charts. Every code from the last year.

Something was wrong.

She just didn't know what—yet. But she was going to find out.

Chapter 2

My Kind of Pain

The Killer

* * *

I stood just inside the door of the Medical ICU family room, watching them fall apart in real time.

They always do.

Shock first—lips parted, eyes scanning for a lie they can cling to. Then the hesitation. Waiting for someone to say it was a mistake. A mix-up.

But the correction never comes. Just the silence that follows a truth no one wants to face.

This family was no different.

The wife crumpled into the vinyl chair, hand to her mouth, eyes wide. Not crying yet. Just... stunned. Like her body hadn't caught up to the information.

The daughter, older than I expected, started pacing. Arms crossed. Mouth moving, but no sound. Her heels tapped a frantic rhythm on the planks of vinyl faux wood - the classy appearance of hardwood with the resilience and cost of linoleum. Sweat gathered at her hairline, despite the cold room. I could see the panic settling in—grasping for cause, for blame, for something to hold.

The son stood frozen. Shoulders stiff. Breathing shallow. The quiet ones always frighten me a little. Grief with nowhere to go curdles fast into something worse.

The resident doctor delivering the news stumbled over the phrasing. Voice cracked—just a little—but enough. Eyes glossy. Chin tense. It was amusing to watch that child pretend to be a grown-up doctor, leading a family through crisis. His white coat was too clean. His shoes still shone. He probably practiced the speech in the mirror—paused for empathy, softened his voice just right. But grief isn't a script. It's a performance. He didn't really care, he was just playing his part.

I almost smiled. Not because of the family. Not really. It was the doctor who fascinated me. The way his hands fidgeted at his sides like he didn't know where to put them. The way he looked at the floor between sentences, probably wishing he could be doing anything else.

They think it makes them human. Makes them good.

It makes them weak.

Emotion clouds precision. If your hands shake delivering bad news, how steady are they in a crisis?

I've never flinched. Not once. That's why I win. That's why they lose.

The doctor kept talking—words like sudden and unforeseen and despite every effort. I stopped listening.

I watched the family.

They whispered names of doctors. Asked questions no one could answer. Said things like "But he seemed fine," and "He was just talking to me last night."

Just enough concern to pass. Enough distance to disappear.

They don't know what to do with suddenness. When death feels instant and irreversible. No decline. No warning.

Just gone.

That's the art of it. Make it look natural. Or at least, inevitable.

I stayed until the sobbing started. Until the daughter finally sat down, and the mother broke into quiet sobs that penetrated the space around her and made the air itself feel heavy.

The mother collapsed inward like something soft had broken. The daughter finally stopped pacing, too dizzy with sorrow to keep moving. And the son—still stone—stared at the floor like he might burn through it.

It was beautiful, in its way. The kind of pain they never forget.
The kind I get to watch, again and again.

I waited one more breath. Let it soak in.
Then I turned and walked away.

Satisfied.

Chapter 3

Front Row Seat

Jamie Lin – Internal Medicine Resident

* * *

Jamie sprinted from the cafeteria across the skywalk to the education auditorium, clutching her lunch.

As she arrived at the massive wood doors, she balanced a takeout container and a Diet Coke in one hand while nudging the auditorium door open with her hip. The metal handle was cool and perfectly smooth—polished by a thousand sanitized hands—and the door groaned slightly on its hinges as it swung wide. The room was half full already—mostly residents and medical students, plus a few attendings—settling in for Grand Rounds beneath the cold, humming buzz of fluorescent lights. The air smelled faintly of coffee, sweat-soaked scrubs, and whatever cafeteria mystery meat had been served that day.

She slipped into a seat near the aisle, the chair's vinyl cushion squeaking as the cotton-poly blend of her scrubs stuck slightly to the backs of her thighs, still damp from running across campus in the afternoon heat. She peeled the lid off her lunch and tried not to spill on her pants. The noodles gave off a whiff of garlic and soy, but it only made her stomach turn.

Her gut twisted—not from hunger, but from the leftover adrenaline coursing through her muscles. She hadn't really wanted to come to Grand Rounds or to eat lunch, but the alternative was catching up on notes, and after the code that morning, she didn't have it in her. Her pager still buzzed from time to time, pulling her back to consults and signatures and routine orders. The ordinary rhythms of the hospital had resumed, indifferent to the man who died that morning. Everyone else had moved on. Jamie wasn't sure she had.

The rest of the morning had passed in a haze of progress notes, IV alarms, the sterile mechanical blast of air conditioning, and the faint hospital-clean scent of alcohol wipes and latex. And beneath it all, the acrid tang of vinegar—the industrial kind used to mop the hallways. She hated that smell. It always made her feel like something had already gone wrong. Her mind kept circling back to that room. That moment.

She had been the last one doing compressions when Navarro finally called it.

The memory came back in staccato beats. Her hands, locked over the sternum. The resistance giving way with a sickening crunch—ribs splintering beneath her palms. The way the chest rebounded like a broken trampoline, gristle and cartilage collapsing with each push. Sweat had dripped from her forehead, stinging her eyes. She'd swallowed hard and kept going, she was acutely aware of how focused and alive she felt—energized.

She loved doing compressions.

The adrenaline that flooded her veins sharpened everything. The room's sterile tang, the click of the defibrillator paddles being charged, the hiss of oxygen, the slurp of suction. The suction made a gurgling rasp as the tubing cleared the airway. The monitor's erratic beeping pulsed like an arrhythmic metronome. Voices overlapped in a staccato shorthand:

"Epi's in!" "Pulse check!" "Charge to 200!" "Resume compressions!"

The commands rose and fell over each other like waves crashing on the same shore, layered over the mechanical sounds of the crash cart drawers opening, plastic crinkling, and the thump of a stool being kicked aside.

And at the center of it all: her.

She had the best view. Leaning over the patient's chest, she could see everyone—the intern fumbling with the crash cart, the nurse drawing up meds with swift, practiced hands, the respiratory therapist squeezing the ambu bag in timed intervals. Every movement. Every expression.

The body beneath her hands had felt wrong. Cold skin. Mottled patches along the limbs. Lips tinted dusky blue. The eyes—half-lidded and empty—still open but seeing nothing. The man had already been gone when they arrived. Everyone knew it.

But that didn't stop her.

This was where the learning happened. Not in conference rooms or simulation labs, but here. In the real moments. A few minutes earlier, and she would have been the most senior one in the room. The one running the code. Life or death. Muscle memory, decision-making, instinct. Her body hurt from the effort, her arms trembled, but she didn't want to stop.

It wasn't about saving him anymore. It was about seeing it all, doing it all, being part of it all. The code room was its own kind of theater—and Jamie loved having the front-row seat.

Dr. Navarro had stood at the foot of the bed, arms crossed, issuing commands in a tone of clipped authority. Calm, collected. Impressively composed. Jamie couldn't be sure. Navarro's face was unreadable, her jaw tight, eyes locked on the monitor like she already knew how this was going to end.

Jamie admired that. The way Navarro never showed her hand, never flinched. It wasn't that she seemed uncaring—more that she had complete control. It was enviable. Jamie made a mental note to learn to project that kind of demeanor. She wanted to be that steady. That unreadable.

The whole thing had lasted less than twenty minutes.

But it lingered in her. What she learned in there would last forever. Next time she would beat death.

"Room Six Fourteen did me a solid," a voice said behind her.

She didn't need to turn to recognize it—Dr. Ravi Patel, a second-year resident with the social awareness of a golden retriever.

Ravi flopped into the seat behind her, tearing open a granola bar. His jet black hair was sticking out in every possible direction. His white coat was disheveled—coffee stains on the front, the collar dark with old sweat and skin cells. It hung severely askew, with the heavy right pocket filled with his phone, stethoscope and a mini textbook far outweighing the empty left pocket. The scent of peanut butter mingled unpleasantly with the lingering garlic from her food.

"I only made it to Grand Rounds because of that Celestial discharge," he added cheerfully. "But off the list is off the list. Doesn't matter to me where they go. Lucky me!" It was the same joke he had made at the nursing station after the code.

Jamie turned halfway toward him, gave a forced smile, then faced front again.

Celestial discharge. Also known as the vertical discharge. It was ICU slang, tasteless even by resident standards. She'd heard it before—more than once or twice—but never with that much enthusiasm. She didn't think he meant it cruelly—not exactly. Gallows humor was part of the job. But there was something in the way he'd said it that felt unsettling. As if it were fated to happen, just to make his life easier.

She'd taken over compressions after Ravi on that patient. Two full inches, steady rhythm, just like they taught in ACLS. She'd locked her elbows and let her upper body do the work, hands stacked over the sternum. And she'd felt it—the distinct, sickening shift of ribs giving way under her palms. Not just once, but again and again. A wet crunch. Like stepping on a branch that wasn't dry enough to snap. Ravi had felt the same thing, but he never flinched. As much as she loved doing compressions, she couldn't ignore that sickening snap.

She looked down at the patient's face: eyes open and bulging, soulless. The bluish-gray tint around his lips, the slack jaw, his head gently bobbing side to side every time she pushed down. His hospital gown bunched on his stomach—the top ripped down to expose his chest for compressions and the bottom carelessly tossed up so someone could keep a finger on the femoral artery pulsing in the groin—his naked body was already mottled.

From that vantage point—leaning over the chest, arms straight—she could see it all—panic, precision, detachment—mapped onto every face around the bed.

Dr. Navarro had arrived like she always did during a code—calm, in control, her voice sharp and surgical. Jamie had watched her scan the vitals, call for the ultrasound, double-check the meds. Nothing she did seemed wrong. Nothing obvious, anyway.

But there was something about her expression in those last minutes. The tightness in her jaw. The way she stared at the monitor, even after the rest of the team had already accepted the inevitable. There was something in her stillness. Like she was calculating something no one else could see.

Not shocked. Not confused. Just… waiting.

It wasn't that she suspected Dr. Navarro of anything. It wasn't even that she thought the patient shouldn't have died. People arrested all the time in the ICU. People coded and didn't come back. That was normal. Expected.

Still, the memory stuck with her. Like a pebble caught in the tread of her shoe—annoying, not painful. But always there.

She glanced back at Ravi, who was now halfway through his granola bar and scrolling on his phone. The smell of peanut butter still lingered between them.

A few rows ahead, an intern scrolled on his phone. Someone behind her was whispering about discharge summaries. The attending near the front kept checking his watch. Grand Rounds was a different kind of theater. Everyone pretending to listen while their minds stayed on the floors.

She turned back as the lights dimmed and the Grand Rounds presenter stepped up to the podium. The static pop of the microphone made her flinch.

She stabbed a forkful of noodles, appetite gone. The food had cooled, turning gummy in the bottom of the takeout tray.

Grand Rounds hadn't even started, and she already had indigestion.

She needed to let it go. But part of her didn't want to. The clarity of the code was gone. No structure. *No purpose.* What was left was this: sticky scrubs, cold noodles, and the blank hum of the overhead lights. She missed the intensity already.

Luckily, it happens all the time.

Chapter 4

In the Name of Mercy

Ravi Patel – Internal Medicine Resident

* * *

Ravi Patel popped the last bite of his granola bar into his mouth as the lights dimmed. He didn't love Grand Rounds, but after the morning he'd had, sitting was a luxury.

The title slide glowed on the projector: End of Life in the ICU: Are We Saving or Suffering?

He let out a quiet breath of appreciation. Finally. A talk worth listening to.

Beside him, Jamie sat motionless, the remains of her lunch pushed to the side. Her face was unreadable, her shoulders just slightly tense. Her fork lay untouched on the tray, tangled in cold noodles. Her jaw was set, but her eyes gave her away—tight at the corners, holding something she wouldn't name.

She hadn't spoken since they sat down. He didn't blame her.

The presenter—Dr. Kline, one of the palliative care attendings—began with a case vignette. A ninety-three-year-old woman with metastatic ovarian cancer. Intubated for pneumonia. On three vasopressors, all maxed. Family still insists full code.

Ravi clenched his jaw, but not in surprise. In recognition.

"Her kidneys failed," Kline said calmly. "She was on continuous dialysis. We escalated antibiotics. She had a midline, then a central line, then a dialysis catheter. She coded twice in a week. Each time we brought her back. Each time she suffered more."

There were no gasps. Just the slow, quiet nods of people who'd seen the same thing a dozen times.

When Kline opened the floor, Ravi raised his hand without hesitation.

"We talk a lot about survival," he said, voice level. "But survival to what? We keep people alive long enough to die slower. Sometimes letting go isn't defeat. It's the most ethical thing we can do."

A few heads turned. Not in judgment. In agreement.

Ravi went on. "If our goal is to minimize suffering, then we have to ask what kind of deaths we're creating. There's a difference between extending life and prolonging dying."

A voice from the far side of the room chimed in. Female. Clipped. Slightly sharp.

"And yet, the family asked us to keep going. They wanted time."

It was Avery Cole, one of the senior respiratory therapists. She was known for being blunt, but never cruel.

"Time for what?" Ravi countered, gently. "For her to rack up more procedures she didn't consent to? For another stranger to break her ribs for a few more minutes of organ perfusion?"

Avery didn't flinch. "Time to say goodbye. Time to prepare. To reconcile. If you haven't watched someone get that chance, you can't understand what it means."

"That family was being selfish" Ravi retorted without hesitation, the tension in his voice growing. This was starting to feel personal. "They couldn't see past their own grief to the suffering of that patient. They put their own needs first."

Jamie spoke up then, her voice soft but clear. "It's not just about how people die. It's about how we show up for them when they do. We train for this. We have tools, protocols, decision trees. And yes—sometimes we can change the outcome. We have skill, not miracles. But that skill means something. Some people want the fight. They want to know that someone stood in the fire with them, didn't walk away. And sometimes... we give up too soon."

A heavy pause settled over the room.

Avery nodded slowly. "I've seen patients come off vents after we thought they'd never survive. And I've seen families who regretted not trying. We don't always know what mercy looks like in the moment. It is easy to say suffering isn't worth it when you aren't the one facing death."

Ravi glanced sideways at Jamie. She didn't meet his eyes. She stared straight ahead, arms folded, as if bracing for impact.

"And I've seen people brought back just to suffer another week," Ravi said. "Tubed, restrained, sedated. No chance at recovery. Just more procedures. More blood draws. More pain. That's not mercy either."

Kline nodded from the front. "This is why we have these conversations. There is no single right answer. But we have to be honest about the choices."

Jamie finally turned to Ravi. "I don't think we disagree."

He smiled faintly. "Maybe not. But I think we draw the line in different places."

"Maybe," she said.

Avery added, "There are worse things than dying. But there are worse things than trying, too."

No one had the wrong answer. Just different truths.

But Ravi wasn't debating anymore.
He was remembering.

"My father had a stroke while we were on holiday in Greece," he said quietly, more to Jamie than the room. "Massive MCA infarct. Hemiplegia. I told him he'd improve. That we'd find rehab, adaptive tools. That he would find purpose again. That there would still be a life worth living."

He looked down at his hands. His fingers curled, not quite fists, not quite relaxed. His throat tightened, he didn't let himself blink. If he made any motion toward grief, he knew he'd never finish the story.

"He believed me. Until the hemorrhagic conversion. Severe deficits. DNR isn't legal in Greece, so they did everything—intubated, trached, PEGed. He was stabilized and flown home to India."

Ravi's voice stayed calm, but there was a tension in it now. He rarely spoke of his father. It took everything to stay composed, but showing emotion in this room felt unforgivable.

"That was eight years ago. He hasn't spoken since. Can't move. Can't feed himself. My dad—who built his life on independence—would rather have died a thousand times than live like this."

Jamie didn't speak. Avery didn't either.

"His wishes were clear," Ravi added. "He begged me not to let him live like that. But the system, the law, and worse, the family—*my* family—they couldn't let go. They wanted time. Closure. They wanted to believe he could come back. But they weren't thinking about him. They were thinking about themselves."

He looked up again, voice steady but colder now.

"We don't serve families. We serve patients. Sometimes, doing what's best means doing what no one else is willing to. And sometimes, doing what's best for them means protecting them from the people who love them too much to do the right thing."

Ravi looked back toward the front.

"None of them were wrong," he repeated. "But that doesn't mean we haven't been part of something cruel."

The silence that followed wasn't disapproval—it was discomfort. The kind that lingers.

He liked that.

Sometimes the truth needed to sting. And if it made people shift in their seats, question their certainties, feel even an ounce of what his father endured—then it was worth saying out loud.

Jamie was still beside him, but she felt miles away. Her arms remained crossed, but her fingers tapped lightly against her bicep, as if counting something no one else could hear. She said nothing. She didn't look at him. But she hadn't pulled away either.

Dr. Kline stepped forward again, calm and steady. "This is what our patients live and die by—our assumptions, our timing, our interpretation of what mercy means. You won't always agree. You have to learn to put your own opinions aside and support a family that you don't agree with."

The screen faded to black.

The projector gave a low whine before it clicked off, leaving behind a soft electronic heat and the echo of silence.

"These conversations are hard because they matter. They're hard for us—and even harder for the families trying to make decisions through fear, guilt, and grief. Be mindful of that. Be honest. And above all, be kind.

The palliative care team will be hosting goals-of-care discussion workshops over the next few weeks. I encourage you all to attend."

Chapter 5

Natural Causes

Dr. Elise Navarro

* * *

"I have a new death to report," Elise said, phone tucked between her shoulder and ear as she pulled up the chart, ignoring the cramp in her shoulder from the awkward angle. The office around her was quiet, its fluorescent lights buzzing faintly. Her office in the critical care wing overlooked the parking structure behind Pavilion H. A ceramic dish of dried lavender and eucalyptus potpourri sat on the windowsill, gently masking the hospital's usual cocktail of sanitizer and stress with something calmer, more deliberate. Beneath it all, the faint bitterness of burnt coffee still lingered.

The voice on the other end belonged to a man who sounded like he'd just woken up—or hadn't slept in days. Gravel dragged behind each word like a cough waiting to happen. "Case number?"

"Leonard Wu. Admitted yesterday with sepsis from obstructing cholelithiasis. Perc chole tube placed, improved overnight. Arrested this morning. No response to ACLS."

A pause. Typing. Fingers clacking faintly through the receiver. "Time of death?"

"06:11."

"Less than 24 hours… Alright. What are you putting on the death certificate?"

Elise blinked, her hand tightening slightly around her pen. "Excuse me?"

"What are you listing as the cause of death?" the medical examiner repeated, flat and impatient. "Septic shock? Acute respiratory failure? Pick something. If it's natural, I don't need to open the body."

"You're releasing him?"

"Unless you're telling me this is suspicious. Are you?"

She hesitated. "The code was on point. The team performed well. But it was baffling. No trigger. No warning. He was awake minutes before, asking about breakfast. It doesn't make sense."

"That's not uncommon with sepsis. They can turn fast."

"No, I know that. But… it was too…abrupt. Lactate was improving. Vitals were stable. Then he was gone. It was like the body just—shut off."

A longer pause. "Doctor, are you trying to say you think this is a homicide?"

The word hit like a dropped scalpel—sharp, alien, absurd. But now it was in the room. In her head.

"What? No," Elise said quickly. "I'm not saying that. I'm saying there might be another explanation. A systems failure. Contaminated medication, maybe. During fellowship, we had dryer contamination from the laundry service—acinetobacter. Three patients died. Then the saline bags from that compounding center—caused toxic reactions. Or that batch of albuterol nebulizers filled with legionella. Two asthmatics and a COPD case. You must remember."

The examiner sighed. "None of that makes this a post case. Not unless you're saying someone did it intentionally. Otherwise, it's a hospital issue. Not mine."

"I'm not asserting anything," Elise said, jaw tight. "I'm saying I don't have a cause of death."

"Then put 'unknown.' 'Natural causes.' Whatever. If it's not a homicide, I'm not taking it. Body's released."

The line went dead.

She lowered the phone slowly, the receiver still humming in her hand.

That was it. No curiosity. No collaboration. Just a bureaucrat in a swivel chair deciding what counted as worth asking about. A man who would never see the bruises on Leonard's chest from CPR. Never hear the way his daughter had wept last night when she called Elise "the one who saved him."
Or how she sobbed this morning when Elise had to call her back and take that hope away.

She wasn't even sure what she'd expected. But it wasn't indifference.

Homicide.

She hadn't thought it. Not really. But now it echoed. She had just met Leonard Wu when she admitted him the day before. It was always worse when they were kind. When you could picture them recovering, laughing, going home. She'd told his daughter he was improving. Now she'd have to call back. He seemed like a kind man. Alert, polite, grateful. She had expected him to be recovering by now, asking about discharge plans—not lying on a stretcher with a toe tag.

She dropped into her chair and woke her screen. If not foul play, it was something. Something real.

The room felt colder suddenly, though the thermostat hadn't changed. Outside the frosted glass, monitors beeped steadily, nurses' voices murmured through the corridor. The hospital never really slept.

She pulled the code data for the past twelve months.

Rows of dates, names, and room numbers blinked back at her from the pale blue screen. The layout was sterile, but to Elise, it looked like a battlefield—each entry a casualty marker. Names she'd said aloud during rounds. Rooms she'd stood in. Each line a moment she hadn't known would matter.

She began to sort by time, then by provider. Patterns began to emerge, faint but rhythmic.

There it was—a rise starting in July. Subtle, steady.

She ran the year prior. The jump stood out.

July. Residency turnover.

Could one of them be a carrier? A Typhoid Mary in scrubs? Someone who passed unnoticed. Who looked healthy. Innocent.
Until it was too late.

But that didn't make sense. There was no incubation period. Infections don't kill this abruptly.

This wasn't slow.

It was instantaneous. Precise.

She started scanning the names. Times. Locations.

Too many rooms. Too many bodies.

If there was a pattern, someone had stitched it together with a surgeon's hand.

She blinked and scrolled again.

Jamie Lin's name appeared. Ravi Patel's, too. Interns Priya Malhotra and Caleb Morse were listed next in the physician column. Trusty ICU charge nurse Danika was there in the next column, along with the bedside nurse, Madison. Two other nurses, Tanya Malloy and Jodie Sung were listed below that in the nurse column. Nilesh Patel from Pharmacy was listed in the third and final column. Avery Cole and Michael Wynn from Respiratory Therapy were listed under Patel's name. All people Elise knew. Most of them she had worked with for years. All names she recognized. All had been in the room that morning.

But that wasn't surprising. They worked long hours. Covered most of the hospital. Their names would be everywhere.

She trusted them.

Didn't she?

She leaned back and rubbed her temples. This wasn't evidence. It was correlation. And as she frequently told her residents, correlation does not equal causation. It could just be a pattern she could be inventing. Maybe it was just the code team doing their jobs and showing up for codes. And yet... she couldn't shake the unsettled feeling. Like the numbers were trying to speak. Like the list itself was a warning.

She considered pulling in another attending for a second opinion. Or going to the Chief of Staff with her concerns. But the thought caught in her throat. They would laugh. What if she was wrong?

They'd call it paranoia. Tell her she was overworked, overthinking. That she was chasing anomalies.

So for now, she'd keep looking. Alone.

Room Six Fourteen wouldn't be the last.

Not if she was right.

And not if no one else was looking.

Just as the thought formed in her mind, it was interrupted by a harsh electronic tone blaring through the overhead speakers. Elise froze, instincts snapping to attention.

She stood quickly, her chair scraping across the floor, and hurried to the doorway.

She paused there, heart already accelerating, listening for the operator's voice to follow—the room number, the location, the urgency. Her body tensed, muscles coiled and ready.

Her pulse thudded behind her eyes, and her fingers gripped the doorframe a little harder than necessary. Part of her was already trying to predict which room it would be. Part of her didn't want to know.

She didn't know if it was adrenaline or dread—only that her feet were already moving.

Another code.

She was already moving before the announcement finished.

Chapter 6

Within Normal Limits

Dr. Ravi Patel

* * *

The code tone blared overhead—one long, piercing note followed by the sterile monotone of the operator.

> **"CODE BLUE, THREE SOUTH, ROOM THREE-THREE-SEVEN. CODE BLUE, THREE SOUTH, ROOM THREE-THREE-SEVEN. CODE BLUE, THREE SOUTH, ROOM THREE-THREE-SEVEN."**

Ravi Patel dropped the saltines and peanut butter he had nabbed from the nurses' station and bolted.

His feet pounded the vinyl flooring as he raced down the hall, dodging a supply cart and nearly wiping out on a freshly mopped corner. His stethoscope bounced against his chest. His coat flared behind him like a cape. The usual flood of adrenaline coursed through him—automatic, electric.

But as he skidded to a stop outside Room Three-Thirty-Seven, he knew.

There was no urgency in the air. No frantic compressions. No sharp commands. Just low conversation and the unmistakable ripple of awkward relief.

The patient was lying on the floor, propped against the wall. Pale but conscious, breathing steadily. A physical therapist knelt nearby, still catching her breath. Jamie Lin crouched next to the patient, two fingers pressed lightly to the wrist, the other hand holding up a penlight.

"Where are we right now?" Jamie asked gently.

"The hospital," the man croaked.

"And what day is it?"

He looked sheepish. "Uh… Tuesday?"

Jamie double checked her watch before nodding. "Close enough," she said, giving a reassuring smile.

Someone snorted softly.

The therapist who had helped the patient down stood up, brushing off her scrubs. "Sorry, guys. I wasn't sure if he had a pulse—I panicked and hit the button." Her cheeks were flushed with embarrassment.

Jamie grinned and stood up. "These lazy residents need the exercise anyway."

Ravi leaned against the doorframe, catching his breath. "Damn, Lin. Do you sleep here or teleport?"

Jamie always managed to be right there, like a shadow that outran you. Like she was waiting for the drama to happen just so she could catch it first.

Jamie glanced over her shoulder. "You're not even sweaty. You take the stairs or just followed the sound of my patients coding?"

A nurse from the desk called out, "You two done flirting, or should we give you the room?"

Laughter broke out in the hallway—half tension release, half the collective chuckle of a narrowly avoided catastrophe. The smell of antiseptic and warm food trays hung faintly in the air, grounding everything in the reality of hospital life.

Ravi laughed with the others, but deep down, he hated always being second.

He stepped into the room, offering the man on the floor a crooked grin. "You know, if you wanted attention, you could've just pushed your call light. No need for the drama."

The patient tried to smile but looked mortified. "I just stood up for PT…"

"Orthostasis," Jamie said quietly. "Looks like a simple faint. The therapist caught him on the way down."

"More graceful than most of us, honestly," Ravi muttered.

The nurse—an older woman named Marcy—shook her head. "Third one this month. Maybe we should start issuing helmets."

Someone in the back said, "Or bedpans with seat belts."

More laughter. Ravi joined in, though his eyes drifted back to Jamie.

She was still kneeling, focused, brushing a strand of hair behind her ear, checking the man's pupils again. Not because she had to. Because she couldn't not. Always the first to arrive, always the last to leave.

"How do you do that?" he asked, his voice lighter, teasing.

"Do what?"

"Get there before everyone. Every time."

Jamie just gave a faint smile and stood up, brushing off her knees.

Ravi shook his head. "You're gonna win the invisible points race, you know that? Attendings love that crap. Makes the rest of us look lazy."

Jamie smirked. "Then get faster."

Behind them, another resident—Sonia Kapoor—entered the room late, holding a portable vitals monitor. "Guess I missed the fireworks." She looked around, then leaned closer to Marcy. "Wasn't he the guy from 17 last week?"

"Transferred from 417 yesterday," Marcy said, glancing at the clipboard.

"Lucky timing," Sonia replied, then looked Jamie up and down—blatantly sizing her up. "Figures you'd already be here." Her tone was too breezy to be friendly.

Ravi caught it, felt a flicker of irritation he couldn't quite place. The hell did that mean?

But he let it go. Everyone was tired. Everything felt weird lately. Probably nothing.

Nothing unusual about that.

He shifted, feeling the faint tackiness of dried sweat at his collar and the ache in his knees from running full tilt. The antiseptic bite in the air made his nose itch. Under it there was a hint of bay leaves. He had been smelling that more often. Probably just homesick for his mother's cooking, he dismissed the thought and refocused.

In the background, Dr. Navarro entered quietly, surveyed the room, then turned away without a word. Just a glance toward the patient, then toward Jamie, unreadable. She walked off down the hallway, hands tucked behind her back. Someone popped open a can of ginger ale nearby with a hiss.

Ravi bitterly noticed. Probably just hovering and judging while they did all the real work.

Still, as the crowd started to drift away and the patient was helped back into bed, Ravi caught Jamie's eye one more time. She smiled.

He smiled back.

He told himself it was nothing. A habit. A reflex. Jamie always stayed a beat too long, saw a little too much. Maybe that's what made her good. Or maybe it was something else. Something harder to name.

Just another non-code. Just another false alarm.

Jamie paused at the doorway, glanced back at the patient, and frowned slightly—as if annoyed it hadn't been a real code. Or maybe she wasn't annoyed. Maybe she was disappointed. Ravi wasn't sure which unsettled him more. Then she turned and disappeared toward the stairwell, headed up to the ICU.

Ravi lingered a little longer. When the room was quiet again, he pulled up the patient's chart. He was covering this one. Mr. O'Hara—68 years old, recovering from pneumonia. Steady vitals overnight.

Earlier that morning, orthostatic vitals were normal: lying flat, 136/72 with a heart rate of 78; sitting, 132/74 with a heart rate of 82; standing, 137/72 with a heart rate of 87. His blood pressure didn't drop when he stood up. No reported dizziness. No meds changed. No fever. Nothing that should've tipped him over.

Ravi frowned. Something didn't add up.

He scanned the timeline again. Not for notes. For gaps. For anything that might explain it—or anything that might need explaining.

He jotted a note and closed the chart. It didn't feel like relief. Not exactly. More like the moment after a missed step—when you're still upright, but something in you knows you almost fell. The fluorescent light above flickered once and steadied. He turned, finally, and headed back toward the stairs, the faint echo of the code tone still humming somewhere in his chest.

Chapter 7

Ringmaster of Stooges

The Killer

* * *

I watched from the far end of the telemetry corridor, where the air smelled faintly of floor wax and maple syrup and felt cool against my skin as the hallway emptied.

No one noticed me. No one ever did.

People see what they expect—scrubs, a badge, a task being done. They don't see me. Not really. Just another body in motion. Just another part of the hospital's hum.

The parade of white coats and clattering shoes faded, the squeak of a cart wheel trailing behind them and the last beep of a monitor lingering in the air, leaving behind the sterile echo of nothing. It looked like a Three Stooges sketch—one intern, in his scramble to look important, yanked his stethoscope out of his coat pocket and launched his pager halfway across the room. He dove for it, smacked his head on the chair rail, then knocked over a pitcher of water on his way back up. Soaked his pants front. He looked like he'd pissed himself. The others barely noticed in the chaos of it all. But I noticed. I had to pinch myself real hard to keep myself from laughing out loud at that one. I didn't need the attention; I would have plenty of time to laugh about that one later.

Another one—a heavyset resident with a sweat-slicked brow—arrived nearly three full minutes after the rest, gasping for air like he'd just run a marathon. Probably waddled from the elevator. This is who people trust for health advice? A man who gets winded walking from radiology to the ICU? Unbelievable. I will have to figure out this guy's schedule so that I can make sure emergencies happen as far from him as possible. I was going to have fun watching him scramble around the hospital. If he didn't have a coronary and get admitted himself!

And then there was the drama queen. A junior nurse, I think—already in the room, but barely holding it together. She hovered near the bed like she'd been dropped into a war zone, hands fluttering, eyes wide, practically gasping with concern. When the patient sat up, she let out a little gasp and covered her mouth like she was about to cry.

No one was even dying.

It's always the same ones. The over-emoters. The breathless hand-wringers. As if panic were a form of competence. Like acting overwhelmed makes them deeply caring.

False alarm. No heroics required today. Just a tired old man who stood up too fast. The code team had burst in, flushed and breathless, ready to save a life. And for what? A nosebleed's worth of drama. A stumble. A faint.

They always ran so fast. Like it mattered. Like they could actually change who lived or died. I almost let him go. Just a little more. But not today.

Today was just for fun.

Jamie Lin was the first to arrive. Annoyance flared in my chest when I saw her. Of course she was. She always was. She must think it means something, being first. That she's the best because she sweats the most. Because she's always watching. Always learning. Always desperate to prove herself. She doesn't understand—it's not her call.

It's not up to the residents.

It's up to me.

They all think they're gods because they hold pagers and talk fast and know how to push the button on the defibrillator. But they don't know anything. Not really. They're clowns. Performing. Scrambling. Gasping under fluorescent lights, flailing for glory.

And I'm the ringmaster.

They need to be reminded. Humbled. Taught.

They act like death is failure. But to me, death feels like proof—like the closest thing to an honest moment this place ever has. Death is truth. The only one that matters. The rest is just ego and paperwork.

What I give them isn't cruelty. It's clarity.

A little chaos sharpens the edges. Makes the world clearer. Makes me feel alive.

I smiled and turned away, feeling the hospital badge lanyard brushing lightly against my collarbone and the cool draft of the corridor on my face, already thinking about the next one.

Let them run.

Let them sweat.

Let them wonder.

One of them would be next. I just hadn't decided who.

Chapter 8

Complications

Dr. Elise Navarro

* * *

The ICU was quieter now. The air carried a metallic tang and the low hiss of oxygen, and the monitors flickered against the walls like small blue fires. Most of the day shift had gone home, and the hallways dimmed to a dull hum of machines and distant footsteps. Elise sat alone at a computer station, the glow of the monitor casting blue shadows across her face. She was deep in the EMR, combing through code records, paging through labs, notes, and vitals with a cold, steady focus.

She had a growing list: patients who had coded unexpectedly over the last twelve months. Jamie Lin and Ravi Patel's names kept surfacing in those records. So did Avery Cole, the respiratory therapist. Interns Priya Malhotra and Caleb Morse. Nurses Madison Tran, Tanya Malloy, and Jodie Sung.

Some of them had been documented in the room. That much was clear—code sheets captured only those directly involved. But what about the people nearby? The ones just outside the door, restocking a supply cart or wheeling a lab sample down the hall. Not documented. Not assigned. Not accounted for. It felt insurmountable.

Who was close enough to harm, but far enough not to be seen? Patterns began to flicker beneath the surface—just enough to unsettle her. But other names surfaced as well—residents, nurses, even a float pharmacist once or twice. Given their hours and the chaos of hospital life, it wasn't that surprising. Still, a pattern was beginning to take shape. Not sharp enough to point, not soft enough to ignore.

There was no single person documented as being at all of the codes. There was no single person who was even in the hospital for every code. Ravi Patel had his clinic rotation in October, and Jamie Lin had her research month in February. The interns were all at a retreat that weekend in August where there were six codes in two days. Avery Cole had a medical leave in December, although Navarro had inside knowledge that she was admitted to the hospital under a pseudonym, so she was still around.

She was not sure if this provided anybody with an alibi, considering she didn't know for sure that each event was a part of the pattern. Certainly some of them were natural. There was just no way of knowing which ones for sure.

A soft voice pulled her out of the screen. "Elise. You done for the day, or are you planning to sleep in that chair?"

She turned to see Dr. Marcus Reilly standing at the end of the workstation row, his tie loosened and his bag slung over one shoulder. The warm tone in his voice softened the stern lines of his face. He'd always looked more like a professor than a radiologist—tweed-blazer energy in scrubs.

They'd been residents together once, long nights and bleary-eyed rounds tying them into an unspoken camaraderie that had lasted through the years.

She leaned back and rubbed her eyes, feeling the dry grit along her eyelids and the dull ache between her shoulder blades. "I'll leave soon. Just wrapping up."

Marcus stepped closer, peering at her screen before arching a brow. "This looks like more than wrapping up."

Elise hesitated. Then, quieter: "Have you noticed anything... strange lately? More codes. More complications. Younger patients. Ones that shouldn't be coding."

He nodded slowly.

"Can you elaborate?"

"I've been seeing more PEs on imaging. Small ones, usually—not the saddle embolisms, not crashing patients. But still… more than usual. A lot more. And not in patients you'd expect. I brought it up at the department meeting last month, but they said it was because I had excellent vision and could see clots that nobody else can see. They completely brushed me off."

Elise folded her arms, her focus sharpening. "What kind of patients?"

"All kinds. Post-op joints. Pneumonias. Even a couple young ones without any risk factors. I figured maybe I was overreading. But it's enough that I started tagging a few cases to double-check."

Her brow furrowed. "You think something's being missed? We are vigilant about DVT prophylaxis."

He shook his head. "Honestly? No. I mean—I don't usually see the meds, or the patients—but there have been so many I have started checking the charts. They have all been on heparin or Lovenox. Weirdly, none of them have been on oral anticoagulants. SCDs are on. It doesn't add up.

And there's something else. I've had to read an unusual number of STAT chest films where a patient who already had a chest tube suddenly needed another one—same side. No trauma. No new procedure. No explanation. The original tube was either gone or malfunctioning, and there's no record of why. I figured it was just bad luck. Or maybe there's a reckless nurse yanking people around during turns or boosts. But now that you are asking about it, I'm not so sure."

Elise didn't answer right away. Her eyes flicked back to the screen. Code after code.

Chest tubes. Now that he mentioned it, she could remember several patients like that. Sudden dislodgements. She had one where the lung re-collapsed within hours of placement, and it turned out the suction hose was cracked. She had never seen that before, but all equipment is at risk of malfunctioning, so she didn't think much of it. Another had been found coiled under the sheets. But she had seen that many times—it wasn't hard to pull out. The tube was secured only by a loop of suture thread wrapped around it, like trying to put a leash around a snake; one good tug and it would slide free.

There were the central lines, too. These tubes had eyelets on the side for suturing in place, they were less prone to falling out. And yet, three patients had lost them unexpectedly in the last six weeks. The notes all said 'inadvertent removal.' In each case, the assigned nurse was Madison Tran. Madison had insisted she just walked in and found the line lying in the bed with a slowly expanding pool of blood on the sheets. Elise hadn't wanted to believe it, but she remembered the last warning from the CNO—one more incident, and Madison would be fired on the spot.

Now, Elise wasn't so sure. How many were real complications? How many weren't? They were realizing the breadth of the problem. They had no way of knowing who the true victims were. No way to separate poor outcomes from routine complications—or from intentional harm.

She checked the vitals. Stable. Medications. Unchanged. Code record. Complete.

But something about it still felt wrong.

Her eyes drifted down the growing list she'd compiled: names, timestamps, unit assignments. It read like a ledger of the lost. She didn't know what she was looking for anymore. Only that she hadn't found it yet.

One case had started it—a woman in her 50s. Elise couldn't even remember the exact diagnosis. Something treatable. She'd coded in the middle of the night, and no one could explain it. Elise had spoken to her husband the next morning. "She was getting better," he'd said. "You told me she was getting better."

That conversation had haunted her. That was the first pebble. And now the avalanche was building. Resuscitation attempts, pulse checks, notes in hurried prose.

"We should keep comparing notes," she said finally. "Because if this is real… if someone's doing this…"

She didn't finish. She didn't have to.

Marcus exhaled slowly. "We don't even know how to identify the victims. Let alone the suspect. When does bad luck stop being bad luck? When does a complication stop being a coincidence?"

Elise stared at the screen again, pulse quickening. "And how do we prove it's not just medicine being messy? We can't call foul without proof. But we also can't sit on our hands if someone's deliberately doing harm."

Marcus's expression turned grim. For a moment, Elise thought he might back away, might tell her it was too far-fetched to keep digging. But instead, he just looked tired, like he'd been carrying the same doubt too long. "Yeah. We should."

They walked out together. Elise felt the weight of it all settle between them, heavy as lead, before they moved again, past the flickering lights and empty stretchers, two old friends trying to find sense in the dark. The corridor outside the ICU smelled stronger than usual of disinfectant. A floor cleaner—the kind that looked like a miniature Zamboni—whirred softly as it rolled past them, steered slowly by a bored-looking custodian. The machine left a glossy trail in its wake, the hum of its motor rising and falling as it maneuvered down the hall.

Elise stepped aside to let it pass, the reflection of its blinking lights momentarily flickering across her shoes.

Neither of them spoke. The hospital was quiet in that eerie, late-hour way—too clean, too still, like a stage between performances.

Just before reaching the elevator, Elise glanced down at her notebook. She'd scrawled a single word in the margin beside the names.

"Why?"

It wasn't enough. But it was a start.

Elise didn't look back at the ICU. The faint smell of disinfectant trailed after her as she walked, mixing with the cool draft from the elevator opening ahead.

Not tonight. Tonight she would rest, if only for an hour. Tomorrow, she would start pulling at every thread.

Chapter 9

Into Thin Air

The Killer

* * *

The sun hadn't risen yet, but the sky was beginning to lighten, bleeding pale lavender and washed-out pink through the small rectangular window. The fluorescent lights buzzed softly, casting a pale flicker across the floor tiles. There was a cool draft in the air above me, mingling with the slow hiss of oxygen through wall tubing and the gentle beeping from monitors that tracked the dull rhythms of life. The hallway carried the faint, clean scent of the special cleanser I always preferred—something crisp and herbal that reminded me of home. Mornings in the hospital were like that—quiet, clean, like the air held its breath before the shift changed and chaos was restored.

I slipped into the room on the fifth floor surgical unit without a sound. For an instant, I let the hush settle over me, the faint hum of the monitors, the plasticky tang of the IV tubing mingling with the antiseptic scent, and the cold air brushing the skin at my wrist.

The patient stirred in the bed, eyelids fluttering before settling again in half-sleep. His chart said he was twenty-six. Post-op day two from an uncomplicated appendectomy. He looked younger. Pale, soft-skinned, and not yet wary of the world. Tousled brown hair curled slightly at the edges, and a faint shadow of stubble gave his face a rugged softness. There was something striking about him—the symmetry of his features, the curve of his lips even in discomfort.

He opened his eyes when I stood beside the bed.

"Rough night?" I asked.

He blinked at me, confused, then gave a weak nod. His voice was hoarse. "Only if you count being serenaded by IV beeps and hallway gossip."

I smiled. I could hear a pair of nurses giggling by the nutrition fridge just feet from the room—something about a surgical intern getting tongue-tied in front of a patient's mother. Predictable. Harmless. Human.

He smiled back, wincing slightly as he shifted.

"Mind if I take a listen?"

He shrugged.

I pulled the stethoscope from my coat pocket and warmed the diaphragm with my hand before pressing it to his chest. The faint rustle of his gown. The quiet thud-thud-thud beneath skin and bone. I moved the stethoscope slowly, deliberately, savoring the soundscape. Then I heard it—a soft, high-pitched systolic murmur.

It was faint, but unmistakable. A patent foramen ovale. Most people didn't even know they had one.

I glanced down at the chart. The resident had written "no murmurs."

I almost laughed.

They never listen properly. They rush. They skim. They write down what the resident before them wrote. They want the checklist done before their coffee cools. Arrogance parading as competence. And then they think they have the right to decide who lives and dies?

No. That choice doesn't belong to them.

It belongs to me.

I made a note on my own pad, not his chart. My hand moved with care. This was the kind of detail they never caught. But it would matter. Competence always matters. Even in death.

He watched me, eyes heavy but warm. "You seem different. Not rushed. Not... like the others."

"I care," I said simply.

He nodded, already drifting off again. "Thanks... you've been really great."

I smiled, small and quiet, feeling a soft bloom of satisfaction—as if I was about to restore some small balance to the world.

I turned to the IV line. The syringe was already in my pocket. I opened the sterile wrapper and drew back the plunger, forcing the syringe to fill with air. I watched the way the light glinted off the barrel. I attached the syringe to a side port in the tubing and pushed the plunger hard and fast. The air vanished into the tubing like it had never been there at all.

They wouldn't notice until they came to wake him for his morning evaluation. Unless the phlebotomist noticed first. Her cart was outside the next room, half-organized and already half-full. She had a habit of humming under her breath while labeling tubes. She never looked at the patient's face.

Or maybe it would be the nurse. Vitals due in thirty minutes. Just another sleeping patient who wouldn't rouse.

I lingered a moment longer than I should have, letting the hush and the warmth of his breath fill the space between us. There was something peaceful about him. Not just in sleep. In the shape of his features, the even slope of his brow—at least the one that hadn't started to droop already. It almost made me wonder if I should have waited.

Almost.

As I stepped into the hallway, the early light gilded the floor in thin streaks. People looked up as I passed. Nurses, a tech, even the phlebotomist arranging tubes on her tray.

They all looked.

But none of them saw me.

They never do.

Chapter 10

Airhead

Dr. Ravi Patel

* * *

The hallway glowed with the gentle blush of sunrise, gold and pink spilling through the tall windows at the far end of the unit. Ravi was hunched over the computer at the nurses' station, pecking through lab results and progress notes, the familiar ritual of pre-rounding. His coffee had gone cold. He didn't notice.

> **"STROKE ALERT, THREE SOUTH, ROOM THREE-FIVE-SEVEN. STROKE ALERT, THREE SOUTH, ROOM THREE-FIVE-SEVEN. STROKE ALERT, THREE SOUTH, ROOM THREE-FIVE-SEVEN."**

The overhead call snapped his head up. His heart dropped. 357—that was his patient. He hadn't been in there yet this morning. This didn't make any sense. He was a young, healthy guy with a simple appy. He told me yesterday the PCA made him woozy. Probably just a little too much medication. It had to be.

He jumped up from the desk and spotted Jamie jogging down the hallway, stethoscope bouncing against her chest. Of course she was already on her way.

He caught up with her just as they reached the room. A neuro resident—someone from the first-year class named Maya—trailed behind, sleep lines still creasing her cheeks.

Inside, the patient looked worse than Ravi had imagined. Pale. Slumped to one side. His face had lost its symmetry. His eyes flicked toward them without recognition. He immediately knew this had nothing to do with narcotics.

His mouth had gone dry, a metallic tang gathering at the back of his tongue. His fingers trembled as he fumbled with the mouse to close the EMR window. The air in the room felt thinner.

"What time was he last seen normal?" Jamie asked.

"I helped him to the bathroom at 4:15. He looked a little groggy but responded appropriately," the nurse said quickly. "He slept through his labs this morning—wouldn't wake up for the phlebotomist."

"I just thought it was because of the morphine," the phlebotomist, who had arrived at the Code Stroke, inserted with just a twinge of guilt.

"I came in to check morning vitals and saw the facial droop. Right-sided weakness, too," the nurse continued. "I called the stroke alert immediately."

Ravi stepped up to the bed. As he leaned over, a faint scent drifted up—sharp and unmistakable, like bay leaves. It reminded him of home in a way that made his stomach clench. His mind spun, a flicker of disbelief giving way to cold dread as he looked at the obvious asymmetry on the guy's face and realized this wasn't narcotics after all. The patient tried to speak, but it came out garbled. Slurred. His right arm lay limp.

Ravi stepped to the bedside and began the NIH Stroke Scale exam, methodically moving through each category, his voice flat with disbelief.

"Level of consciousness: drowsy but arousable with constant stimulation—two Points.

Orientation: unable to answer the current month or his own age correctly—two points.

Commands: 'sir, can you squeeze my hand?'—nothing. 'Open your eyes.' His lids flitted open to reveal clear blue eyes before fluttering back closed—One point."

He moved on.

"Gaze preference: forced deviation to the left—two points.

Visual fields—difficult to score with this level of responsiveness, but he doesn't flinch when I come from the right, so I am going to give him one point. No, two points." Ravi debates with himself while glancing at Maya for confirmation.

"Facial palsy—clear severe droop on the right—three points.

Motor arm—left arm drifts slightly—one point.

Right arm, flaccid—four.

Left leg, mild drift—one point.

Right leg, no movement—four."

He gently lifted the patient's arms and legs as he scored them, every motion clinical, detached.

"Limb ataxia: you have to be able to move to have ataxia—zero points." Ravi seems almost amused by this irony of being too bad to score points.

"Sensory:" he wakes the patient up for the sixth time during this exam. "Do you feel me touching you on the left here?" The patient weakly nods and grunts. "How about the right?" He asks while stroking both legs. Nothing. "Two points"

"Speech—unable to name objects or follow prompts. Two points.

Dysarthria—speech so distorted it was nearly lost. Two points.

Extinction and inattention:" Ravi does his best to get the patient to look to the right, but his eyes won't cross midline. It was as if anything to the right of the midline didn't even exist. "Clear neglect on the right. Two points"

His tally was rapid but certain. He glanced at Maya.

"NIH thirty," he said grimly. Severe. He has bilateral deficits; he must have had a showering of strokes for some reason.

Maya's hands fumbled slightly as she updated the stroke team and radiology. She lowered the phone, eyes wide. "Should we push tPA before imaging?"

Ravi hesitated. His tone was steady, calm. "Let's see the scan first. What if it's a bleed? This guy should not be having an ischemic stroke."

Minutes later, they were pushing the gurney down to CT. Ravi gripped the cold metal side rail, the wheels squeaking across the tiles, fluorescent lights glaring off the frame. His heart pounded. It wasn't just the pattern anymore. It was this patient—healthy, young. He'd been joking with Ravi just yesterday.

The CT angiogram came back negative—no occlusion in the large vessels. But the CT perfusion scan lit up with a clear area of hypoperfusion in the left hemisphere, along with scattered smaller areas of restriction. Tissue in trouble, no visible clot to target.

"There's no blockage to remove," Maya said, frowning. "No clot retrieval. But it's a salvageable penumbra. We should give tPA."

Ravi nodded. "Do it."

The medication was hung. Despite the clot-busting medication, the patient showed no improvement in his stroke symptoms or neurologic deficits.

Later, an MRI was ordered to clarify the findings. Ravi stationed himself at a workroom computer, clicking refresh at least once a minute. He wasn't expecting much. His stomach felt sour. He checked in on another patient just to move, but couldn't stay away long. He kept refreshing the imaging tab on the EMR. Then one time, it refreshed and it was suddenly there. A live link to click on. Another ten seconds to load.

The report stopped him cold.

Multiple tiny foci of susceptibility artifact primarily in the left and less so in the right cerebral hemisphere consistent with air embolism.

Air? Ravi thought distantly of another patient—one with sudden hypoxia and no clear cause—though he tried to push the memory aside and focus on the case at hand.

No central line. No surgery this morning. Nothing that should've put air into this man's brain.

Ravi didn't say anything. A twist of dread and helplessness coiled under his ribs, the certainty that somehow he should have seen this coming. Just reread the sentence. Again. And again.

He tried to tell himself it was nothing—some rare, freak occurrence. A fluke. He must have a PFO for this to happen. But even if he did, so did a third of the population. There still had to be a source of air to travel across that hole in his heart and up to his brain. The body is as predictable as the direction of a highway.

He closed the report, his stomach rolling with nausea and a cold flush creeping up his neck. There was nothing else to do—but it didn't feel finished.

He stared at the screen a moment longer, the glow reflecting in his glasses and the ache tightening his jaw. This man would never walk again. Might never speak. Ravi thought of how he'd laughed about discharge plans just yesterday, the memory so fresh it felt like a punch. Part of him wondered if it was cruel to let him live like this—trapped in a body that no longer answered.

Chapter 11

Patterns in the Chaos

Elise

* * *

Elise sat in the corner of the dimly lit radiology reading room, feeling the cold from the bank of monitors seep into her arms and the hard edge of the chair digging into her shoulder blades, the only glow coming from the bank of monitors where Dr. Marcus Reilly clicked through axial images of a brain MRI. The room smelled faintly of burnt coffee and static. She had never liked this room. Too still. Like stepping into someone else's brain.

"There it is again," he muttered, zooming in. "Third time in a year. Before that, I'd only ever seen one of these in my entire career."

Elise leaned closer, peering at the small clusters of black flecks scattered across the left hemisphere.

"Air embolism," she said under her breath.

"Yep. No surgery. No central line. Nothing that should explain this. Just like the last two." He glanced at her. "Young patient, too. And you know what's even more unnerving? All three had PFOs. Otherwise, the air never would've made it to the brain. Which makes me wonder how many others we missed—patients without PFOs who got air in the venous system and had sudden hypoxia or cardiac arrest before anyone suspected what had happened."

She frowned. "You're thinking intentional air emboli? Sudden arrests?"

He nodded. "Exactly. The ones who coded too quickly for anyone to understand why. CTA would have been ordered to rule out PE—"

"But air doesn't show up on CT angiography of the lung. It's invisible," Navarro took over his thoughts.

"And the only way to confirm it would be with a V/Q scan—"

"Which no one orders unless there's a contrast allergy or you're already suspecting a PE. And even then—"

"Then no one ever knows," he finished.

Elise crossed her arms, tension growing in her jaw.

"When you mentioned the uptick in PEs, I started paying closer attention. I've been seeing more, too. Not just the big ones that get flagged—small, almost-missed ones. And now this... It feels like there's something we're not seeing."

Reilly turned back to the screen. "Whatever it is, it's not subtle anymore."

Elise stared at the monitor a few seconds longer, then looked away. A memory surfaced—one she hadn't thought about in months. A young woman, early thirties, post-op from a hysterectomy. No complications. Healthy. Until she wasn't.

The code had come out of nowhere. No arrhythmia. No warning. She'd died within minutes. Elise had stood in front of the family, hands folded, voice steady, and told them it was a tragic, unforeseeable event. At the time, she'd believed it. Now she wasn't so sure.

She jotted a note in her pad, a flicker of doubt crossing her mind—what if she was wrong, what if she was seeing patterns that weren't really there?—just a name, a date. Another thread to pull.

* * *

An hour later, Elise found herself in the Chief of Staff's office. Dr. Abrams was a kind-faced man in his late sixties with neatly combed silver hair and a framed photo of his grandchildren on the bookshelf behind him. He listened patiently as Elise laid out her observations—her suspicions.

"You're saying someone is deliberately harming patients?" he asked gently, almost patronizingly so.

"I'm saying there's been a rise in adverse events—especially iatrogenic ones—that can't be explained by coincidence. I think we need to conduct a more thorough audit. Look for patterns."

Dr. Abrams leaned back in his chair. Elise felt her stomach tighten, bracing for the answer she already suspected he'd give, sighing. "Elise, this is a teaching hospital. If our rates of complications are rising, it may be because we're failing as educators. Residents have always made mistakes—it's part of how they learn."

She opened her mouth to argue, but he held up a hand.

"I'm not dismissing your concerns. But instead of launching a full investigation, I think it's time we focused on education. I'm forming a new committee to review how we can enhance supervision and training. I'd like you to chair it."

Elise stared at him. "You want me to chair an education committee?" A pulse of disbelief flared in her chest, mixing with something that felt like resignation.

"You've always been one of our strongest teachers. And if there's any truth to what you're seeing, maybe the problem is that we've let things slip."

She forced a smile. Nodded. "Fine," she said, slowly. If that's what it took to keep looking, she'd play along. "I'll chair it. However, I would like to form a subcommittee. One that looks specifically at these educational mistakes. I can't improve the teaching if I don't know the full extent of the problem."

Abrams hesitated, then gave a slow, thoughtful nod. "Fair enough. Just... keep it constructive. We don't want to scare people."

This wasn't about supervision. This was reconnaissance.

She'd need help—but it had to be the right kind of help. Marcus, for sure. Maybe Danika. And Naomi from Infection Control. She briefly considered the chief resident—the resident who took an option fourth year to fill a prestigious, well-respected position that involved overseeing the teams. But then she shook her head. Still one of them. Still tied too tightly to the group under scrutiny. Once a resident knew, the rest would know within hours.

Outside, she walked silently beside Reilly toward the parking garage. The halls were quieting down as the evening shift took over, and the slow hum of the floor cleaner echoed in the corridor. A janitor drove the Zamboni-like machine methodically down the hallway right on schedule, its rotating brushes leaving a glistening path behind, the scent of disinfectant sharp and clean in its wake. She didn't look up as they passed. Just kept steering the machine, humming something low and unrecognizable.

"So what now?" Reilly asked.

"Now?" Elise said, watching the cleaner pass by. "Now you're my co-chair on the new investigative subcommittee of the educational committee."

He raised an eyebrow. "That's a mouthful."

"Our first order of business will be to change committee to unit so we can call ourselves ISeeU." She dryly retorted. "We have to find proof," she continued without missing a beat. "Because no one's going to believe this until we do."

"What are we even hoping to find?" he asked.

"Something we can't dismiss," she said. "Something they can't ignore."

She wasn't even sure what she was looking for anymore—just that it was growing.

They stepped out into the cooling dusk, the sky streaked with burnt orange and plum. The parking lot lights flickered on, catching in Marcus's hair and casting long shadows across the pavement. A breeze sighed through the trees, stirring the leaves and muffling the distant sound of traffic.

"Let's just… keep our heads down until we know more," Marcus said quietly. "This could still be nothing."

Elise didn't answer right away. She should've felt vindicated. Instead, she felt watched. Like the hospital itself was holding its breath. Like the walls were listening.

She exhaled slowly, unlocking her car. Her heartbeat felt too loud in her ears, and the cool air pressed heavy against her skin. A part of her wondered if she was truly alone, or if someone was still watching from the shadows. The day wasn't done—it was just changing shape.

As she turned to leave Abrams's office, she glimpsed the Communications Director slipping in behind her, already smoothing the front of his suit. She didn't have to hear their conversation to know it would be about controlling the story.

Chapter 12
The War Room
Elise Navarro

* * *

Elise sat in her parked car, the engine ticking softly as it cooled. Her hands gripped the steering wheel, unmoving. The sky was getting dark, the last remnants of daytime loomed on the horizon. Instead of driving home, she turned off the engine and stepped back into the hospital.

She walked the silent halls like a ghost, unacknowledged by the few night staff trickling in. Her steps echoed as she reached a rarely used second-floor conference room, where the air felt stale and smelled a trace of old cleaning chemicals. Dust swirled in the weak beam of light from the single window. She turned on the overhead lights and sat heavily at the long table.

She let the moment settle, feeling the weight of the task ahead.

She opened her laptop.

By 8 p.m., after hours of watching the light outside fade from pale gray to ink-black and the hallway clocks tick slowly forward, she'd found someone from the EMR support team—an affable young woman named Jenn who agreed to help her extract data. Jenn had a colorful tattoo sleeve winding down one arm, a riot of vivid ink—bright peonies intertwined with snakes, circuit boards morphing into tree branches, a koi fish arching around a stylized anatomical heart. It was a mesmerizing work of art. There was a silver bar through her eyebrow, a small hoop in her nose, and a cluster of ear and cartilage piercings that jingled softly when she moved. Elise suppressed a twinge of jealousy. For a moment, she felt the old ache of everything she'd set aside to be taken seriously—the art, the color, the parts of herself she had buried to survive. She had conformed, sacrificing self-expression to maintain the respect so often denied to professional women. Beneath the punk aesthetic was the girl next door—freckles dusted her cheeks, and her curly auburn hair was tied back in a high ponytail, with stubborn wisps curling free around her temples and ears. Her dark brown eyes were earnest and calm. Jenn had a bounce in her step and an easy laugh that contrasted with Elise's intensity. When Elise told her she wanted every patient admitted in the past two years, Jenn blinked.

"That's... massive," she said, squinting at the screen. "But alright. Let's filter it down so we don't kill the server."

Together, they refined the list. They removed patients discharged within 24 hours, those without major interventions, and those with uncomplicated courses. What remained were patients with crashes, strokes, PEs, heart attacks, unexplained bleeding or sudden deteriorations. As the list formed, Elise's chest tightened. Row after row of patient data populated the screen, the green glow of the monitor reflecting in her glasses and the cursor blinking like a metronome. She scrawled notes, cross-referenced charts, pulled scanned documentation. The noise of her own thoughts blurred with the clatter of keystrokes and scribbles.

Jenn's energy shifted as the night wore on. Her chatter slowed, her eyes narrowed. Elise caught her staring at one case longer than the others—a patient who had coded in the middle of a quiet afternoon, two days after being transferred out of the ICU.

"This isn't just data," Jenn said quietly, glancing over her shoulder. "These are people. People with families. With children. With hopes and dreams and full lives."

Elise looked over. Jenn's expression was serious now, her easy charm faded into something steely. A mix of disbelief and resolve.

"You know if you push this too far, they'll shut you down," Jenn murmured.

She watched Elise pin printed cases to the wall, her voice dropping to a whisper. "I've never seen this many in one place."

She was organizing them by type: patients who had been recovering but suddenly coded, those with rare complications they were unlikely to develop, all recent strokes, all recent PEs, all unexpected hemorrhages. She collected minor adverse events, too. Patient falls, tube dislodgements, self-extubations. She could think of two patients in the last month who had pulled their own breathing tubes. Both times the nurse had sworn the restraints were tied, but both times they were found dangling off the bed. Elise pinned those to the wall. As she tacked them into place, her eyes brushed across the nurse's name—Madison. Both times. A pattern was taking shape, one she could almost see.

By midnight, Jenn stood with arms crossed, staring at the now paper-covered walls.

"This is... a lot," she murmured.

"It's not everything yet," Elise said, her voice dry. "But we're getting there."

"You're really doing this?"

"Yes. And I need help. Join the team."

Jenn grinned. "Oh,—I'm already on the team. I got off two hours ago."

After Jenn left, Elise stayed. Her hands trembled slightly, whether from fear or exhaustion, she couldn't tell, as she moved cases around and reorganized the categories. Names, dates, symptoms—all of it began to blur. Her mind spun in tight circles, unable to rest, unable to process. Sleep deprivation was starting to hollow her out. She felt almost manic, wondering for a moment if she was losing perspective completely, like her brain was jelly—too full, too soft, too scattered. Thoughts sparked too fast and fizzled out before she could catch them. Details overlapped in her mind—faces with the wrong names, birthdays she couldn't match, symptom timelines that slipped through her fingers.

Still, she kept reading. She knew she wouldn't sleep anyway, whether out of resignation or a fierce, exhausted determination to see this through.

Some names stung more than others. She paused over one: Gloria Martinez, remembering how Gloria had complained of a strange metallic taste hours before she crashed—a detail Elise had dismissed at the time and now couldn't stop replaying. Elderly, but recovering well from pneumonia. Alert, talkative, joking about her grandson visiting with a therapy dog. Then, out of nowhere, she crashed. Elise had been the one to call time of death. No clear explanation then. And now, staring at the chart again, she wondered how she had let it go.

Sometime around 3 a.m., Elise pulled out a notepad and began a different list—names of people she needed on her team. People she could trust. She jotted down:

- Marcus Reilly — Radiology. As the only other person who had seen the pattern, he was her second-in-command, whether he wanted the role or not.
- Jenn – EMR support. She was capable of doing things no clinician could—discreetly, efficiently, and without raising suspicion. Indispensable.
- Infection control — Naomi Hart. There were only two infection control officers. The other guy, the weekend coverage guy—Bryce something. She did briefly consider him. He only worked weekends, making him an unlikely suspect. But he had a reputation for cutting corners and showing up late to morning meetings. He was actually kind of useless. The choice was clear.

- Pharmacy — Nilesh Patel. There were a few good clinical pharmacists she could have picked, but Nilesh had just returned from a six-week trip to India over the holidays. That made him an unlikely suspect—unless, of course, this was a partnership or team of perpetrators. But Elise wasn't ready to go that dark...yet.
- Danika Moore — ICU nurse manager. She'd considered the night supervisor and two seasoned charge nurses. But Danika had the best system-level awareness and wasn't too close to the residents. Elise couldn't quite put her finger on it, but Danika just felt like the right choice.

She considered someone from the legal team, then scratched the idea out. She had no doubt they'd smile and promise to help, only to quietly alert administration and spin up the PR machine the moment she found something that couldn't be buried. Their job was to protect the hospital. If this investigation led somewhere uncomfortable, they could become a barrier.

Then she added another person to the list.

- Security – TBD

She hesitated, tapping her pen against the paper. She had gone on a few dates with someone from the security team—Logan Dean something. It had been casual so far, nothing serious. He struck her as solid. Honest. He'd only started at the hospital four months ago, which meant he couldn't be involved in the pattern she was seeing. And he had access to what she needed—security footage outside patient rooms.

This is too important, she told herself. I'll reach out to him tomorrow.

If I build this team wrong, I'll lose before we start. The real danger wasn't just the killer—it was the institution's willingness to pretend nothing was wrong, she thought.

The paper-covered wall loomed behind her like a crime scene—disjointed moments of tragedy, pinned and highlighted, begging for meaning. Jenn had called it a lot, but Elise saw it as something more: a map of something sinister. The pattern wasn't clear yet, and for a moment, she wondered if she was imagining it or if she should be terrified that she wasn't. Either way, the shape of it was forming.

By dawn, sunlight bled through the window. She felt a quick, irrational fear that someone might walk in and see what she had been doing all night, paper chaos littered around her. Elise sat cross-legged on the floor, surrounded by files and printouts. Her eyes were red, her hair unkempt, but she was awake. Alert. Drowning in data, but alive with purpose.

Outside the window, the light turned golden. The glass was cool against her temple, and the papers piled around her smelled of toner and old files when she leaned her head back, exhausted. Below, the parking lot glistened with dew. A bird cried out from somewhere on the roof. In the distance, a delivery truck rolled over the asphalt with a low hum. Elise took a deep breath. The hospital was waking up again.

She reached for another chart.

Somewhere down the corridor, a code tone echoed—faint, distorted by distance. Elise didn't move. She stared at the chart in her lap and the wall in front of her, covered in names and dates and symptoms, and knew: the pattern was still growing.

The sun continued to rise.

Time seemed to stretch thin, every second heavy with the dread that the pattern was still unfolding beyond her reach.

Chapter 13
Sleep is for the Weak
Elise

* * *

By noon, Elise had been awake for over 30 hours. She never went home after yesterday's shift—just stayed in the second-floor conference room, poring over chart after chart until morning bled into daylight. Her brain buzzed from too much caffeine and too little sleep. A sour burn settled in her stomach, her hands jittering with every movement. Her mind was stuffed with timelines and symptoms that refused to fit.

As dawn broke, Elise forced herself to take advantage of the hospital's quietest hour. She left the room for the first time in hours, rubbing bleary eyes, and made the rounds—not with her patients yet, but with her mission. If she was going to investigate this, she needed allies.

Marcus Reilly was already at his workstation in the radiology suite, hunched over glowing monitors. Tall and wiry with silver-threaded dark hair and deep-set eyes, he had the sleep-deprived look of someone who had stared at too many scans for too many years.

"I'm in," he said without looking up. "You wouldn't be here otherwise."

"Obviously," Elise responded with a dry smile. "We keep you radiologists in the basement for a reason—and it's not just so we can get our steps in."

Naomi Hart from infection control, her voice carrying the smooth, melodic cadence of her Guyanese roots that contrasted with Elise's ragged exhaustion, was sipping her first cup of coffee when Elise found her. She was a tall Black woman in her forties with skin the color of polished mahogany and keen, observant eyes the shape of perfect almonds. Her natural hair was swept into a high twist, and she wore her badge and ID with the same precision that defined her meticulous work. Naomi exuded a calm, steady presence, but her sharp mind and unyielding standards made her one of the most respected—and occasionally feared—figures in the hospital.

Every day, she checked on every patient with a line or a tube in place and challenged the staff on whether it was still necessary. It's a crucial intervention for reducing line-related infections, and it takes a special person to challenge providers, especially when those lines and tubes make patient care more convenient. But it isn't her job to make life easy for anyone. She was perfect for this team.

After flipping through Elise's annotated chart samples, Naomi gave a low whistle. "Alright. You've got my attention. Let me pull some of my own data. I'll have it before lunch."

Danika, the ICU nurse manager, was reviewing staffing assignments near the nurses' station. Broad-shouldered and solidly built, she moved like someone used to handling chaos. Her brown hair was pulled back in a messy braid, and her face bore the calm of a woman who had seen too much to be easily rattled. She was the most senior nurse in the unit, at a ripe old 55. Most nurses don't last that long in the ICU. Everyone in the unit called her Mama Dane. Every ICU had a fifty-something-year-old nurse called Mama Something.

"Crap. I just thought the residents were getting dumber and the nurses were too green to catch it. These aren't random codes," Danika muttered. "Yeah. I'll help."

In the pharmacy, Dr. Nilesh Patel barely glanced up before nodding. He was slim, with neatly trimmed facial hair and dark, expressive eyes that always seemed to be doing mental math. His white coat bore a faint coffee stain on the pocket, which was almost the exact color of his skin; however, his attention to detail regarding drug interactions was legendary.

"Meet at noon?" he asked.

Elise nodded, a flicker of guilt catching in her chest—she was asking them to take a risk. If this turned out to be nothing, or if the wrong person found out before she had proof, the fallout could be brutal. They would all be blamed for stirring up trouble without cause.

"Conference Room 2C. I'll bring coffee and sandwiches."

Last was Jenn, her EMR ace, who was already logged in and running queries when Elise stopped by her corner of IT support. She was younger than the rest—late 20s, with a shaved undercut and a bright, impatient energy that contrasted with the quiet, humming machines around her. The T-shirt under her hoodie read: *Ctrl + Alt + Del your ego.*

"Need data?" Jenn asked without preamble.

"I'll bring lunch," Elise said, managing a faint smile.

By the time morning rounds started, Elise was running on fumes. She moved like she was underwater, every step a dull pull against her limbs and a heaviness in her chest, forcing herself to focus as residents presented patient after patient. Her eyes stung, her thoughts blurred, but she said all the right things—checked the notes, corrected the doses, reviewed the imaging. She was well-trained in this kind of exhaustion. Residency and fellowship had taught her how to think on no sleep, to make critical decisions with a heart rate of fifty and a bloodstream full of caffeine. It wasn't healthy, but it was familiar. Muscle memory took over where clarity faltered. All while half her mind buzzed with the growing horror pinned to the walls of that dark conference room. Everywhere she looked, all she saw were suspects. Every patient lost felt personal now—especially those she'd looked in the eyes and promised they'd be okay.

Her fingers were ink-stained and cramped, her eyes dry from too many hours of scanning charts, parsing timelines, and rearranging cases like puzzle pieces. A hollow hunger gnawed at her, but the thought of leaving the building felt impossible.

Instead, she sent a few messages. One by one, her selected allies agreed to meet her for a quick lunch—those who were off-cycle or could skip the noon conference. By design, most of the residents and senior staff were attending the weekly morbidity and mortality conference downstairs. It was an irony not lost on her. Today's M&M wouldn't include any of these cases. Those were the cases where the errors were visible, the ones someone had admitted to. These... these were ghosts. Missed patterns. Hidden harm.

She laid out sandwiches with the sharp tang of pickles and the crinkle of the paper bags, coffee, and bottled water in the same dim conference room—whatever she could scrounge from the cafeteria. By 12:05 p.m., they started to trickle in.

Marcus Reilly was first. He looked tired but intrigued, rolling the stiffness from his shoulders as he settled into a chair.

"I still can't believe those air bubbles," he said under his breath as he crossed the threshold to the conference room.

Next came Jenn carrying her laptop and a second coffee. "Hope I'm not late. The query is still running—I'll have more data by tonight." Jenn's fingers flew across the keyboard, crafting queries Elise couldn't even begin to decode. It felt like magic—or maybe witchcraft.

Then Naomi Hart, the infection control specialist. She had a clipped efficiency to her that Elise respected. Naomi reviewed the early data Elise handed her, her brow knitting.

"Some of these shouldn't have gotten infections. Not with their risk profiles," she said.

Elise nodded. "Exactly."

Danika arrived still in scrubs, a badge clipped to her collar, sleeves streaked with dried saline and a faint orange tint from chlorhexidine. She had seen everything. When Elise showed her the list of patients who had coded unexpectedly, Danika's mouth tightened.

"That many? You're sure?"

"Still verifying, but yes."

Dr. Nilesh Patel arrived last. He reviewed a short list of medication errors, timing mismatches, and unexplained dosing.

"Someone knows how to hide this," he murmured. "It's not sloppy. It's careful." He glanced at one of the files and added, "This one feels familiar—like something I've seen before.""

When they'd all arrived, Elise stood beside the paper-covered wall and took a breath. Her voice was low, intense.

"I need you to help me investigate this. Quietly. These aren't just isolated incidents. There's a pattern here. Someone's hurting patients. And I think they're getting away with it because no one's looking at the big picture."

No one spoke for a moment.

Then Jenn said, "You think it's a doctor?"

"Probably. Or maybe a nurse. I don't know what it means. But I don't think it's random."

Naomi folded her arms. Danika gave a humorless little snort. "It means the CMO will bury it unless you hand them undeniable proof. If this is real, you know what it means, don't you?"

Elise nodded. "I know."

Her phone buzzed. A new message. She glanced at it—it was Logan.

She hesitated, then looked at the team. "There's one more person I want to bring in. Someone from security."

Marcus raised an eyebrow. "Is that wise?"

"I've gone out with him a couple of times," she admitted. "But I trust him. And he only started four months ago, so he can't be behind this. We'll need video access if we're going to match movements and room entries. Plus he will have access to the lock data. He'll be able to see who badged in and out of different hospital areas. This could help us catch someone in the act."

No one objected. Elise trusted everyone in this room—she had to. But wasn't trust exactly what had allowed this problem to grow unchecked?

Elise exhaled, thinking how trust felt dangerous now, a liability that had already cost lives. "Alright. We keep this between us. No residents. No legal. No administration. Not yet. Because right now, everyone is a suspect—and even if they aren't, gossip is like oxygen in this place. The wrong rumor could kill this before it starts."

As the others filtered out, Elise lingered, reviewing one more chart as the conference room emptied. She stared at the paper-covered walls—the lives lost, the patterns almost visible. It was no longer just an instinct. It was a case.

And she finally had a team. Almost.

Instead of resting, she made her way down to the security office, tucked beside the loading dock. Logan was behind the monitors, sipping from a dented thermos and scanning the overnight logs. He looked up, surprised but not displeased to see her.

"Elise," he said, straightening. "Everything okay?"

Logan was former Army, early thirties, with a square jaw, close-cropped sandy hair, and a quiet steadiness that made him easy to trust. His hazel-green eyes held hers as he studied her for a long moment. Elise didn't let herself get distracted by his rippling biceps stretching the sleeves of his uniform or the way his tight shirt clung to the sculpted lines of his torso—you could practically see the six-pack beneath it. She hesitated, aware of the thin line she was crossing—part of her ashamed for mixing personal and professional motives, and part of her relieved to have someone she trusted. But she needed him. Needed those logs.

"I need your help," she said. "Off the record."

He raised an eyebrow. "What kind of help?"

"Video access. Badge logs. A lot of things I probably shouldn't be asking for."

He studied her again, slower this time. "You got it. But only if you promise me something."

"What?"

"Promise me you'll take a nap. You look like you're about to collapse."

Elise smiled for the first time all day. "Deal."

Chapter 14

Cry for Help

The Killer

* * *

Midnight is the best time. The halls are quiet—too quiet. Fluorescent lights flicker above, emitting a faint, high-pitched hum that vibrates in the ceiling tiles above like tired stars, casting everything in sterile shades of blue and gray. Each footstep echoes faintly against polished linoleum, cold and hollow in the empty corridor. Even the machines seem to hum more softly, like they're whispering secrets to themselves. The air is thick with the scent of bleach, overcooked vegetables from the evening trays, and the faint, ever-present tang of something metallic. The cool draft from the ventilation brushed against my skin, raising a ripple of goosebumps. Blood, maybe. Or fear.

The demented woman in 517 is still screaming. "Help me! Help me!" Repeating it like a prayer. Or a curse. She's actively being helped—two nurses are in there right now, adjusting her lines, calming her. But her mouth doesn't care. Her brain is long gone, and her body just remembers the words. Like muscle memory. She'll keep screaming them long after they stop making sense. Long after anything makes sense.

I pass her room without looking in. I used to believe hospitals saved people. Now I know better. They're factories. Production lines. And I'm here to disrupt the flow.

At the workstation, a resident is logged into the charting system. He should be working an admit. Instead, he's scrolling through social media, thumb flicking lazily while he smirks at something stupid on his screen. He doesn't even notice me.

A few steps later, I pass an intern trying to flirt with one of the night shift nurses. He's leaning too close over the counter, flashing his dimples, pretending to listen while she twirls her pen. So cliché. She should be ashamed. This is a place for the dying, not a high school hallway. And yet, no one ever tells them that. No one expects professionalism from people like them. Just warm bodies to fill the gaps in the schedule.

I keep my steps light. No one stops me. No one sees me. There are no alarms. No questions. Just the hum of the hospital and the steady, numbing rhythm of complacency. They never learn. Residents scrolling, nurses flirting—blindly trusting habits, protocols, each other. It's a chain of ignorance.

The med room is locked. It always is. I wave my badge past the sensor, and the lock dutifully clicks open. Hospitals are so proud of their systems, their little layers of control. Badges, locks, cameras—they see safeguards. I see invitations.

I slip inside and catch the door before it locks behind me. The latch clicks—clean, final. The hum of the refrigeration unit vibrates faintly against the cabinets.

I open the controlled meds drawer. Type in the code with a practiced hand. They think those locks mean something. They think a log sheet and a warning label can prevent harm. They can't.

I pull out three vials of enoxaparin. One dose a day keeps clots at bay. Miss more than three? Bad things start to happen. I pull them out and line them up like soldiers. The rubber seals shine dully under the overhead light. I pop off the plastic safety cap that is going to reassure the nurse that this bottle has not been tampered with. I slide the needle in through the rubber top cleanly, extract the anticoagulant one milliliter at a time.

Footsteps echo outside.

I freeze, hand gripping the needle.

They pass.

Another close call they'll never know about.

I refill each vial with sterile saline, watching the clear liquid swirl as it settles. No bubbles. No residue. Just precision. The rubber top reseals itself when the needles pulls out, there is no mark of my sabotage. I use just a dab of surgical glue on the edges in 3 miniscule spots. If the lid is too hard to pop off, they will be suspicious.

I step back and admire my work.

Then three more.

And three more after that.

Nine vials now, perfect replicas of deception. Better make it twelve for good measure.

I line them up again, shoulder to shoulder.

My silent army.

Not just sabotage—art.

A flicker of pride moved through me, proof that I could do this perfectly, without error. No trace. No flaw. Each seal smoothed like glass, each syringe stroke a signature.

I pause, eyes drifting over the collection like a gallery. How many will it take to sabotage a life? Three? Four? Maybe none. Maybe they'll catch them in time. Maybe not. That's the delight of it—the randomness, which also conveniently hides that sometimes the choosing isn't random at all. This time, I won't even know which of these pitiful people I'm hurting. There's something liberating about that. It feels as if randomness lifts any burden of responsibility—like the outcome is out of my hands. Like the way it always was back then, in that other place, in that other life. Not everyone deserves to be saved. Some are just occupying space. Wasting time, resources, breath. I'm making room. Trimming the fat. Maybe one day they'll thank me—not that they'll know why.

And from an investigative standpoint? It's brilliant. If even I don't know the pattern, how could they ever hope to find one?

I return the vials to their place. Exactly where they were. The drawer closes with a soft hiss.

I step back out into the hall.

The woman in 517 is still crying out. "Help me!" Over and over. Like a mantra.

Before the door locks behind me, I slip my hand into the shrinking opening and go back into the med room.

I open the patient med fridge and pull out the tray labeled 517, rifling through its contents. Insulin. She's on a standard U100 regimen. Nothing remarkable.

But then the vial in the neighboring tray—516—catches my attention. U500 insulin. Five times the potency. Rare. Dangerous. Perfect.

I take my kit back out. I remove the regular U100 insulin from 517's tray, drawing it out one cc at a time and squirting it into the sink. Then I extract U500 insulin from 516's vial and carefully refill the empty U100 vial with it. Finally, I drain the remaining U500 insulin from its original vial, refilling it completely with sterile saline and sealing it again. Room 516 will get no insulin at all. Room 517 will get five times the intended dose. Dangerous hyperglycemia for one, severe hypoglycemia for the other. Perfect symmetry.

I turn and leave, satisfied that I've helped.

The woman in 517 is still crying out. "Help me!" Over and over. Like a mantra.

I step into her now-deserted room and gently fluff her pillow. The slick plastic cover crinkles under my fingers, the pillow oddly weightless in my hand. She barely stirs—won't remember this moment, not even long enough for me to reach the door.

Let it never be said I ignored a cry for help. A small, quiet satisfaction settles in my chest, echoing words I once heard a charge nurse say: "We do what we can."

Chapter 15
Insulin Exchange
Dr. Leilani Kealoha, Third Year Internal Medicine Resident

* * *

The overhead fluorescents buzzed softly above the nursing station, their harsh glow casting a sterile chill across her skin and bathing 5 North in that same flat, timeless brightness that blurred day and night in every hospital.

It could have been dawn or dusk—or anything in between. A third-year resident—Dr. Leilani Kealoha—sat beside Ravi Patel, flipping through the labs from the overnight sign-out. She was tall and athletic, with warm brown skin and a mess of black curls pulled back into a low bun. Her features bore the calm determination of someone raised in big waves and bigger families, and her expression was unreadable except for a tiny flicker of amusement in her dark eyes. Her scrubs were clean and crisp, the fabric just stiff enough to rasp against her skin, and the badge lanyard tapping lightly against her chest. Around her neck hung a worn pendant—a tiny carved honu turtle her grandmother had given her for protection during med school.

Leilani looked like she could still be in high school—smooth skin, a round face, and no trace of makeup. It didn't help that she was younger than most of the interns. She had skipped a year in high school and completed a combined six-year undergrad/med school program, making her just twenty-two and barely past the legal drinking age—an anomaly among third-year residents. Her youth often surprised people, but her sharp mind and calm demeanor silenced doubters quickly. Somehow, she managed to command authority from her team and her subordinates despite being the youngest on any given medical team.

"Did you see 516's glucose this morning?" she asked, frowning.

Ravi leaned in, brow furrowed as the glucose value registered. His expression twisted. "Hey!" He chortled. "Her glucose is the same as her room number!" But his amusement quickly passed as the more serious implications settled in his mind. His face made a smooth transition from a smile to a frown. "She was on U500. That makes no sense."

"She got every dose, too. Plus her long-acting. I triple-checked the MAR," Leilani said. Her voice held a note of tension, but her posture stayed relaxed. "I even went back through the orders. No missed doses."

Ravi sipped his coffee with a grimace. "That's not how DKA happens. You think someone hung D5 by mistake? Or there's a dextrose rider in one of her meds?"

"I looked. No amio, no heparin, no sneaky dex. It's not there."

"Look," Ravi said, pointing at a small cake pictured next to her name and birthday, "it was her birthday yesterday. Anybody sneak her in some cake?"

"She was NPO for cath today. So only if they smuggled it in."

Leilani glanced up from the MAR and flagged down the nurse stepping out of 516. "Hey, did she have any family visiting recently? Anyone staying overnight?"

The nurse gave a short laugh, not unkindly. "Family? They dropped her off in the ED last week and haven't been back since. Told us she was having chest pain—knew that'd get her admitted. Real story? They wanted free elder care while they went on vacation."

Leilani's eyebrows lifted. "Seriously?"

"Swear to God. They're on a cruise. They call and check in at every port."

"How noble."

"She doesn't even remember who they are. And since they claimed she had chest pain, we admitted her. Doesn't matter how much she denies it now. She wouldn't remember the chest pain anyway."

Leilani didn't answer. There wasn't one. Not really. Just a sour taste in her mouth that no amount of coffee could wash away.

She tapped the side of her monitor, looking at the trends. 517's sugars had been stable all night, and the MAR had a nurse's initials she didn't recognize. She didn't just double-check meds—she double-checked the people administering them. Her throat felt dry, a dull ache blooming behind her eyes from the hours of focus. She had learned that trust in medicine was earned, not assumed. "She's on U500. Scheduled. That's a lot of insulin. She shouldn't be anywhere near DKA."

She leaned back slightly, arms crossed, a dull dread stirring in her chest that maybe, despite all her vigilance, she had still missed something critical. "When I was an intern, I missed a guy's steroids. I had ordered them, but the pharmacy hadn't verified the dose. He went into an adrenal crisis. I swore I'd never overlook another med order again. This isn't that. I've looked at every box. This doesn't make sense."

Ravi gave a half-nod. "That's what scares me. This doesn't feel like an error. It feels like we're missing the part that makes it make sense."

Leilani exhaled slowly, letting her eyes drift to the board. Her brain kept replaying a lecture from her second year—iatrogenic DKA, rare causes, how things slip through cracks. But this wasn't a crack. Nothing was missed.

He leaned back, thoughtful now. "That's going to be a fun conversation with Dr. Warren."

She smirked. "Good luck with that. This is your fire to walk through."

He groaned dramatically, slouching deeper into his chair. "I hate you."

She reached over and stole a sip of his coffee. "No you don't."

The unit buzzed with the usual low chaos—monitors pinging, supply carts creaking. Somewhere, a med pump chimed in three-second intervals.

The overhead speaker crackled.

Then came the moderate-pitched tone that warned staff an announcement was coming. Everyone froze, eyes lifting toward the ceiling where the voice was projecting from, waiting to see what color code it would be.

"C'mon, red," Leilani muttered while crossing her fingers and closing her eyes tight. "Just be an early morning fire alarm. Just be someone smoking in the stairwell."

> **"CODE BLUE, FIVE NORTH, ROOM FIVE-SEVENTEEN. CODE BLUE, FIVE NORTH, ROOM FIVE-SEVENTEEN. CODE BLUE, FIVE NORTH, ROOM FIVE-SEVENTEEN."**

Leilani bolted upright, her stomach dropping in a cold rush of fear that she'd been right all along from her stool. Her jaw clenched. Her body snapped into motion before her mind caught up—muscle memory forged in three years of chaos. Gone was the cool sarcasm and banter. What remained was precision, speed, and instinct. Her sneakers squeaked across the linoleum, and for a moment, she thought she caught the faint scent of bay leaves drifting through the air, evoking memories of her mother's kitchen. It was gone before she could be sure, and her thoughts snapped back to the present, adrenaline tightening her chest as she matched Ravi's pace.

Ravi was already moving, and for a moment, she felt a surge of relief that she wasn't alone in this, that someone else saw how wrong it was.

Chapter 16
A Good Death

Jamie Lin

* * *

The nursing station erupted in motion—scrubs flying, shoes squeaking on the polished floor, crash cart wheels shrieking as it barreled down the hall. Overhead lights seemed to pulse with urgency.

Jamie stopped just inside Room 517, the warmth of the room in contrast to the cool hallway, the faint smell of vinegar rising around her, chest heaving, sweat slick on her back. She'd beaten Ravi by a full step, despite running three times as far, just in time to grab the ambu bag from the nurse and start ventilation. The patient was unresponsive, her skin cool and clammy under Jamie's gloved fingers as she checked for a pulse, eyes open but vacant, her skin already starting to gray.

The bedside nurse stood outside the room, pale and trembling. Her voice cracked. "I thought she was asleep. She screamed all night. I just... I thought she was finally resting."

Inside, the patient lay limp in the bed. Her skin had the waxy sheen of someone who'd been gone longer than minutes. A nurse was already peeling back the hospital gown as the respiratory therapist took over the ambu-bag from Jamie, holding the mask tight around the patient's mouth.

"Start compressions!" Leilani shouted. Ravi was already stepping up to the bed without hesitation, starting hard, fast pumps to the chest.

The woman's ribs cracked like dry wood, and later, the sternum gave way under her palms with a soft, sickening collapse.

It always did, but it never stopped feeling gnawing.

The crash cart arrived seconds later. Someone shoved an intubation tray toward Jamie. She grabbed the laryngoscope with her gloved left hand, twisted it into her palm, took the tube in her right, and went in. She pried the mouth open with the blade. The airway was wide open—she slid the tube in cleanly, even as compressions continued, the airway bouncing in and out of view.

A respiratory therapist detached the ambu bag from the mask and connected it to the tube. Ventilation resumed immediately, one therapist bagging while another secured the tube—moving in perfect concert.

The body—small, birdlike, hollow—jerked with each compression. Limbs flopped. Her head lolled.

"No color change," the therapist bagging said, worry creeping into his voice. A misplaced tube—into the esophagus instead of the trachea—would seal her fate.

"Capnometry won't change without circulation," Leilani reminded him calmly. "Do you feel resistance when you bag?"

"Yes."

Leilani nodded.

Jamie disentangled herself from the cords that had wrapped around her during the intubation and stepped into the line of compressors, ready to rotate in at the next pulse check

Leilani grabbed the trembling bedside nurse and made her stand next to her. She softened for a second. "I know this is hard, but you are the only one here who knows what just happened. I need you to stay right here and fill me in."

Eighty-nine years old. Severe dementia. Bedbound. Full code.

"Has anyone gotten a glucose?" Leilani shouted before turning back to the bedside nurse for more information.

A nurse stabbed a lancet into the paper-thin skin of the patient's fingertip and squeezed.

The glucometer beeped.

"Fifteen," came the answer.

"Push D50," Leilani shouted.

"Rhythm check!"

"Asystole."

"Resume compressions. Give an epi."

A nurse had already replaced Ravi, poised and ready to start compressions.

The massive syringe of dextrose was uncapped but then set down so the epi could be given first.

"She's only got one IV!" another voice called.

"We tried three times last night—blew every vein," the unit charge nurse replied calmly, as she pulled out a small toolbox and handed it to Jamie.

Jamie suppressed her excitement at needing to use the toolbox. An intraosseous device—the quickest and most brutal way of obtaining access to the human circulatory system. She grabbed the small drill and the smaller of the two sharp bits—the patient had no subcutaneous fat to get through. She felt around the shin for the top ridge of the tibia bone. She held the drill against that bone, her heart pounding. She pulled the trigger, feeling the smooth whir in her hand as the bit slipped into the tibia. "I/O's in!" she yelled.

The glucose was quickly pushed into the freshly established I/O. Jamie pictured the lifesaving sugar flowing through her metal drill bit directly into the marrow, then into the bloodstream the same way fresh blood cells did. Grotesque, but elegant in its brutality.

Jamie took over compressions, her arms piston-steady. This lady didn't even know her own name. But someone—probably a son, maybe a daughter—had decided she deserved everything modern medicine could throw at her. Jamie felt a pang of something between sadness and frustration—a visceral guilt that she no longer believed in the code the way she once had, and a flicker of anger at the futility of pretending this was anything but the end—this wasn't heroism, it was futility wrapped in protocol.

Navarro stepped in then—sharp-eyed, taking in the scene in one sweep.

Epinephrine. Compressions. No pulse.

The team moved like a machine. Chest compressions for two minutes. Rhythm check. Pulse check. Epi. Repeat.

Round after round, they fought for a heartbeat that refused to return. Time stretched and distorted, every second feeling thick and treacherous, a fleeting dread settling under Jamie's skin before each rhythm check. The patient's ribs began to creak and deform under Ravi's hands. Jamie took over again, her palms already bruising.

Jamie had no idea how many minutes had passed—it could have been five or fifteen. Codes warped time like that.

"Recheck glucose."

"Twenty-eight."

"Push another amp of D50."

By now, the I/O port had begun to ooze slightly around the edges, the skin fragile and pale like rice paper. The woman's body was failing in every visible way, but the team persisted.

The woman's sternum gave way early, and with every compression after that, her chest seemed to cave deeper—soft, broken, unresisting. The thud of bone on bone. The sickening squelch of tissue tearing under force.

"Still asystole," the lead nurse said, glancing at the monitor.

"No shockable rhythm. Resume compressions."

Jamie took her turn again. She planted her palms and counted silently—one, two, three—feeling the brittle cage deform under her hands. Sweat rolled down her back. Her shoulders burned with fatigue. Her excitement had long since turned to mechanical effort. Just doing what needed to be done, even when it felt pointless.

Then the smell hit. Her throat tightened, and for a second, she thought she might gag. A wave of sweet, rotting, almost metallic stench—unmistakable. The final loss of control. The famed death poo.

"There it is," Ravi murmured.

The floor beneath the bed darkened slowly. Still, the team worked.

"Push another epi," Leilani said. Her voice had taken on the hollow timbre of repetition.

"V-fib!" someone shouted.

"Charging to 200."

"Clear!"

The patient's body arched grotesquely off the mattress as the shock snapped through her. The smell of scorched adhesive filled the room. Then she collapsed again—silent. Lifeless.

"Resume compressions!"

A nurse bagged air into the woman's lungs, and Jamie caught a glimpse of froth at the corners of her mouth—pink, bubbly sputum from ruptured capillaries in the lungs.

"Hold compressions."

"Still no pulse. Asystole."

Leilani looked defeated. "Any last ideas? Any objections to calling this one?"

Silence.

She finally called it. "Time of death: 7:42."

The room deflated. For an instant, all motion stopped, a heavy stillness settling over them like a suffocating blanket. The silence that followed was deafening.

The son had arrived during the code, still wearing a floral cruise ship shirt, sunglasses pushed back on his head. A rolling suitcase clattered behind him as he stopped short in the hallway, eyes wide and watering.

"We just got back," he whispered, dazed. "She wasn't even supposed to—"

Jamie stepped toward him. But he brushed past her into the room, dropped to his knees beside the bed, and began to sob.

"You can't let her go!" he screamed, voice cracked and raw.

Jamie felt a surge of exhaustion so deep it hurt. Not just from the code. Not just from the sweat and strain and hollow ache in her arms. But from the relentless weight of it all. The fighting. The failures.

She couldn’t listen to his pitiful sobs anymore.

She slipped out before anyone could stop her, before she had to deal with the son’s grief. He had his own resident. Someone else could carry that burden.

Jamie left the room without signing the code sheet, pulling off her gloves, and feeling the sting of hand sanitizer she didn’t remember using. Her body moved automatically toward the resident lounge. She had fifteen minutes before rounds. She needed water. She needed to breathe.

From the hallway, she heard the son start to wail.

Dr. Kline from Palliative Care was walking down the hall toward the room, his gaze somber as he passed her. He didn't try to stop her, just dipped his chin in quiet acknowledgment before turning to the family. Jamie didn’t look back.

Chapter 17

Out of Frame

Logan Dean, Security

* * *

Logan leaned back in his desk chair in the security office, scrubbing a hand over his buzzed hair as the last clip finished rendering. He'd pulled the footage from 5 North—everything from the three hours before the code in Room 517. He knew what he was seeing, or rather, not seeing. No unauthorized personnel. No suspicious activity. Just nurses coming in and out, soothing the old woman as she moaned through the night. The only people entering the room were the expected ones. Still, something felt wrong. Something he couldn't quite put his finger on.

He turned in his chair and stared at the black monitor wall for a moment, watching the sterile, fluorescent-lit halls of the hospital unfold in silence. One nurse lingered outside 517 for nearly three minutes, just standing there. Another figure—Ravi Patel, he thought—walked into the frame, paused briefly, then pivoted away from the camera and vanished down a side hall. The timing was odd.

This was bigger than he could handle alone.

He grabbed his phone and sent a message to Navarro.

Logan: Got the footage. You're gonna want to see this in person.

Her reply was short and immediate.

Navarro: Can't talk about it here. The walls have ears.

That part was true. Gossip moved faster than Jamie Lin running to a code.

Logan: Come to my place tonight. I'll drop a pin to the team. I also want to loop in someone—my roommate. Former Army buddy. He's a homicide detective now. Totally off the record, but I think we need help.

Navarro: A cop?

Logan: Not officially. Just an extra set of experienced eyes. We're not filing reports or tipping anyone off. But I've been through this footage frame by frame and came up with nothing. We need help if we're going to catch whoever's doing this.

The typing bubble blinked. Then stopped. Then started again.

Navarro: Send the pin. I'll be there.

Logan exhaled. She hadn't said no to the cop. That was a win.

Logan: 8 PM. I'll order food.

He wrote to the group, "My place. 8 PM. Bring open minds and closed mouths," and dropped a pin in the thread labeled Policy Review Committee—their placeholder for something that had long outgrown plausible deniability—and leaned back in his chair.

At 7:58 PM, the doorbell rang.

Logan tossed a handful of napkins onto the table and padded over in socked feet. Just as the Thai delivery guy handed him two bulging paper bags, the warm, savory smell of basil, garlic, and fried shallots hit Logan like a gut punch. His stomach growled so loudly it startled him. He was suddenly very aware that he hadn't eaten since leaving the house that morning, and suddenly the hunger felt like a second pulse.

He was still setting the cartons down when the second knock came—short, sharp, impatient.

Navarro.

He opened the door, and she stepped in wearing jeans, a windbreaker, and the expression of someone expecting bad news. She had an understated glow about her, even lit by the warm gloom of the apartment. Logan wished, fleetingly, that she were coming over for dinner with just him.

"You live here?" she asked, glancing around.

"Better than the barracks. It even has hot water." He smiled widely and gestured to the living room, where the lights were low and his roommate's neatly arranged military memorabilia lined the shelves. "Help yourself to food. The others should be here any minute."

Navarro set her coat on the back of a chair but didn't sit. "So. The detective."

"Tyler. We were deployed together. He's smart, discreet, and he knows how to ask the right questions. And he's not looking to blow this open—just help us see what we're missing."

Navarro nodded slowly. "We'll see how he handles himself."

She moved toward the table, reaching for a bottle of water from the cluster of drinks he'd laid out. The soft rustle of her jacket sleeve, the brush of her hair as she turned—Logan caught all of it. And suddenly, the air between them felt charged.

This was the first time he'd had anyone over that mattered. The first time since coming back from deployment that he'd felt something unfamiliar and sharp tug behind his ribs. Attraction, sure—but also nerves. He liked her more than he probably should, more than he'd let on. Maybe more than she realized.

She glanced at him again with those focused eyes that always seemed a step ahead, and Logan wondered—*should he kiss her?* He took a half-step forward before catching himself. *Don't be an idiot.*

The front door opened without ceremony and Tyler stepped inside like he owned the place—which, to be fair, he half did.

"Evening," he said, giving Navarro a measured nod as he scanned the room like it was a new sector.

Navarro's eyes narrowed slightly. "You're the detective?"

"Tyler Grayson," he said, offering a hand. "I'm just here to listen. Not wearing a badge tonight."

"I can see the badge that you are literally wearing," Navarro retorted, returning his steady stare but ignoring his hand.

Logan gave her a look. "He's solid. Trust me."

Navarro nodded and stepped aside to let Tyler into the circle.

By 8:15, the rest of the team had arrived—Reilly with his laptop bag slung over one shoulder, Naomi in a blazer with her ever-present clipboard, Danika with a bottle of wine she jokingly called her coping mechanism, Nilesh carrying a neatly tabbed folder and a look of exhausted curiosity, and Jenn with a portable drive and a frown that meant business.

They gathered around Logan's living room, pushing aside takeout containers and sharing knowing glances. Logan dimmed the lights and connected his laptop to the TV.

Jenn started them off. "We've been seeing an uptick in codes. Last year, we had maybe 10 to 12 a month. Since July? That's jumped to 20 to 30. All floors, all shifts. And our survival rates are tanking, too. We used to save about 23%. Now we're down to 7%."

Naomi added, "Sepsis deaths are rising. Most of these are DNRs, so they don't trigger reviews, but we're seeing way more sudden declines. Quiet deaths that no one expected."

Nilesh leaned forward. "Antibiotic failures have spiked. Last year, we had one case where the antibiotics failed despite culture sensitivity. This year? Thirty-seven. These drugs should've worked. Someone's interfering."

Reilly tapped a few keys and pulled up a graph. "DVTs and PEs are trending up. We've had literally two inpatient DVTs since the hospital revamped the protocol four years ago. The last year, six. Which makes it twelve times higher this year than the four years prior. We've had three ischemic strokes from suspected air emboli, which is more than most doctors see in a career. That's not a coincidence."

Danika crossed her arms. "What about the guy who collapsed from orthostatic hypotension? He'd just had normal orthostatics. Vitals were stable, no signs of volume loss. But that kind of event—we don't track that. It's too minor. If this includes stuff like that, we'll never see the full scope. There's no paper trail for half of it."

A heavy pause settled over the room. For a moment, it felt like the walls were closing in, like they were all teetering on the edge of something they couldn't take back.

Logan clicked on the final tab.

Navarro stepped forward. "Patterns?"

Logan nodded slowly. "Yeah. At least one. Jamie Lin."

A stunned silence followed.

"She's at or near almost every single one. Codes, antibiotic failures, sudden declines. I know she works a lot—but there are a hundred internal medicine residents. How is it always her? On the other hand, the trends also don't dip when she has outside rotations or vacations."

Tyler raised an eyebrow. "Would she be in the hospital on her off days?"

Navarro's jaw tightened, a flicker of dread tightening her chest as Jamie's name came up. "It's possible. During certain rotations—like outpatient or procedural electives—residents are often expected to attend noon didactics in person. Even during vacation, it wouldn't be unheard of. Some residents use that time to come in and catch up on discharge summaries, update patient messages, or write notes in the library. Others show up just to use their meal cards."

"Would people notice?"

"Not necessarily. It wouldn't raise any red flags."

"It would honestly be weird not to see that one in the hospital," Danika added.

"That sounds disconcerting, given the current context," Tyler replied.

"And Ravi?" Navarro's eyes narrowed.

Logan's expression darkened. "He's not listed on the documentation from the last two codes. But I saw him when I was reviewing the video."

Reilly muttered, "That's not a mistake. That's erasure."

"It doesn't mean anything," Navarro interjected. "I saw Lin walk away from a code without signing the code sheet today."

"To be honest," Danika added, "a lot of the nurses get the minimum number of signatures. There are so many people in the room, and they scatter as soon as it's over. The nurse will just grab a few of the participants."

The room went still again, the weight of implication heavy in the air.

Navarro's voice dropped. "Then we need to decide what to do. Carefully."

Tyler spoke up. "If this is sabotage—and from what you've shown me, I think it is—you're not just dealing with a medical mystery. You're standing in a crime scene that hasn't been taped off yet."

He looked around the room, letting the words sink in.

"This isn't just about who's in the room anymore. It's about intent. And that means it's time to start building a case."

Logan nodded, stealing one last glance at Navarro, a flicker of guilt tugging at him that his feelings were surfacing in the middle of an investigation before turning back to the screen. "This is just the beginning."

Chapter 18
Pattern Recognition

Detective Tyler Grayson

* * *

Tyler leaned against the living room wall, feeling the unsettling contrast between the warm familiarity of the apartment he shared with Logan and the grim purpose that had brought them here. His arms were crossed, and he scanned the faces around the coffee table. The room still smelled of Thai food and tightly wound nerves, the takeout containers still radiating a faint warmth against the cool air. Lemongrass, basil, and spice still lingered in the air, absurdly pleasant for a conversation about death.

The team looked exhausted, wired, and silently bracing for what came next. He studied them like a crime scene photo: Reilly's hands clasped tight in his lap, knuckles blanched; Jenn's neatly tabbed folder stiff in her lap, like a shield more than a tool; Danika leaning back but arms crossed, her tension contained but not softened; Elise—Dr. Navarro—sitting forward, her eyes burning with calculation, but her foot tapping just enough to betray the adrenaline underneath.

He cleared his throat, calm but steady. "You've all done something extraordinary. You spotted a pattern nobody else has. I understand why you didn't go through channels. You were trying to protect people, trying not to tip your hand. That's brave. It's also dangerous."

Navarro's eyes narrowed, wary but listening.

Tyler held her gaze. "I'm not here to lecture you. And I'm definitely not here to tell a room full of clinicians about HIPAA. You all know more about that than I ever will. However, you need to understand your current situation. This isn't just about bad outcomes or red flags. What you're looking at is systematic, deliberate harm. It's criminal. Which means things are about to get complicated."

He took a slow step forward. "I promised Logan I wouldn't tell anyone. And I haven't. But that was before I saw the data—before I realized there might be dozens of people dead and hundreds more hurt. That changes the math. I can't not investigate what you guys have told me."

He paused. "Also, my mother was admitted to this hospital last week. On one of those same units."

That landed like a weight in the room. Reilly looked away, jaw clenched. Jenn lowered her folder to her lap, blinking as if she were recalculating everything. Danika muttered something under her breath and shook her head slowly.

He hadn't planned on mentioning his mother. He'd meant to stay detached—helpful, analytical. But watching their faces now, seeing the horror of recognition begin to creep in, he knew it had to be said. That this wasn't theoretical. It wasn't an algorithm. It was personal.

"I'm not here to hijack what you've built," Tyler went on. "But you've hit the edge of what you can do alone. If you want to stop this, if you want justice, you need to take the next step."

Reilly frowned. "You mean go to the police?"

"As the police, I would say definitely. But as your friend and confidential informant, not yet," Tyler said. "This is going to be a lot easier if we have the hospital administration on our side, holding doors open for us. First, you loop in the legal team."

Danika looked skeptical. "Hospital legal? Aren't they just going to tell us to shut this down?"

"Maybe," Tyler said. "But not if you frame it right. And not if they are ethical lawyers. You don't file a complaint. You request legal guidance on potential liability. Frame it around patient safety. You're not pointing fingers—you're asking how to protect the hospital. That's what makes them listen."

Navarro nodded slowly. "And then?"

"Then you take it back to the Chief of Staff. You make sure he hears it directly. Not filtered through a report. Not delayed in a chain of command. Sit him down, walk him through the evidence, and make him see the pattern. Just remember, he'll be thinking about liability and optics more than accountability. They always do."

Jenn folded her arms. "He's a good man. But he sees the best in everyone. He won't want to believe any of this. He already didn't believe it the last time Dr. Navarro tried to tell him."

"When we are in secret clandestine meetings, feel free to call me Elise," Navarro broke the tension with an uncharacteristic joke. Tyler noted the smile didn't reach her eyes—but the effort counted.

"Exactly," Tyler said. "He's not corrupt. He's just trusting. That's why it has to come from you, not from some external report. He has to see the faces behind the numbers."

Reilly asked, "What if we never get past legal? What if it dies in a boardroom?"

Tyler shook his head. "That's where I come in. I'll make sure the official police report lands on my desk. Quietly. Directly. No alarms. But you've got to build it airtight. No speculation. Just facts."

Logan gave a short nod. Not gratitude—trust. The kind forged in heat and blood. They'd pulled each other out of worse than this. But this? This was the quiet kind of war. Slower. Trickier.

They'd first met in Kandahar, sharing a plywood bunkroom and ducking mortar fire between patrols. Logan had been sharp then—an intuitive tactician with a sixth sense for finding threats before they surfaced. He'd saved Tyler's life more than once, though he never talked about it. Seeing him now, posted up in hospital security, checking badge logs and surveillance feeds—it felt like watching a sniper relegated to a parking meter. The man had instincts built for more than catching med students stealing yogurt from the resident lounge.

A long silence followed.

Logan looked around the room, then back to Tyler. "So legal first. Then the Chief. Quiet, steady, careful."

"Exactly," Tyler said. "This isn't about panic. It's about precision."

Navarro exhaled and nodded once, her eyes flickering with dread and determination. "All right. We do this the right way. Together."

Tyler glanced toward the darkened window, then back to the group. "You've been brave. Now it's time to be smart."

Outside, the city kept breathing—horns honking, lights blinking, people moving through their lives unaware. Inside, the team shifted. No longer just survivors of a growing crisis. Now they were strategists.

It had started with suspicion. Now it was a case. And soon, it would be war.

Tyler lingered at the window a moment longer. His reflection stared back at him in the glass, cool against his fingertips as he rested them lightly on the pane at him in the glass—older than he remembered, tired, sharper around the edges. He thought of his mother again. Thought of the nurse who had smiled at her like nothing was wrong. The chart that looked fine. The vitals that were "normal." He thought of how close it would be—how easy—to miss the sign, to miss the moment that ended it all. And about how many sons never even knew to look. He clenched his jaw. Whatever it took, he wouldn't let her become one more quiet death on a spreadsheet.

Chapter 19

The Quiet Ones

Jamie Lin

* * *

The buzz of the fluorescent lights in the resident workroom was louder than usual. Or maybe it was just that Jamie couldn't stop hearing it, couldn't stop noticing the way everything felt a little too bright, a little too sharp. Like a world where the contrast had been turned up to maximum, every edge cutting a little too clean, every whisper brushing too close.

She was sitting at a computer terminal, pretending to scroll through labs. Her fingers hovered above the keyboard, twitchy and restless. Her chest felt tight, like she couldn't quite get a full breath. Every few seconds, she glanced sideways—not obviously, but enough to track the subtle shift in body language around her. The edge of a whisper. The flicker of an expression. Her heart beat faster than the situation warranted, a steady thud-thud-thud she could feel behind her eyes. The muscles in her jaw ached from how long she'd been clenching them. Her stomach churned, a bitter taste rising in her throat—not from hunger, but from a tension so deep it had settled into her bones. In reality, she was watching people. The glances that lingered half a second too long. The shift in tone when she entered a conversation. The way Ravi paused when she walked up to the charting station, his voice catching just a little before resuming. Even the nurses, who normally greeted her with casual nods, now seemed to look through her.

She told herself it was fine, though for a flicker of a moment, she remembered the first time she'd felt this—singled out, when an attending questioned her judgment in front of everyone, the heat in her cheeks and the certainty she'd never belong. They were just stressed. Everyone was. It didn't mean anything.

But still—she felt it. The eyes. The doubt. The pressure of a spotlight she hadn't earned, hadn't asked for.

Ravi sat beside her now, typing progress notes. He didn't look at her, but he hadn't moved away either. That had to mean something.

They had each other's backs. They always had. From the awkwardness of intern year to the long nights of call, to the mistakes no one else had seen. They were a unit. Weren't they?

Jamie returned her gaze to the screen, though she wasn't reading. Her mind was elsewhere. On the woman in 517. The code. The way her ribs had caved in beneath relentless compressions. The soiling, the smell, the chaos. The son screaming. The way Jamie's hands had moved—precise, practiced, almost detached. Almost.

You have to live!

Jamie's lips pressed into a tight line.

That poor old woman had begged for rest all night long. She'd screamed and cried and begged for someone to help her. Jamie had helped her. Jamie had given her what she wanted—peace.

And her son… her son hadn't even seen her. All he saw was his own grief. His own fear of being alone. As if that gave him the right to demand more suffering from a woman who'd already had too much.

He was the reason they broke her ribs. The reason her frail body was pummeled, jabbed, shocked, bruised in death. If he had even a sliver of compassion, he would've signed the DNR order. He could've spared her.

But no. People like him never saw the patient. Only themselves.

She tried to tell herself it was just one case. Just one moment. But it wasn't. The pattern was undeniable. She saw it every day—the quiet suffering no one else wanted to look at, the patients languishing in bed after bed, forgotten by families who had already moved on. The ones who lingered not out of hope, but inertia.

Jamie exhaled sharply and stood. She needed to move. To get away from the workroom, from the eyes, from the noise in her own skull. Her body felt hot, sweat prickling along her skin, and still somehow cold, a chill creeping up her spine—like her blood couldn't decide whether to rush or retreat.

She made her way off the unit and ducked into a quieter med room on an underused floor without much traffic. She swiped her badge without thinking. The door clicked open with a dull mechanical sound. Familiar. Comforting.

Inside, she leaned against the cool metal of the refrigerator and let her eyes close. The artificial chill crept into her skin, grounding her.

It wasn't about death. For a moment, she felt a pang of guilt, something sour and uninvited, before she shoved it ruthlessly aside. Not really.

It was about winning.

It was about balance.

Death was the opponent. The natural conclusion. But she could beat it. She could call it off when it came too soon—or coax it forward when it stayed too long. Medicine loved the illusion of control. Jamie had the real thing.

No one blinked when doctors withdrew care, stopped meds, turned off ventilators. No one called it murder when you gave a little extra morphine to ease the end.

But if you saw the suffering coming—if you had the vision to act before the agony set in—suddenly it was wrong?

The outcome was the same. The only difference was timing. And intent.

She opened the fridge and stared at the vials. Neat rows of precision and promise. Little glass vessels of control. She could feel the hum of the refrigeration unit, soft and steady, the cold air brushing her face, condensation beading on the vials and the smooth metal racks cool under her fingertips and the faint medicinal scent of sterile vials hanging in the air. A metronome of potential.

Every day she saw patients wasting away in agony. Families clinging to the idea of miracles. Doctors afraid to say the truth out loud.

She wasn't afraid. She had learned that in a place where supplies were scarce and no one came when you called for help.

Some people were too damaged to be saved. Some lives too tangled in pain to be worth prolonging. And yes, maybe some weren't dying. Maybe some were just… offensive. Dangerous. Toxic. They hurt others. They wasted resources. They played the system.

Jamie blinked slowly. Her pulse steadied.

She could help. She was helping.

She was two steps from the door when it opened.

Ravi stepped in, his face unreadable, eyes flicking to her then back to the fridge. The room felt suddenly smaller, tighter.

"Forgot something," he mumbled, stepping toward the shelves without meeting her gaze.

Jamie gave a tight smile. "Late for a dose?"

He shrugged. "Inventory check."

They stood there for a beat too long, silence stretching taut between them.

"You okay?" she asked finally.

Ravi hesitated. "Yeah. Just tired. You?"

"Same."

He glanced around the room, then muttered, "Thought I left my notes in here."

Jamie raised an eyebrow. "You mean those notes sticking out of your scrub pocket?"

Ravi looked down and let out a sheepish laugh. "Damn. Left pocket strikes again. I swear I need a map to my own pants."

He gave a casual wave and slipped out, his tone light, but his shoulders just a little too tense.

Jamie watched the door long after it closed. Whatever he was doing, it wasn't inventory. And whatever she had been about to do—she wasn't sure anymore.

Not yet.

They wouldn't understand. Not yet. Maybe not ever.

But she wasn't the villain.

She was the cure.

No one had ever questioned her when she wrote 'comfort care' in the chart, she thought, and maybe they never would.

She smiled faintly as she closed the fridge and walked out, steps measured, calm. Each movement deliberate, each breath controlled.

She just needed to stay one step ahead.

And she always had.

Chapter 20

Rat Park

Dr. Ravi Patel

* * *

The on-call room stank of sweat, sanitizer, and the stale tang of microwaved food. The sheets on the cot were stiff, scratchy polyester that clung to the body with static. Somewhere in the corner, a vent rattled, coughing out lukewarm air that never quite reached the far wall. A metal folding chair had been shoved haphazardly under the desk, and Ravi's foot kept brushing its cold leg every time he shifted.

He stared at the ceiling, eyes burning from lack of sleep. The fluorescent light above the door buzzed with a faint hum, even though the switch was off. He hadn't even bothered to take off his shoes. There was no point. He wasn't going to sleep anyway.

Second year was supposed to be easier. Familiar. But the truth was, it was harder. Relentless. The stakes were higher, the hours longer, the mistakes more haunting. They were expected to handle double the patient load on top of managing an intern or two.

He couldn't shake the memory of that teenage girl who coded on the CT table. The septic old man whose blood pressure bottomed out in front of his daughter. The patient with sickle cell who begged not to be discharged—and was dead two days later. The cancer patient whose labs had been flagged too late.

His brain flipped through them like flashcards on fire. Mrs. Chan with the bowel perforation leaking stool and bacteria into her bloodstream. Mr. Ochoa, who wouldn't stop seizing. For days. The baby who coded in the ED—he hadn't even been on the case, but he heard the screams from the hallway. He barely conjured a memory before another one would push its way into his brain. That 35-year-old woman in the car accident with her three kids crying over her body as the life drained away. The old lady with the tension pneumothorax. He got the chest tube in, but not quick enough. Her heart stopped seconds later, before he had a chance to stitch the thing in.

Too many codes. Too many long nights. Too many questions. He tried to remember if anyone ever checked to see if he was OK. They hadn't. And he wasn't.

He sat up and scrubbed his hands over his face, feeling his stubble scratch his fingers. He used to shave religiously, kept a clean jawline—one of the few things he could control. But lately, even that had slipped.

He needed something to take the edge off.

It wasn't always like this. He used to pride himself on control—keeping the pressure at bay, managing the grind without ever letting it show. But somewhere along the way, the weight had shifted, and now it was pressing down too hard. He couldn't just keep covering it with jokes.

The first time he pocketed a vial, it had been out of desperation. He'd told himself it was just temporary. Just to get through that one impossible stretch of nights.

But it had gotten easier. Smoother.

Now, it was a ritual.

As he made his way down the hallway toward the 4 North med room, Ravi spotted a nurse outside one of the rooms wrangling a demented elderly patient. The man was clearly delirious and combative, flailing against her attempts to take vitals.

"Need a hand?" Ravi asked, flashing an easy grin.

The nurse blew a strand of hair out of her face, her arms full, trying to keep the man from pulling out his IV. "I'm good. We're just getting our nightly exercise. Right, Mr. Boland?" she said, turning back to the patient, as if he could appreciate her joke. He tried to spit at her in response, but his mouth was too dry to muster up the required saliva.

"I'll grab the Tylenol," Ravi offered, nodding toward the reading of 102.1 on the screen of the mobile vital cart glowing between the nurse and the patient.

"Thanks," she said, clearly relieved. "My badge is right there on the COW."

"Does he need a little vitamin H to go with it?"

"Nah," she shrugged him off. "We'll be OK. He just doesn't like to be touched. If he doesn't calm down when I'm done with cares, I'll grab the Haldol."

Ravi grabbed the laminated badge off the computer-on-wheels and it held up. "He broke it off you?," he half inquired as he fingered the broken clip, slipping it into his coat pocket as he walked toward the med room, not waiting for her answer.

The door clicked shut behind him. The Pyxis stirred to life, humming like it didn't care.

The cold air of the med room made the back of his neck prickle. His palms were clammy. He wiped them on his coat, fingers twitching with adrenaline. Every sound—every creak of the hallway floor, every groan of the HVAC system—felt magnified. He listened hard, heartbeat pulsing in his ears.

He swiped the nurse's badge and keyed in the patient's name. Navigated to the acetaminophen on the itemized list of medication contents. The drawer popped open.

In one fluid motion, he grabbed the Tylenol and, with a sleight of hand, feeling the cool glass pressing against his palm with a deceptive, fragile weight, palmed a vial of fentanyl tucked just behind the blister packs. His fingers trembled slightly.

The fentanyl vial was small, almost weightless, but it might as well have been a grenade in his pocket.

Before closing the drawer, he manually adjusted the count. A couple of keystrokes. Justification typed in without hesitation. A loophole in the software. Everyone was aware of it, and everyone assumed the individuals accessing it were trustworthy.

The first time he pocketed a vial, it had been out of desperation. He'd told himself it was just temporary. Just to get through that one impossible stretch of nights.

But it had gotten easier. Smoother.

Now, it was a ritual. A habit. A hidden crutch that felt equal parts medicine and moral failure.

He paused, listening again. The hallway was silent.

He hated that he needed it. Hated that he'd crossed a line he used to think was unthinkable. But the shame had dulled over time, replaced by a hollow kind of practicality. This was survival. Nobody was checking on him. Nobody was helping him hold it all together. If the system wouldn't protect him, he'd do it himself.

He remembered reading once about the Rat Park experiment—how caged rats overdosed on morphine, but when given a rich, social environment, they rarely touched the drug. The implication was simple: it wasn't the drug, it was the cage. He wondered what that meant for doctors trapped in hospitals like this.

He closed the drawer and exhaled slowly, slipping the vial into his coat pocket.

He told himself he wasn't an addict. He didn't crave it. He didn't chase a high. He just wanted to feel less. To sleep. To breathe without the weight pressing down on his ribs.

And maybe—just maybe—he was entitled to that.

Back in the hallway, he handed the Tylenol to the nurse with a smile.

"Still in one piece?" he asked.

"Barely," she muttered. "Thanks, doc. You're the best."

He gave her a smile polished over years of charm and distraction, the kind that used to open doors and cover sins in the same breath. The nurses still bought it. Most of them. For now.

She chuckled, distracted, already turning back to her patient.

Ravi walked away, smile fading and jaw tightening.

He wasn't a bad person. He used to judge doctors who crossed this line, told himself he was better than that, but here he was. And now he wondered if he was lying to himself when he said it was different. Not really. He cared. He worked hard. He saved lives. Some of them, at least. He just needed help himself sometimes—and the hospital didn't exactly hand out medals for burnout.

Besides, nobody had ever noticed. Not the Pyxis. Not pharmacy. Not the nurses. Not Jamie.

Jamie.

He frowned, a flicker of unease twisting low in his gut—a fear that maybe he was seeing her clearly for the first time.

Lately, things felt… off. He wasn't sure when it had started. The tension, the strange silences, the look in her eyes. But they were still on the same team. Weren't they?

They were the ones who understood each other.

At least, he hoped they did.

They'd witnessed the same horrors. Done things no one else could stomach. Held secrets like weapons in their palms. If that hadn't broken her, what could possibly be rattling her now?

They were bound by bloodless crimes, and he remembered the way she never flinched after that last code, how she'd walked out with her face too calm, her voice too steady and whispered understandings. Whatever game she was playing now, he'd figure it out.

He had to.

He clenched the vial tighter, feeling the smooth glass edges bite into his palm, a sour shame rising in his throat even as part of him insisted this was survival in his fist. Just in case.

Just something to take the edge off.

Then back to work.

Back to codes and chaos.

Back to Jamie.

As if nothing was coming for them both.

Chapter 21
Rupture
Elise Navarro

* * *

Elise sat at the end of the long, polished conference table in the administrative boardroom, her hands folded tightly in her lap to keep them from fidgeting. The chairs were too stiff, the air recycled and dry enough to parch a throat after a single sentence. The scent of lemony disinfectant failed to cover the undertone of old coffee and nerves. The room was too cold, too bright, and smelled faintly of sweat and fear.

Tyler stood at the head of the table, flanked by Jenn, Reilly, and Danika, each of them looking more like whistleblowers than doctors. They were here for the reckoning.

Across from them sat the hospital's legal team—two attorneys with tablets, wary eyes, and pale expressions. They weren't criminal lawyers. They dealt in routine malpractice claims, bickering families disputing DNRs, and legal gray zones around withdrawing care. This? This was uncharted territory. They looked like they were trying to disappear into their suit jackets.

One of them, a balding man in his fifties, kept pushing his glasses up his nose and glancing at the other as if begging her to speak instead. The younger woman, with tight curls and a power suit that looked more aspirational than representative, tapped nervously on her tablet and bit the inside of her cheek every time a new case was mentioned. They were used to filing paperwork—not uncovering serial crimes.

Dr. Abrams, Chief of Staff, sat between them. His white coat was pristine, but his posture had sagged since the meeting started. He'd gone from polite disbelief to anxious silence in under ten minutes. It even seemed like the edges of his bowtie were starting to droop.

"We're not saying this lightly," Tyler said, voice even but firm. "What we're looking at isn't a few bad outcomes. It's a pattern. Multiple, coordinated assaults on patients that appear to be happening inside this hospital."

Jenn flipped through her printed charts. "The spike in codes and survival anomalies began nine months ago. Look at the run charts. It's not random. It's targeted."

Reilly added, "And the complications—PEs, DVTs, air emboli, hemorrhages, hypoglycemia, hyperglycemia—all started rising around the same time. These aren't just sicker patients. At least half of them have been young and healthy, they were low risk for complications."

Danika leaned forward, her expression grave. "Not all of them died. Some had minor events, like near-syncopal episodes and unexplained hypotension. Those don't trigger investigations. But they're just as suspicious if you know what you're looking for. I've been in this hospital twenty-seven years. You don't get this many young, low-risk patients crashing without something rotten going on."

The attorneys exchanged a glance, and the older one cleared his throat, clearly flustered. "These are serious allegations," he said, tapping his stylus against the desk with a sharp, anxious rhythm. "But—well—these aren't yet criminal charges. They could be… system errors. Or maybe—anomalies in documentation? We'd need to notify risk management immediately. And consider whether this could impact our liability coverage."

The younger attorney jumped in, voice a little too high. "Or there could be environmental factors, statistical clustering, even a problem with the EMR flagging—"

Tyler cut in. "If we don't act, people keep dying."

Dr. Abrams cleared his throat. "We've always trusted our staff. If someone were intentionally harming patients…" He trailed off, looking dazed.

"Someone is," Elise said quietly. Her voice surprised even herself. "You don't have to believe it yet. Just help us stop it."

There was a long silence.

Finally, one of the attorneys nodded slowly. "You have our permission to proceed with a confidential internal investigation. Legal will coordinate. But nothing leaves this room without going through us first."

Tyler folded his arms. "That's not enough. I'll be opening a criminal investigation as well. I'll keep it off the books for now, but it's happening. These aren't theoretical victims. These are patients in your care. My mother was just admitted here last week. On the same unit where two unexplained deaths occurred in the past month. I moved her to another floor last night. Quietly."

The room stilled at that.

Elise watched as Dr. Abrams looked down at the tabletop. He wasn't a bad man. Quite the opposite. He was someone who still believed everyone else was as good as he was. And now he was realizing that faith might have been misplaced.

When the meeting ended, the plan was set: legal first, then bring it back to Dr. Abrams with formal findings. And now that the official police report was going to be filed, Tyler would make sure it stayed on his own desk—so he'd be assigned as lead detective and could guide the case from within.

An hour later, Elise stood in the security office with Logan. The monitors flickered in the dim light, a wall of silent, pixelated windows into every corner of the hospital. She had come to review footage, to calm her nerves by doing something useful. It felt wrong to sit still.

Logan handed her a cup of coffee, their fingers brushing briefly. There was something electric in the way her hand lingered against his. Her eyes lifted to his, hazel with flecks of amber and green that caught the light like sparks. Their gaze lingered for a heartbeat longer than necessary. Then her eyes drifted downward, tracing the sharp line of his jaw, the curve of his lips. Something was growing between them, a current neither of them had named. But the guilt hit her almost instantly. Thinking about romance in the middle of a crime spree felt selfish. People were dying. Now was not the time.

Her pager buzzed as the familiar overhead tone sounded.

> **"CODE BLUE, SURGICAL ICU, ROOM FOUR-OH-SEVEN. CODE BLUE, SURGICAL ICU, ROOM FOUR-OH-SEVEN. CODE BLUE, SURGICAL ICU, ROOM FOUR-OH-SEVEN."**

She stared at her pager screen displaying the same information. The alert hit her like a slap.

It was her patient.

She'd admitted him six hours ago after a tumor was removed from his neck. Stable, improving, unremarkable.

Before starting her sprint to the unit, her eyes desperately scanned the monitors. She flipped between angles, switching from hallway to hallway, pausing on every figure that moved. She searched the halls in and around the ICUs for anyone that didn't belong. Anyone who looked suspicious. Anyone who stood out in any way. Nothing.

Logan turned to the monitors. "I'll watch the feeds. Go."

* * *

Logan

* * *

He watched Elise sprint down the hallway on the live feed. Controlled. Efficient. Unshaken.

She reached the trauma bay just as the doors burst open. A flurry of motion followed—nurses, residents, blood.

This one was bad.

Carotid artery rupture.

He'd seen blood before. He'd seen arterial spray in combat zones, in places with no running water and no anesthesia. But this? This was like a horror movie come to life.

Blood spattered the ceiling. It painted the walls. It soaked into the scrubs of everyone in the room, pooling on the floor like a scene from a massacre.

In Kandahar, he'd seen medics work with one hand and shoot with the other. He'd seen men bleed out into the dirt. But nothing had ever looked like this—this polished room, this flood of color, this sharp smell of iron and antiseptic. This was war, but disguised in fluorescent light.

But Elise—she didn't flinch. She issued orders. She grabbed a resident's hands and placed them firmly over the wound, then grabbed them by the shoulders and moved their body into a position they would be able to stand in for a while. The poor kid just looked relieved to know exactly what they were supposed to be doing.

Someone in scrubs ran into the room, grasping a red picnic cooler with a white handle. They quickly popped it open, revealing 4 burgundy bags of blood. Elise grabbed one and quickly checked the bag to make sure it was the correct unit, uncrossed trauma blood. O neg. Perfect. She handed it to Danika, who started loading it into a plastic pod mounted to a pole—the rapid transfuser. That unit would be in in fifteen minutes. She grabbed a second unit from the cooler, checked the label, then handed it to a resident. She spiked the bag, then moved the resident's body near the top corner of the bed, where she would be out of the way. She lifted the resident's arms as high as they would go in the air and had them start squeezing the bag. Makeshift rapid transfuser—the army medics would be proud of the field maneuver. Two units of blood infusing in under two minutes—impressive.

After this, the team seemed to calm a little and develop the rhythm he was used to seeing in the codes. She had them running like clockwork. But she didn't stop moving. She grabbed a blue package from a cart and cracked it open. She rubbed a swab on the groin. She went through the tedious steps of putting on sterile gloves, but did not bother with the full gown, cap and mask he usually saw them don for procedures. She didn't bother with that sterile drape, either. She didn't have even a minute to spare. This was usually a resident's job, but she wasn't about to count on them getting it on the first stick in a crashing patient with no blood in his veins and compressions still rocking the target back and forth. There wouldn't be time for a second chance.

She plunged a fat needle into his groin and almost immediately drew back a syringe full of blood. She threw the syringe aside and a few drops of blood spilled from the hub of the needle that remained in the groin. She pushed a flimsy wire through the hub and then stuck the needle back in the blue kit. As she was bringing her hand back from the needle to the groin, she picked up a scalpel on the way without wasting a second. She made a quick tiny cut where the wire was going in to make room for the line. She retracted the scalpel and tossed it back in the kit. Then the line. It was short and fat and had the fattest IV he had ever seen hanging off the side of it. It was in the groin and the wire was removed before he realized it. She tied it with a suture faster than he could tie his boots and put a bandage over it. She moved the blood infusion over to this fancy new line.

"Hold compressions" rang out just after the blood was moved over.

They got a pulse back. Eight minutes. Maybe he would be OK.

Then they lost it.

Then got it again.

Stabilized. Barely.

A third unit was hung in the rapid transfuser, the portable monitor was moved from the crash cart to the foot of the bed, and the patient was wheeled back to the OR being trailed by a respiratory therapist pushing the vent, a nurse pushing the bed, another nurse wheeling the IV pumps and rapid transfuser, and a wide-eyed intern still squeezing blood in as fast as possible. And there was Elise, pockets lined with code meds giving calm instructions to everyone.

Suddenly, the room on the monitor was empty. Blood everywhere, epi boxes and tubing scattered around the room.

Logan leaned back in the chair, heart hammering. She was extraordinary. Braver than half the soldiers he'd served with. Steadier than most combat medics. He had meant to watch for suspicious activity, but she was just captivating. Then the thought chilled him: what if he'd just watched the killer in action?

When she returned to the security office, her scrubs soaked with sweat and blood, she didn't speak.

She just collapsed into his arms.

"I don't even know if it was a crime," she whispered. "This kind of rupture—it's a known risk. He had surgery last week. They reconstructed the muscle around the carotid."

Logan didn't try to answer. He just held her tighter.

She didn't cry.

But her whole body trembled like the adrenaline hadn't drained, just curdled into something colder. Her hands, usually so sure, hung at her sides like she didn't quite know what to do with them anymore.

She pulled back after a moment, eyes unfocused, and sat heavily in the nearest chair. Her gaze drifted toward the bank of monitors, not really seeing them. The gnawing uncertainty of whether she'd just pulled someone back from the brink… or arrived a minute too late to stop another murder.

"What if this one wasn't part of it?" she said softly. "What if I've been chasing shadows and seeing patterns that aren't there? What if we're wrong?"

Logan crouched in front of her, meeting her eyes. "And what if you're right?"

Elise didn't answer. She stared at the screen where the ICU room was now quiet, empty—just a red slick on the floor, like the scene had been erased except for the blood.

She felt like she was still there, hands inside the wound, trying to stop a river with her fingers, heartbeat pounding through her knuckles.

Chapter 22

Free Fall

Jamie Lin

* * *

Jamie sat hunched over her half-eaten sandwich in the call room, the overhead light too bright, the silence too heavy. The room smelled faintly of bleach and old coffee, and the upholstery of the call room couch scratched against the back of her legs through her scrubs. Her stomach churned with nausea, a sour tang rising to the back of her throat. Her heart thudded too fast, erratic and fluttering like a trapped bird. There was a bitter, metallic taste on her tongue—the taste of anxiety. She had missed it. Again. Another code, another story traded in low, reverent voices—about arterial spray on the ceiling, blood pooling like oil on a garage floor, Elise Navarro strutting the room like a field general.

She should have been there. That was her patient. Typical. The resident does all the admission work and the attending gets all the glory.

Instead, she was one floor down, performing a manual disimpaction. That's right. While everyone was upstairs in what might have been the most glorious code of her life, she was just out of earshot, literally digging shit out of a 90-year-old's ass.

She tried to brush it off, but the disappointment gnawed at her. That was the good kind of adrenaline—the kind that reminded you you were alive, that you were useful. Not like this emptiness. Her thoughts drifted to jumping out of a plane on her eighteenth birthday. That moment, standing at the edge of the aircraft, the earth stretched below her like a quilt of green and gray, cars no bigger than ants, people invisible. Two miles up, the wind howling past, adrenaline surging so hard it drowned out every thought but one: jump. Her heart thundered in her chest, her palms slick with sweat inside her gloves, but it wasn't fear—it was clarity. And then she made the easiest decision of her life. She jumped.

For a full sixty seconds, she fell. Free-fall. The air tore at her jumpsuit, her face, her soul. She wasn't constrained or restrained. No family expectations, no academic pressure, no patient lists, no alarms. Just sky and speed. Just freedom. Then she pulled the ripcord, and her body jerked mid-air. The descent slowed so abruptly that it felt like she'd stopped moving entirely. Floating. Suspended in the sky. Only as the ground rushed closer did she realize how fast she was still going. Her feet slammed into the earth and her legs instinctively ran forward, absorbing the impact. A safe landing. Exhilarating. Life-changing.

She'd been chasing that high ever since. Her heart had pounded with clarity, with purpose. This code would've been even better. Oxygen from the wall instead of wind from the sky. Telemetry monitors instead of altimeters. Blood instead of gravity. So much blood. Controlled chaos instead of chaotic control.

She closed her eyes and let herself imagine it—the scream of the monitor, the flurry of gloved hands, blood gushing in perfect, synchronized spurts with each faltering heartbeat. Arterial spray arcing like choreography. The gasps. The panic. The art. It must've looked like a painting in motion. Red and chaos and human determination. And Navarro, moving through it all like a conductor.

She let herself believe she could have put that venous sheath in as fast as Navarro did.

God, she wanted to be that calm. That controlled—that emotionless.

Maybe it had never really been about helping people. Perhaps it had always been about chasing that same rush—the illusion of control in the middle of absolute chaos. Of falling and pretending it was flying. Perhaps she had a hero complex; maybe that was all medicine ever meant to her. Being the one who gets to decide who lives, who dies. And no one would admit that aloud, but maybe they all thought it sometimes.

Second year wasn't what she thought it would be. Everyone warned her it would be harder, but no one told her how much it would change her. How the constant grind would erode pieces of you until you didn't recognize what was missing. She had thought it would get easier—more competence, more confidence—but it felt like she was being peeled down to bone.

Her thoughts bounced like a pinball—her intubated CHF patient in the ICU; that brittle diabetic with the foot ulcer; the guy in the ED who kept insisting he was dying even though all his labs were fine; the patient in 3 West with the mystery fevers who probably had endocarditis; the kid post-op day two with tachycardia and borderline urine output. She couldn't hold on to a single thread of thought anymore. Her brain flitted from crisis to crisis, unable to settle—one endless to-do list stitched together by guilt and caffeine.

She rubbed her eyes. Her head hurt. Her skin felt too tight. Her white coat suffocated her.

And Ravi—God, Ravi looked terrible.

She'd seen him in the hallway earlier. Pale. Sweaty. Like he hadn't slept in days. He hadn't, she realized. Neither had she, not really. But it was more than that. He wasn't just tired. He was unraveling.

She stared at her phone for a moment, thumb hovering over a text that never got written.

Was he going to tell someone? Was he going to break?

Her jaw clenched.

Almost a year. It had been nearly a year since the patient in May. Her first. Not the first death she witnessed—she'd seen plenty by then—but the first one that was hers. Her name on the admission orders. Her face the patient had seen during that long hour in the ED, answering questions no one wants to ask. Questions about intubation, resuscitation, and feeding tubes. All of it theoretical, until it wasn't. They talked about where she used to work, her children and grandchildren, and her hobbies. Not that Jamie had cared about those things—she was more interested in any potential factors that might have led to her respiratory viruses. But motivation aside, she had gotten to know the lady.

Jamie's stomach churned. That moment wasn't something she could ever talk about. Not the real version. Only two living people knew what happened in that room that day.

She and Ravi had made a choice. Together. And now they carried it like a shared scar.

At the time, she'd told herself it was mercy. That she'd been brave. That she'd seen what needed to be done and hadn't flinched. But now, a year later, that certainty had begun to fray. Maybe it had always been about control. Maybe it had been about proving she was strong enough to do what others couldn't. Or maybe—maybe it had been wrong.

She didn't know anymore. And that scared her most of all.

It had felt right at the time. Maybe it still did. But now Ravi looked like he was falling apart, and if he started talking—if he couldn't hold it together—

Jamie exhaled slowly.

She might have to do something about that.

Something permanent.

A knock at the call room door startled her. A nurse peeked in. "Dr. Lin? 3 West wants you to sign off a pain med order."

Jamie nodded and forced a smile. "Be right there."

As the door clicked shut, she noticed her hands were shaking.

She might've fooled the nurse. But not herself.

She looked down at her half-eaten sandwich. No appetite now. She dropped it in the trash and stood, feeling the weight of her pager like a ticking bomb on her hip.

She paused at the door. Her reflection in the narrow windowpane looked off. Eyes too wide. A faint sheen of sweat across her forehead. Hair a little too unkempt.

She smoothed her coat. Painted on composure like it was part of her uniform.

Only two people knew the truth.

And Ravi was one of them.

Time to check on her patients.

Before someone else did.

Chapter 23

Out of Frame

The Killer

* * *

ICU codes are chaos distilled—pure, visceral, and uncontrollable. The air reeked of bleach, sharp and searing, but beneath it lingered something worse—something rancid and unmistakably human. The metallic bite of blood, yes, but also the acrid stench of bowel release, the infamous "code brown" that clung to the floor and crept into your sinuses. Under fluorescents, every droplet shimmered like something sacred. But this last one was a masterpiece. A movie director could not have created a more beautiful scene.

SICU 407—just another glass-fronted box filled with too many machines and not enough hope. I watched from the hallway, out of frame. The beauty of modern hospitals is that chaos doesn't discriminate. And this? This was a surgical storm. Screaming vitals. Arterial spray. Blood so bright it looked artificial under fluorescents.

I watched Elise Navarro in the center of it. Calm. Cool. Collected. I saw her barking orders like a general in combat, her eyes missing nothing, her gloved hands confident and sure. Just like she'd been at all the others.

But this wasn't just a tragedy. It was a gift. A front-row seat to carnage so exquisite, it made my pulse throb with delight. I hadn't planned this one, hadn't laid a single hand on the patient—and yet, here it was, a reward for my vigilance. Fate tipping its hat. I considered myself lucky, blessed even, to have witnessed it. I love watching blood and panic and the glint of fear in seasoned eyes.

* * *

Later, I waited until the halls were empty—nearly midnight. The silence was thick, almost tangible, broken only by the occasional hiss of an oxygen valve or the distant clatter of a medication cart. The chill in the air felt colder than usual, as if the building itself knew what was coming. The overhead lights flickered once, casting long shadows down the corridor, stretching like fingers across the polished floor. Even the smell was different—less like antiseptic, more like stale air and latent dread, a tension coiled tight around every corner. Most residents were catatonic by then, running on caffeine and trauma. I took the back stairs—no cameras there, just echoing concrete and the hum of distant ventilation. Once the door shut behind me, I reached into my scrub pockets and pulled out a surgical cap, a mask, and one of those blue scrub jackets the anesthesiologists hoard in the OR. With each piece I put on, I erased a little more of myself. By the time I reached the ground floor, I was just another body lost in the monochrome blur of exhausted staff. I moved as silent as fog.

Navarro's office was dark. I slipped inside like I belonged there. The letter was already in my pocket, but it wasn't the only thing I brought.

The IV tubing was tucked inside a sterile package—crisp, white, unopened. A match for the one that had failed during the September code. Of course, it wasn't the same one. That line was long gone, buried or incinerated with the rest of the case they'd filed under "equipment malfunction."

But this one? This one was just as damning.

Same model. Same flaw.

And this time, I was the one delivering it—clean, untouched, and placed with surgical precision beside her sealed envelope. A calling card in shrink-wrap. A warning dressed as a gift.

She wouldn't be able to prove anything from it. Not yet. But she'd recognize it. She'd remember. She'd understand what it meant to find it waiting for her, deliberately placed, impossibly precise.

She would know it was me. She needed to know it was me.

She needed to be sure this wasn't chance.

She needed to know it was a pattern.

Let that keep her up at night.

I slipped back into the hallway and descended the back stairwell. As soon as the door closed behind me, I pulled off the cap and mask and stuffed them into the pocket of my scrub jacket. The staircase was still empty, but the moment I stepped back onto the patient floor, a voice called out.

"Hey! Hey, miss! Can you help me?"

Room 211. A man in his thirties, gaunt and sunken-eyed, missing several teeth. Spider veins branched across his nose—a classic sign of a long, slow war with alcohol. He was drenched in sweat, tremulous. Withdrawal was eating him alive. But what caught my attention was the perfectly round lump jutting from the side of his scalp. At least four inches in diameter, with no bruising or discoloration. Smooth and symmetrical. It almost looked sculpted.

"Can you get me something to eat?" he barked. "I'm fuckin' starving over here."

I glanced at the dry-erase board in his room. NPO for pancreatitis.

"I'm sorry," I said, keeping my tone warm. "You're NPO right now. I can't get you anything."

"Goddamn bitch," he muttered, eyes narrowing. "Fuckin' tease. You come in here all sweet and helpful, but won't do a damn thing." He tried to spit at me, but his mouth was too dry.

I ignored the bile in his voice and nodded toward the lump. "Can I ask what happened to your head?"

His expression darkened. "None of your fuckin' business what I do on the street. Probably got jumped. Or maybe I fell. I don't know. Don't remember." His words were slurred, greasy with hostility.

He tugged hard at his restraints and then tried a sudden switch in tone. "Can you untie these?" he asked, trying to lift his arms with futility.

"I'm sorry, but I'll have to check with your nurse first."

"C'mon," he said with an oily grin. "I just need to scratch my balls. Nobody else is gonna do it."

When I didn't respond, he sneered. "You could do it for me, if you're feeling helpful."

I turned to leave, done with him.

"Hey!" he yelled after me. "If you won't untie my hands, at least come suck my dick!"

I didn't flinch. I didn't stop. But my pulse quickened, not with fear—but purpose.

I made my way down to the micro lab. The guy at the desk barely looked up, nodding absently as he kept reading his MCAT flashcards.

In the back, the samples were incubating beneath softly glowing heat lamps inside steel incubators, their dials blinking with quiet precision. The room was warm and close, saturated with the tang of agar and disinfectant. Stainless steel racks lined the counters, cradling rows of petri dishes and blood culture bottles, while bulky machines hummed in the background—centrifuges spinning quietly, PCR thermocyclers blinking with rhythmic light, and laminar flow hoods casting a sterile breeze over everything beneath their glass panels. The fluorescent lights above gave everything a pale, antiseptic glow. I moved among the labeled samples with surgical precision until I found his.

Blasto. No doubt. That bump was unmistakable. The idiot didn't even realize it. He didn't know that it had just grown overnight. With all his blackouts, he assumed it was trauma. And the residents? They wouldn't question it. Not when he kept saying he was mugged.

They'd miss it entirely. And that, more than anything, was the thrill. Being seen by no one, shaping outcomes from the shadows—it was control in its purest form. Each oversight validated the craft. Each miss proved their blindness. The system wasn't broken—it was malleable. And I was the only one with the hands steady enough to mold it.

I switched the labels with a sleight of hand, as easy as changing a name tag. Then I turned to the rack of urine samples to double check—no one had ordered the blasto antigen. Of course they hadn't.

Let them chase the wrong diagnoses. This guy doesn't deserve treatment.

I smiled and slipped away into the dark.

Chapter 24

Leaning In

Logan Dean

* * *

The house was quiet but not still. Video files hummed on Logan's laptop, the fan making a soft whir as it rendered another segment of ICU hallway footage. Navarro sat beside him on the couch, eyes fixed on the screen, her posture slouched with the kind of fatigue that goes bone-deep. Tyler had excused himself an hour ago—some development in a body found by the river case. Logan hadn't asked. He just nodded, grateful for the privacy.

They were watching the third angle on the carotid code. It was a corner room, so it could be seen from multiple hallways. And like the others, it showed nothing unusual. Just chaos. Doctors rushing in. Elise commanding the room. Blood. But no one out of place. No one slipping out a side door or lurking at the edge of the frame. The whole thing was awful and mesmerizing, and Logan couldn't look away.

"Back it up a few seconds," Elise said, voice low.

He rewound. She squinted at the screen. "That nurse. Left of frame. Is that Katie or Melissa?"

"Melissa," Logan said without hesitation. "Katie's the one with the streaks in her hair."

"Right."

It had been hours. They'd reviewed the hallway footage from 9 of the 28 code events and innumerable rapid responses recorded in the last 30 days—code strokes, sepsis alerts, rapid response calls, massive GI bleeds, post-op hypotension, sudden hypoxia, bradycardia on telemetry, cardiac arrest in dialysis, and more. Every case they could still retrieve. Every name that mattered.

Elise had scribbled notes across a stack of takeout bags, the ink bleeding through a smattering of oil stains. Napkins, receipts, the backs of paper menus—it looked like a madwoman's paper trail. With 28 code events and even more rapid responses, the notes were piling up faster than they could organize them. Every time they thought they had something, it turned out to be a glitch, a shadow, or a false lead. The system only stored 30 days of footage—which meant most of the suspicious events were already lost to time.

Until Logan saw something.

"Wait," he said, sitting forward. "Go back. Stroke unit hallway. Right after the code was called. See that? Someone is coming out of the room. Not a nurse. Not anyone else we know."

Elise leaned in. "Scrubs, badge, head down. Could be anyone."

"But it's not anyone I've seen before. And they didn't come back. They just walked out the south stairwell door."

"Can you enhance it?"

"Only so much," Logan said, already adjusting the contrast. The figure remained stubbornly nondescript. The kind of person your brain files away immediately.

"Like someone from housekeeping," Elise murmured. "Or maybe transport. Or even dietary. Someone with access."

Logan glanced at her. "You think?"

"I don't know. Maybe. But they timed that exit perfectly. They left exactly seven seconds after the code was called. Almost like they were waiting for it."

They watched the clip again. And again.

Logan's stomach flipped. He didn't recognize the figure, but something about the movement—too deliberate, too clean—made his instincts buzz.

He finally leaned back, rubbing his eyes. The clock on the wall read 3:17 AM. Elise yawned beside him, barely bothering to stifle it.

She shifted slightly, then leaned into him, resting her head on his muscular shoulder. His arm moved around her without thinking, a quiet gesture of protection and comfort. Logan didn't move. Didn't breathe for a second. He could feel her heartbeat, slow and steady, syncing with his own. They both kept their eyes on the screen, pretending to still watch the footage.

But the warmth seeped in. The exhaustion won. Her breathing slowed against his side, and her eyes began to drift close.

Elise was asleep before the next video ended.

Logan stayed awake longer. Watching the monitor fade to its screensaver. Listening to the quiet tick of the kitchen clock. Elise's head rested against his shoulder, and though the exhaustion had dulled his senses, the scent of her hair—cinnamon and vanilla—rose faintly with each of her steady breaths. It was oddly comforting. Intimate.

When he finally drifted off, it was with his arm pinned beneath her, the weight of her body a grounding pressure that anchored him in sleep. Even in that awkward position, he slept better than he had since the day he deployed.

He woke with the sun bleeding into the room, a soft golden haze that edged across the hardwood floors and over the blanket draped across Elise's legs. His arm was still trapped and tingling, but he didn't move. Instead, he inhaled again, catching the lingering scent of her hair. His mind, usually alert and scanning, was still. His body relaxed in a way it hadn't in years. The hum of morning traffic, the chirp of birds outside the window—it all faded into background noise.

Elise stirred beside him, stretching with a quiet sigh. She stretched slowly, spine arching, limbs unfolding like she was shaking off armor instead of sleep. It took her a second to place herself. Then she smiled.

"Morning," she said.

"Morning," Logan replied.

She didn't move away. They stayed like that, frozen in some brief, stolen moment where none of the hospital existed. No codes. No killer. Just the warmth of her body against his and the way the sunlight caught the edge of her lashes.

It was the first moment Logan could remember in years when he wasn't thinking ahead or looking behind.

He leaned in.

So did she.

The kiss was soft. Unhurried. Like slipping beneath still water after a storm. The moment their lips touched, Logan's world fell silent—no intrusive memories, no perceived dangers, no surge of adrenaline. Just her. His pulse slowed. The constant tension in his chest, the twitch in his fingers—gone. Elise quieted the noise in his head. His senses, usually sharp and scanning, dulled to a warm hush. He didn't feel hyperaware or on edge. He felt still. Safe. Understood.

Then her pager beeped.

The sound sliced through the quiet, jarring and mechanical.

She pulled back, breath catching. Logan blinked, coming back into himself, the moment already slipping away like steam off cooling skin.

"I have to go," she said, already standing.

He nodded. "Of course."

She paused at the door, her hand on the frame.

"Logan?"

"Yeah?"

"Thanks for... all of it."

He just nodded again, already reaching for the laptop.

Because whatever that kiss was, it couldn't stop what was coming next.

The door clicked shut behind her.

For a few seconds, he stayed still. The warmth of her body had faded from his side, but the quiet she left behind lingered.

And then, like floodwaters breaching a dam, the noise came rushing back.

Chapter 25

Tangible Proof

Elise Navarro

* * *

Elise arrived at her office just after seven in the morning, dragging herself through the mostly silent hallways of the hospital. Her scrubs were rumpled, her hair barely tied back, and her feet ached in protest. She had barely slept, but she felt invigorated. Her mind kept going back to that kiss, his hand cradling her cheek, his lips pressed into hers. Then a wave of guilt passed through her as she remembered all the victims, that there might be a new one decompensating right now. Someone could have been sabotaged while they were making out like teenagers without a care in the world.

Her keycard buzzed against the office reader. She hesitated for half a beat before opening the door—something felt off. The room was silent and still, the air faintly stale in a way that suggested no one had been inside for hours. It was ordinary, and yet her skin prickled with unease.

She stepped inside and closed the door behind her with a soft click. The early morning light filtering in through the blinds fell on a single object placed in the center of her desk: a brand-new, sealed central line kit. Her stomach dropped.

Her eyes immediately locked on the front pouch, to the clear sterile compartment where the instruction booklet usually sat. But this one didn't contain a booklet. Instead, there was a handwritten note folded neatly inside. The handwriting was tight, deliberate. Not rushed. Almost careful:

"You were right to be suspicious."

She didn't touch it. Her hand hovered above her desk before pulling her phone from her pocket.

"Logan. Tyler. My office. Now."

Tyler had been at the hospital early already, preparing to begin staff interviews. Both men arrived within five minutes.

Elise handed them gloves from the dispenser by her desk. All three snapped them on in tense silence. Logan closed the blinds, his jaw tightening.

Elise lifted the central line kit carefully, turning it over to confirm the sterile seals were intact. A sealed kit meant it had never been opened. Never been touched. Which meant someone had found a way to tamper with it before it ever reached the unit. That level of access—it was terrifying. Then she opened it.

Inside was the typical sterile blue disposable towel, folded around a tower of equipment. They unfolded it corner by corner, like a picnic blanket, leaving them with a square blue sterile workspace. Next came the perfectly folded sterile gown—arms tucked inward, ready to be slipped on. Elise set it aside, heart pounding.

Then the drape. A pale blue sheet with a transparent square with an oval cut out of it to expose the work site. It was folded in a way that arranged for fast, sterile unfolding. And beneath that, the molded plastic tray.

The tools gleamed under the overhead light: guidewire, introducer needle, scalpel, suture, dilator, syringe—and in its fitted ridge at the bottom of the tray, the catheter itself. Long, curved, flexible. Even from above, she could see it was broken.

There was a clean, sharp fracture right through the catheter. Anyone flushing medication or fluids through this line would be delivering it directly into the patient's chest cavity.

Elise stared. Her stomach twisted. This wasn't an accident. It was a message. The room buzzed with her rising pulse.

"Last September," she said. "I remember this. My resident presented it at the M&M conference. The patient coded after a central line was placed. They said it was a manufacturing defect. I reviewed that case when we started this, but dismissed it. The catheter was sealed. Sterile. I thought no one could have tampered with it."

She looked at Tyler and Logan. "I heard the family was suing the manufacturer."

Tyler leaned over the tray. He hesitated before speaking, his expression dark. "But this... this is proof. Someone tampered with a sealed kit. And they wanted you to know it."

Logan muttered something under his breath and scrubbed a hand down his face. He looked as shaken as she felt.

The clinical memory came back in full color:

A young woman with septic shock. Initially responsive to fluids and norepinephrine. But over the next four hours, she deteriorated. Vasopressin was added. Then epinephrine. Her blood pressure dropped further.

Something wasn't right. Elise had brought in her handheld ultrasound. A STAT echo showed a pericardial effusion. Tamponade. She called the residents over, teaching in real-time.

The patient was rushed to the cath lab for pericardiocentesis to remove the fluid surrounding her heart, literally crushing it from within. The fluid was thick and bloody, with flecks of necrotic tissue.

She was rushed straight to the OR.

The CT surgeon came out, his scrubs stained, shaking his head.

"I've never seen anything like it," he said. "The SVC was eaten through. Like it necrotized from the inside out. Lung tissue was dying. The pericardium looked like ground beef. There was nothing left to sew together."

They brought her back to the ICU so the family could say goodbye. She died twenty minutes later.

Elise had felt helpless, like she'd done everything right and still lost. The autopsy revealed a fractured catheter, and everyone blamed the equipment. Not a killer.

Until now.

Tyler broke the silence. "I know it's horrifying. But this—this is gold. This is the first piece of physical evidence that proves there's a perpetrator."

He sounded hopeful. Energized.

Elise couldn't match it. She could barely breathe. The rules had changed. This wasn't pattern recognition anymore. This was a declaration.

But deep down, she knew he was right.

They weren't chasing shadows anymore. They were hunting a killer—with proof in hand.

Chapter 26

Portrait of a Killer

Tyler Grayson

* * *

Tyler stepped out of Elise's office, the door clicking softly behind him. He stood in the hallway for a moment, letting the gravity of the evidence settle in. The sealed kit, the fracture, the message—'You were right to be suspicious'. Written in thick red marker. Block letters. Handwriting analysis would be useless.

But before he could dive headfirst into interviews and surveillance logs, there was one place he had to go.

He took the elevator down to the third floor and slipped into a quieter wing of the hospital. His mother's room was tucked into a corner, just far enough from the nurses' station to feel like a private little island.

When he entered, she was sitting up in bed, flipping through a magazine with a pair of dollar-store readers perched on her nose. The beeping machines at her bedside were quiet, stable. Her face lit up when she saw him.

"Tyler! What are you doing here in the middle of the day?" She looked up and smiled. "What's the matter, someone trying to steal my Jell-O?" She smiled at her own joke, then, more seriously, "You're not working graveyard shift again, are you?" she eyeballed him suspiciously.

He smiled, stepping forward to kiss her forehead. "Nope. Just figured I owed my favorite old lady a visit." He said it lightheartedly. If he didn't tease her a little, she would know something was wrong instantly.

She squinted at him, suspicious but amused. "You're up to something. You always get soft when you're hiding something."

"I'm not hiding anything," he lied smoothly. "You're just more important than anything else I could be doing."

She reached out and squeezed his hand. "You're sweet. But don't think this gets you out of bringing me that lemon cake from Molly's."

He chuckled. "Deal."

He stayed for ten minutes, just enough time to chat about her physical therapy, the food, and the cute nurse on the night shift. Then he left, jaw set.

From there, he made his way to the Neuro ICU.

The stroke patient's room was not quiet. Alarms chirped in distant syncopation. The soft hiss of oxygen mixed with the beeping of monitors, the shuffle of shoes on tile, the low murmur of nurses exchanging updates outside. It was the usual ICU chorus—sharp, clinical, never still.

Tyler stepped inside and introduced himself.

The kid—who looked to be around twenty—was propped against his pillows, a tray of untouched food beside him. It looked like gruel. No wonder he hadn't touched it. His left arm worked fine. His right side, not so much. A thick bandage wrapped around his forearm holding an IV line in place.

His speech was worse than Tyler expected—halting, garbled, and often just plain wrong.

"You... pole... blue?" the boy managed.

"Police? Yes. Detective Tyler Grayson. I'm here to help. I have a few questions, if that is OK."

The boy nodded. It took more effort than it should.

"Were you awake before the stroke?"

Another slow nod.

"Do you remember someone coming into your room?"

The boy nodded slowly. He took a long breath, gathering strength.

"Girl... woman... short... hair... candy..."

Tyler crouched beside the bed, voice gentle. "Wait—do you mean the woman was short, or just her hair?"

The boy's brow furrowed. He pointed vaguely to the top of his own head, then mimed a haircut with his good hand.

"Hair," he rasped. "Short. Bun. Not... her."

"Got it. Short hair. Not a short woman."

A tiny nod.

"Did she say anything?"

The boy's face twisted again. His lips moved, but nothing coherent came out. He tapped his forehead, clearly trying to conjure a word, then gave up and slapped his palm gently against the sheet in frustration.

A thin sheen of sweat had broken out across his brow, his whole body rigid with the effort of pulling words from broken circuitry. His left hand trembled—not from weakness, but rage.

"It's okay," Tyler said gently. "We can come back to that."

"Had you seen her before?"

The boy shook his head.

"You don't recognize her as one of the residents? Nurses? Respiratory therapists?"

Another shake.

"Did she touch you?"

This time, the boy shook his head no, then made a quick motion with his left hand—fingers forming a circle and tapping against his chest, like mimicking the placement of a stethoscope. Then he mimed placing fingers against his IV site.

"She listened to your chest? Then gave you something?"

Nod.

Tyler noticed the sketchpad beside him. Charcoal smudges darkened his fingertips.

"You draw?"

The kid nodded faintly.

"May I?"

He handed Tyler the pad. Dozens of faces filled the pages—staff, patients, nurses. Hyper-realistic. Astonishingly detailed. Tyler flipped through until he reached a blank page. "Is this from today? Can you still draw?"

The kid smiled for the first time—just the left side of his face lifting in a crooked grin. It revealed a perfect row of teeth on one side, bright and youthful, while the other side remained slack, still drawn down in a stroke-scarred frown. He raised his left hand to his forehead, wiping imaginary sweat from his brow.

His saving grace was that he was a lefty. The kid still had something.

"Could you draw the woman who came in? The one who was there before you got sick? Just close your eyes and try to remember."

The boy hesitated.

"You don't need to speak. Just draw."

"But...sleep see..."

"Are you saying you were sleeping? I thought you were awake."

"Sleep awake."

"I'm sorry, I'm not catching this one." The guy was starting to look frustrated again. "Let's slow it down and act it out. Did you play charades as a kid?" Tyler asked.

A slow nod. Then he closed his eyes and let his head loll to the side, like he had fallen asleep mid-conversation. Then, without moving his head or opening his eyes, his left hand moved to his chest as he shook himself awake. His eyes fluttered half open. His hand moved around his chest like he had a stethoscope again, then over to the IV for the injection, and then his eyes drifted back closed.

"Got it," Tyler said with a smile. "She woke you up, so you didn't have a great look. The lights were probably off, too."

The left side of the kid's face looked relieved. The right maintained its sad demeanor.

"Don't worry about that," Tyler encouraged him. "Just close your eyes and see what comes back to you. It doesn't have to be as detailed as this notebook of masterpieces."

The boy relaxed for the first time since Tyler entered the room. He closed his eyes, took a few slow breaths, then opened them and reached for the pad.

The charcoal pencil moved slowly at first, his hand trembling slightly. Then with more confidence. The strokes became more defined. He was steady. Focused.

Tyler didn't interrupt. He sat quietly, watching.

Five minutes. Ten. Fifteen.

Finally, the boy handed it over.

The drawing showed a woman in scrubs and a blue jacket, posture upright, hand on the door like she belonged there. Her mask obscured the lower half of her face.

"This is great. Better than anything our sketch artist could come up with, if you're ever looking for a job."

The right side of his face looked proud.

"Do you have any idea how old she was?"

His left shoulder raised and dropped.

"Did you notice any wrinkles around her eyes?"

Another left-sided shrug. "Dark." He looked pleased with himself for getting the right word the first time.

"Did she say anything?"

The boy's face twisted with frustration. He pointed to his mouth. Then tried again. "Talk talk..."

Tyler waited.

"Talk talk...Talk talk...Talk talk..." he repeated like a broken record that couldn't make it past that first word.

The boy shook his head violently, then grabbed the pencil again. He drew a crude outline of a continent. Labeled it.

"Europe?" Tyler guessed.

The boy nodded. Then pointed to the right of the map.

"Eastern Europe?"

Another nod.

"You couldn't understand her well?"

A frown. Then a shrug.

Tyler tried one more time. "She had an accent?"

The boy hesitated, then nodded again.

It wasn't much.

But it was something.

Every fragment mattered now. Tyler had seen cases cracked on less. A name. A scent. A word half-formed in the mouth of a dying witness. This was more than a clue—it was a start.

He thanked the boy, promised to keep him in the loop, and took the sketch with him, carefully sliding it into a folder. Out in the hallway, he stared at it again.

The eyes haunted him. Even half-covered, there was something deliberate about the posture and stance. Like she owned the room. Like she knew she'd never be caught.

She was getting bolder.

They were closer than ever.

But so was she.

Chapter 27

The Eyes Have It

The Killer

* * *

I spotted him the moment he stepped out of the ICU room—Detective Tyler Grayson, still wearing that tired, upright posture like it proved something. A single sheet of paper was in his hand, held flat and carefully like it mattered more than it should. I didn't need to see it up close. I already knew.

It was me.

Not fully, of course. The mask still did its job. The jacket, the posture—generic. Swappable. But the eyes… the eyes were mine. Exact. Sharp and knowing. The kind of detail only an artist could conjure from memory.

For just a breath, it made me still.

But then came the shrug.
Let them see my eyes.
Let them memorize them.
I'd been right there under their noses for months. They didn't recognize me. This changed nothing.

If anything, it was flattering. Almost tender. Like being seen by someone who could finally appreciate my work. There was an intimacy to it—a recognition that went beyond suspicion. A connection. The artist had captured me, seen me, and somehow that made him feel like mine.

He glanced both ways down the hall. Never saw me. Typical. Nobody ever saw me. I was counting on it.

I'd been careful. The boy in that room was a mistake—not the event itself, no, I'd planned that one beautifully. But I hadn't expected him to remember so much.
Still, no real harm.
He was an art student, not a goddamn surveillance drone.

I conjured a memory of the drawing. No doubt it was good—maybe even beautiful. But it wouldn't matter. A mask. A jacket. Scrubs. I'd worn three different hairstyles that week alone. Wigs made everything easy.

As I walked down the hall and passed through the supply closet—a room as big as any patient room, filled with racks of supplies needed to care for patients—I moved from the ICU door through to the hallway. I walked right past a nurse getting IV supplies. Without hesitation in my gait, I silently reached out and grabbed a pair of tweezers and then exited to the hallway.

Let them play detective. Let them chase shadows in hallways and click through grainy footage until their eyes bled. It wouldn't help. They were playing chess on a board that I had already set on fire.

And yet, something about Tyler made me pause.

He didn't rattle easily.
Didn't waste time.
Didn't ask questions he didn't already know the answers to.

He was the dangerous one.

As I locked myself in an employee bathroom and started patiently reshaping my eyebrows, I made a mental note to keep him busy. Maybe something dramatic. A new incident.

Something messy.

Something loud.

Something that would chew up their attention for days.

The fluorescent lights buzzed above me, casting a pale flicker across the mirror. I stared at myself—not the real me, of course, but this version. This avatar of convenience. I plucked with slow precision. The tension in my shoulders eased with each hair. I wasn't just changing my appearance. I was erasing their progress.

He was a good kid, that artist. Too good. And it made me almost sentimental for a moment. Almost. If the world were fair, he would be drawing in a gallery somewhere. But the world wasn't fair. It was mine.

I looked at my new thinner eyebrows and judged the women who waste their time doing this routinely. As soon as my shift was over, I would go get some lashes from the drugstore across the street. And maybe after the hospital quiets for the night, I can go borrow some brown contacts from the ophthalmology clinic. By tomorrow, I would have nothing in common with that masked woman in the picture.

I began walking again, slow and steady. A nurse passed me and offered a quick nod. I returned it with the perfect expression—neutral, pleasant, forgettable. I made a quick stop near the staff lockers and swapped out my badge for a clean one. I had a half-dozen more stashed in my things. Residents were always leaving them behind—at nursing stations during a rush, outside code rooms, dropped after cafeteria scans, or still clipped to the lab coats draped haphazardly over chairs. Careless. And convenient.

On my way out, I passed the volunteer desk. The girl there didn't even look up.

Good.

The sketch wouldn't matter.
The badge logs wouldn't matter.
But that boy…

He remembered too much.
He was a loose thread.
And loose threads needed cutting.

Chapter 28
Violation
Elise Navarro

* * *

Elise stood in the security office, arms crossed, posture rigid. The air was stale, with the faint scent of burnt coffee and plastic from the old keyboard covers. The hum of the monitors blended with the soft clicking of the surveillance controls, a mechanical symphony that only added to Elise's growing unease. Logan sat at the main monitor, rewinding footage from earlier in the week, while Tyler leaned against the filing cabinet, tapping a pen against his leg in a slow rhythm.

"Residents are talking," Elise said finally.

Logan looked over, eyebrows lifted.

"They've noticed the 'real' cop wandering around the hospital."

"Ouch." Logan clutched his heart, feigning heartbreak.

Tyler didn't react, just let the pen tap twice more before slipping it behind his ear. "They were going to figure it out when we start the interviews."

Logan clicked into a new feed. "Let's get through this footage of your office so Tyler can get to those interviews."

The screen blinked, then loaded footage from early that morning. Elise stepped closer, eyes narrowing.

A lone figure walked into frame. Blue scrub jacket, surgical mask, cap. Probably a female, from the curve of the hips. But other than that, the scrubs and mask hid any defining features. A central line bundle was tucked under her left arm, and a badge was in her right hand. She waved her badge in front of the sensor. Elise could almost hear the door unlock.

Logan paused the video as the figure stepped through the door. The timestamp in the corner read 01:09:47. With a couple of taps on his keyboard, Logan pulled up the badge log. Avery Cole. Next to it was her thumbnail ID picture, looking even younger than she did ten years ago, when Elise first met her.

Logan rewound again. The grainy video showed a scrubbed figure walking down the hallway—no clear face, nothing actionable.
They watched the figure approach Elise's office. Swipe the badge. The door clicked open.

Then nothing.

The figure disappeared inside.

A timestamp in the corner ran for forty minutes before she emerged, empty-handed.

Elise's stomach clenched. "Forty minutes?"

Logan nodded. "Yeah. Sixty seconds to drop a kit. So… what the hell was she doing in there?"

They watched the figure slip away and walk off camera like a phantom. No one noticed. No one looked twice.

Elise stepped back, hand running through her hair. She felt stripped bare. Exposed.

The office had already been sealed—taped off and labeled as under construction. They had to inform Facilities that there was a leak in the ceiling tiles to keep people away. The paper sign looked flimsy now, a poor excuse for the truth it was hiding. However, the rumors still managed to spread.

Elise stared at the screen, watching the footage loop.

"I feel violated," she said quietly. "Like she crawled inside my life and just... lingered."

Logan met her eyes. "We'll find her."

Elise moved closer to the screen. "She's careful. But the message she left in my office—that was arrogance."

Tyler's phone buzzed, and he glanced at the screen. "Time for the first interview," he said, already halfway out the door.

As the door closed behind him, Logan remained seated, eyes still flicking across camera feeds. Elise leaned over the back of his chair, her posture finally relaxing.

Then Logan said, almost offhandedly, "I've got an idea."

She watched him through the monitor as he slipped out of the office and made his way down the hallway. He passed a maintenance man balancing on a ladder and smoothly plucked the measuring tape from the cart parked underneath. A few seconds later, he snagged a black Sharpie from the nurse's station like he belonged there.

Elise blinked. "What are you doing, Logan Dean?" she muttered under her breath, unable to suppress the small smile tugging at her lips.

Logan stopped outside her office door—the very same one the intruder had entered at 01:09. He flicked out the measuring tape, bracing it vertically along the frame. Carefully, he began marking off height notches in black Sharpie, inch by inch, from 4'6" to 6'6". Twenty-four dark slashes against pale beige paint. Each one exact.

Then he turned and walked back toward the camera, and Elise—watching on the feed—let her eyes linger a little longer than necessary. The purposeful stride. The clean lines of his profile. His broad shoulders. Her stomach fluttered, and she shook her head, half amused, half irritated with herself. Were these murders drawing them closer—or just blurring the line between trauma and intimacy?

Her thoughts scattered as the door swung open again and Logan walked back in.

"I want to try something," he said. He pulled up the footage again—1:09 a.m.—and split the screen. On one side, the scrubbed, masked figure. On the other, the current live feed of the hallway, with the new height markers now visible.

Logan paused the video on the frame where the masked woman passed through. He aligned it side by side with the current live feed, showing the Sharpie lines on the doorframe.

The woman's head lined up perfectly between the marks.

Elise leaned in.

"Five-seven," he confirmed. "Exactly."

A thrill prickled at the back of her neck.

They finally had something measurable.

Chapter 29

Mercy

Tyler Grayson

* * *

Tyler had commandeered an unused storage room tucked behind radiology—bare walls, no windows, and just enough space for a folding table and two mismatched chairs. It wasn't an official interview room, but with the overhead light flickering and the faint smell of antiseptic clinging to the air, it served the purpose. Tyler sat in one chair, calm and professional, a legal pad resting in front of him. A steaming cup of black hospital coffee sat half empty beside it. He preferred cream, but black was more intimidating.

Across from him, Ravi Patel fidgeted in his seat. His leg bounced beneath the table, jittery and constant. One hand twisted the edge of his white coat, the other tapped sporadically on the tabletop. There was a slight tremble to his fingers—barely noticeable, but telling.

Logan and Elise watched from the security office, the feed streaming in real-time on one of the corner monitors. Elise leaned forward, her eyes locked on the screen. Logan had his arms folded, watching Tyler with quiet interest.

Tyler started gently.

"Thanks for coming in, Dr. Patel. I appreciate your time."

Ravi gave a faint nod. "Of course. Happy to help."

"I know this investigation feels heavy," Tyler said, his voice soft. "But I want to start by acknowledging how hard this job is. Especially for someone like you. I've heard you're a deeply compassionate physician."

Ravi blinked. "I try."

"Compassionate physicians see a lot of suffering," Tyler continued. "And sometimes... they feel it more than others."

Ravi's expression didn't shift, but his fingers tapped once on the tabletop.

"There are people who struggle to see patients in pain. Those who feel like the system fails them. Like their hands are tied. Have you ever felt that way?"

Ravi hesitated, then gave a half-shrug. "Everyone feels helpless sometimes. Doesn't mean we get to play God."

Tyler nodded slowly. "But you understand the impulse. To ease someone's pain."

Ravi looked at him for a beat too long. "If you work here and you don't, you're either new or a psychopath."

Tyler offered a small smile. "Fair enough."

He flipped a page on his legal pad. "I want to ask about the med room. We have logs showing you entered it quite a few times over the past few months. More than most physicians."

Ravi's jaw tightened. "Sometimes I grab Tylenol or Zofran for patients. Saves the nurses a step."

"Of course. Do you always log the withdrawals under your name?"

"No. Doctors don't have access to the Pyxis. I use the nurse's badge if they ask me to grab something. It's not a big deal. I'm not hiding anything. Everyone does it."

Elise and Logan exchanged a glance.

"It's not a crime to be in the med room," Ravi said, more defensive now. "I wasn't stealing anything."

Tyler made a note. "I didn't say you were."

Ravi rubbed the back of his neck. A sheen of sweat had formed at his hairline. His eyes flitted between Tyler and the door.

"What about some of the codes you've attended recently?" Tyler asked. "You weren't listed as the responding physician for some of them. But you were there."

"This is a teaching hospital. Everyone responds to codes."

"Not everyone. And not that many."

Ravi exhaled through his nose. "I like to be there. Learn something. Help if I can."

Tyler leaned back, folding his hands. "Tell me about Jamie Lin. You two are close."

Ravi's face closed off. "She's a colleague. We work a lot of the same shifts."

"Word is, you two are closer than that. Whispered conversations. Teamwork, even when you're not assigned to the same cases."

Ravi didn't respond. He just looked at the tabletop.

"Are you two romantically involved?"

"No. Did someone say we are?" Ravi asked, taken aback by the accusation.

"Not at all. Just that you spend a lot of time together and are often in the corners whispering about something. I have heard the term 'colluding' more than once."

"That's nonsense. We don't get out much. Gossip is the only form of entertainment around here."

"Do you think Jamie would do anything to hurt a patient?"

"No. Never." He was trying to sound confident, but there was an involuntary hesitation in his voice as he remembered that patient they let die right in front of them.

"Would you?"

Ravi looked up. His eyes were glassy now. "I became a doctor to help people."

"That's what everyone says."

Tyler let the silence stretch. He tapped his pen twice against the pad, then glanced back up.

"One more thing. We have footage of you outside Room 517 just before the patient coded. Can you tell me what you were doing there?"

Ravi's face tensed. "That was part of my pre-rounds. I was seeing patients. That's exactly where I was supposed to be."

Tyler didn't answer, just jotted something down.

Then he stood.

"That's all for now. Thanks, Dr. Patel."

Ravi stood slowly, his movements stiff. "Let me know if I can help."

When he left, Elise and Logan continued to watch the screen.

"Something about him feels off," Elise said.

Logan nodded. "He's unraveling. But he's too disorganized for this."

Elise agreed. "He's hiding something. Maybe he knows something. Or is covering for someone."

Elise stared at the screen long after Ravi's image disappeared. Her gut told her the real killer wouldn't have looked that scared. Sociopaths rarely look scared.

Chapter 30

Vengeance

Tyler Grayson

* * *

Tyler sat across from Avery in the same sparse storage room he'd used to interview Ravi. But unlike Ravi, Avery looked far more comfortable in the deliberately uncomfortable space. She sat with her back straight, shoulders squared—a woman seemingly with nothing to hide. Or, Tyler mused, the demeanor of a complete sociopath. He was about to find out which.

Avery sat stiffly, arms folded across her chest, her ID badge clipped to her scrub top and retractable lanyard wound tight. Her expression was guarded.

"You probably know why I asked to speak with you," Tyler said, keeping his tone neutral.

She gave a flat shrug. "Not really. I've been working a lot of doubles. If this is about missed documentation—"

"It's not," Tyler interrupted gently. "Nothing disciplinary. We're conducting a quiet investigation into some irregularities following recent codes. Just connecting some dots."

Her posture stiffened further. "I'm RT. I show up when people crash. That's the job."

Tyler nodded. "And you do it well. This isn't about your clinical work. We noticed a badge swipe into Dr. Navarro's office yesterday morning. It was yours."

Avery blinked. "Bullshit."

"It was registered to your badge at 1:09 a.m."

"Still bullshit." Avery retorted without hesitation. "You can make up as many details as you'd like. I know I have never entered that office without an invitation." She hesitated a moment and then added, "Or when Elise wasn't there."

"Elise? Most people around here call her Dr. Navarro."

"Most people around here are weak residents who need to learn to respect the hierarchy. Elise and I have spent a lot of years making life-and-death decisions together. Our bodies are often pushed up against each other, crowded around a code patient. I wouldn't say we were friends, we don't call each other on our days off, but we are very close."

Tyler was reminded of his brothers-in-arms. He got this. There were a lot of guys who he didn't like very much, but trusted with his life. He would do anything for those assholes.

"So then, where were you at 1:09 a.m.?"

She hesitated. "I was at home, asleep. And alone. I haven't worked a night shift in years."

Tyler nodded slowly. "Your badge says otherwise. Could anybody else have used it?"

Something flickered across her face—a brief moment of understanding. "It was clipped to my lab coat, hanging in my locker in the RT department. Where it always is when I am off."

"In a locked locker?"

"No. The lock is hanging there, and it looks locked. But I can never remember the combo, so I don't spin the numbers to set the lock. "

"So anyone passing by could've grabbed it."

She rubbed her temple. "Yeah. Shit. I guess if they thought to check. I didn't even think…" she trailed off.

Tyler let the silence linger. "Do you know what was found in Dr. Navarro's office?"

Avery looked up, cautious. Her emboldened demeanor was fading. "Something bad, I assume."

"Something incriminating. We have already pulled prints from it." Tyler lied. Forensics told him this morning that it was clean. "Are they going to match yours?"

She paled. "No. I mean, I didn't know. I swear to God, I don't know anything about that. Can you tell me what it is?"

Tyler watched her oscillate from defiance to visible distress. Her voice lost its edge.

"I know how this looks," she said. "But I wouldn't hurt anyone. Not on purpose. Not ever."

Tyler nodded. "We're just gathering facts. Is there anyone who can verify your alibi?"

Avery's eyes widened. She started to shake her head, then paused. "Nobody was with me...my...my husband died a year ago... but maybe—maybe my Ring camera picked me up? I mean, if I came in or out, it would have caught it."

She was scrambling now. "Or my phone location data. You can check that, right? I never left the house. You'll see."

Her voice was higher pitched than before, brittle at the edges. Tyler didn't respond immediately, just scribbled another note. That panic—that shift—told him more than words ever could.

"Can I ask… was this about me?" she added after a long moment. "Do you think I did this because of what happened to my husband?"

Tyler met her eyes but didn't answer.

Her expression cracked. "I was angry. I am angry. But that doesn't make me a killer."

"As I said—we're just gathering facts."

As he walked her out, Avery looked back at him with a hollow stare. There was fear in her eyes—not fear of being accused, but fear that she was somehow part of something she didn't understand. That someone had used her name to commit a crime. Her usually impeccable posture was starting to round forward.

"One last question, if you don't mind. How tall are you?"

"Five seven. Why?"

Tyler just smiled gently, placed a hand on her upper back and told her she could go, his voice calm and steady as he thanked her for her time.

Tyler returned to the office, unfolding the drawing from the stroke patient beside his notebook. Two things now linked to Avery Cole. The sketch wasn't too far off, if you looked at her from the right angle.

He wasn't sure if it meant she was involved.

Or if the killer had access to endless identities.

Chapter 31
Debrief
Elise Navarro

* * *

Tyler sat alone in the repurposed interview room, jotting a few quiet notes between interviews. His posture slouched with fatigue, the only sound in the room the faint hum of the air vent above.

Logan and Elise entered, each balancing a takeout container—Thai food tonight, fragrant and warm. Tyler looked up, a tired smile tugging at the corner of his mouth.

"You're a lifesaver," he muttered as Elise handed him a container. They sat in mismatched office chairs, a makeshift table between them formed from an unused supply cart.

The silence between them was companionable, punctuated only by the clink of chopsticks and muted chewing. It wasn't until Logan broke open a packet of soy sauce that Elise spoke.

"Avery didn't feel right at first," she said. "Too stiff. But the second you mentioned the badge swipe, she cracked. Not like a guilty person. More like someone blindsided."

Tyler nodded, mouth full. He swallowed. "She was scrambling by the end. Offered to give us Ring cam footage, location data.

"Maybe she was being defensive," Logan countered. Those aren't exactly airtight. She has a back door, and phones could be left at home."

"I know. She seemed panicked more than defensive."

Logan added, "If she didn't do it, then someone used her badge. That means someone's collecting them."

"That's what we have to figure out," Elise said, leaning forward. "But that could be anybody. People don't treat their badges as secure property. Except the residents who have meal cards on them. Who else would want them?! They have no street value."

They moved to the security station in the corner of the room. Logan tapped the keyboard and brought up the footage of the person entering Elise's office.

The timestamp read 01:09. The figure in the video wore a blue scrub jacket, cap, and surgical mask. From a distance, the build matched Avery's, but something didn't sit right.

"Pause it," Elise said.

Logan did.

"She doesn't move like Avery," Elise murmured. "Her gait's wrong."

"You see that?" Logan pointed at the slow drag of the left foot. "There's a limp. A pretty noticeable one."

"Avery doesn't limp. Never has."

"Could be faked," Tyler offered, wiping his mouth with a napkin.

Logan tilted his head, studying the frame. "Posture's different, too. Shoulders set wider. Might be padding under the scrub jacket."

Tyler pulled up Avery's employee records on the tablet. "She travels often. Uses her vacation days. Takes time off. Not around enough to match the killer's timeline."

Elise nodded slowly. "If anything, she avoids the hospital. That doesn’t fit the pattern."

The trio sat in silence for a beat longer.

Finally, Tyler stood and crumpled the food wrappers into the bag. "Time for the next round."

Logan clapped a hand on his shoulder as he passed.

Elise stayed behind, her eyes fixed on the paused image.

Avery's badge. Someone else's body.

The figure stood frozen on the screen.

Elise stared at it, unsettled, her food forgotten.

Chapter 32
Just Because

Tyler Grayson

* * *

The interview room was quiet, a pocket of sterile calm in the middle of a hospital swirling with tension. Tyler sat across from a tall, wiry woman in light blue scrubs. Her badge read Tanya, and she nursed a steaming cup of coffee like it was the only warmth she'd known all shift.

She looked at ease, but only superficially—her shoulders held just a little too tight, her eyes sharp and restless.

"Thanks for meeting with me," Tyler said, his tone easy but direct. "I know you've already been helpful, but I wanted to follow up."

Tanya offered a shrug. "Happy to help, I guess. Things have been... weird lately. Everyone's on edge."

Tyler nodded. "You were present for several of the recent codes. I want to ask you a few questions about them."

"Right. I did compressions on the kid in 514. I was at the bedside for the guy who bled out from the neck thing. And I helped set up the rapid infuser for that old lady with the GI bleed. And that was just this past week. It's kind of what we do here."

"Why were you involved in codes outside the ICU? Isn't that where you were assigned?"

"No. I was the rapid response nurse those days. It would have been my responsibility to evaluate anybody decompensating on the floor and to respond to any stroke alerts or code blues."

Tyler tapped his pen against his notebook. "Did anything stand out to you? Any odd behavior, misplaced supplies, people where they shouldn't be?"

Tanya sipped her coffee, brow furrowing. "Hard to say. We float so many nurses in and out now, sometimes I barely know who I'm working with. There was one float nurse—I can't even remember her name. Seemed jumpy. Always showing up in rooms she wasn't assigned to. Said she was helping, but... I don't know... maybe I am overthinking it."

"When was this?"

"A few weeks ago, maybe. It wasn't a code, just a patient who decompensated suddenly. But now that you ask..."

Tyler made a note.

"What about any odd behavior from ancillary staff?" Tyler asked. "Anyone from respiratory? Pharmacy? Security? Central supply?"

Tanya tilted her head. "I mean, Madison's had some bad luck lately—patients pulling lines, that sort of thing. People have noticed. But she seems wrecked about it, like she's taking it personally. Avery… she's been kind of standoffish since her husband died, but that's been going on a while. Nothing really jumps out at me."

She paused. "Housekeeping and central supply are always around somewhere in the background, but I don't know them very well."

"Can I ask something?" Tanya said. Her voice dropped and she leaned in almost imperceptibly; her fingers tightened around her cup.

"Of course."

"Is Ravi under suspicion?" Her eyes searched his face. "People are talking. He's been acting strange."

"Should he be under suspicion?"

"Isn't that your job to figure out?"

"It is, but you work closely with him. Anything strike you as suspicious?"

"I don't want to speak badly of him. He's a good doctor. And he seems like a good guy. He is always taking extra time with families who need it. He gives his pager to the nurse so he isn't interrupted, which is definitely a rarity. He looks those families in the eyes and is honest with them. He listens better than most doctors. It is hard to imagine a guy that compassionate doing what you're talking about."

"But?" Tyler questioned the hesitation in her voice.

"But…I'm not sure… he's been off lately. Taking losses too hard. He has been getting really upset when families won't sign a DNR or withdraw care. I mean, we all get frustrated delivering futile care, but he has been getting actually angry. As if it were personal."

"Anything else unusual with Ravi?"

"Nothing abnormal. He is deteriorating—run down, bloodshot eyes, distracted. That is kind of normal halfway through training. By this point, they are all sleep deprived and stressed out."

"You also mentioned you once saw Dr. Lin enter a room just before a code?"

Tanya hesitated. "Yeah. Room 446 two months ago. I was on the floor at a rapid across the hall. It was a young guy, admitted for a Crohn's flare. She went in, and maybe five minutes later, the alarms were going off. She said she found him unresponsive and called the code, but that would have taken less than a minute. What was she doing in there for the other four minutes?

Could be nothing, but... Lin is always intense. Like, really intense."

Tyler nodded again, keeping his expression neutral. "Thank you. That's helpful context."

They spoke for a few more minutes—routine questions, nothing dramatic. Tanya seemed honest, but she was definitely nervous. Tyler left the door open for another conversation if needed.

After she left, Tyler's phone buzzed. A message from Logan: "You get the vibe she was trying to be helpful, or trying to nudge you toward Jamie?"

Tyler exhaled. Could be both, he typed back. Or could be someone else planting seeds. Either way, worth keeping an eye on.

She's got no motive. Logan pointed out.

Does a psychopathic serial killer need a motive? Maybe she thinks it's fun. Or thrilling.

Logan agreed. I guess someone thinks it's fun. We'll keep her on the radar.

Tyler leaned back and stared at his notes.

It was starting to feel like everyone had a theory.

And none of them were the truth.

Chapter 33
The Thrill
Tyler Grayson

* * *

Tyler was sitting in one of the two mismatched chairs in his commandeered storage room, back pushed against the wall to make room for the chair on the other side of the folding table. The single overhead light gave it the feel of a cinematic interrogation room. Tyler stared at the empty walls, a legal pad resting in front of him, lost in the memories of his most recent interviews.

Dr. Leilani Kealoha stepped through the door, the only thing that broke up the monotony of the wall, coffee in hand, her white coat crisp over pale blue scrubs. Her dark hair was braided and looped into a bun, a pen clipped to the edge of her V-neck, and her badge angled just-so at her hip. She looked, in a word, together.

She gave Tyler a wary but polite nod and sat without waiting for permission. "So," she said, arching an eyebrow. "Am I a witness or a suspect?"

Tyler smiled, keeping his voice light. "I won't know until after the interview. For now, you are just someone whose insight might help us make sense of some patterns. I appreciate you taking the time. I know things have been... a lot."

Leilani gave a dry little laugh. "That's one way to put it. Half the hospital is too sleep-deprived to think straight, and the other half is busy trading rumors like baseball cards. I'm sure you've heard some of them. Gossip is like currency around here."

"I have," Tyler admitted. "I'm hoping to get a clearer picture. We've been cross-referencing badge swipes, code logs, and security footage. Your name came up quite a few times."

"Not surprised," she shrugged, "I gravitate towards action. I'm starting my critical care fellowship in the fall. I do as many ICU rotations as I can - this year I've done a month each of medical ICU, surgical ICU, neuro ICU, and cardiac ICU. Plus, a trauma rotation and an anesthesia rotation. And when I'm not doing critical care, the other residents come to find me for help. Most of them hate being in the unit."

"So you've been present for a number of the recent codes."

"Too many."

He gave her a moment. "Any of them stand out to you?"

Leilani stared at her coffee, thinking. "A couple of patients declined faster than I expected. One in particular—a middle-aged man recovering from a routine post-op. Vitals stable, pain controlled, eating breakfast. Then, thirty minutes later, he was unresponsive. No sign of infection, no obvious complication."

"Do you remember who was already at the bedside?"

"Jamie. She said she found the patient unresponsive."

"She said? You don't believe her?"

Leilani scrunched her brow, looking conflicted. "It isn't that I don't believe her. We've all walked in on a pulseless patient. Last week, I was walking out of the hospital when I passed a room just as a patient went into VTach. I ended up doing two rounds of CPR before I took my backpack off."

"I understand. These things happen around here. So what gave you pause on this occasion?"

"She had been in there five minutes. We were discussing the labs at the nursing station, then she went in, and five minutes later, she called that code. It should take less than a minute to figure out someone doesn't have a pulse and call for help. I've always wondered what she was doing in there for the other four minutes."

Tyler nodded slowly. "You know her well?"

"Well enough. She's brilliant. Focused. Comes off arrogant sometimes, but honestly? She's earned it. I've never seen her falter in a code, never seen her unsure. She's always first in the room, first on the chest. Most residents hesitate—compressions are brutal, and frankly, a little traumatizing—but not her. She doesn't flinch. Lately though… I don't know. She's been wound so tight I'm afraid she's going to snap. And her eyes—there's this… excitement. Like she's not just reacting to chaos. Like she's waiting for it."

"What about Dr. Patel?"

"Ravi? He's a mess. I say that with love. He's sharp, but he hasn't been sleeping. Always has that thousand-yard stare. I once caught him in the med room late—said he was grabbing Tylenol, but the drawer he had open was controlled substances. He made a lame excuse about a glitch in the software and the wrong drawer popping open."

"You didn't report it?"

"I wasn't sure. It was just a second. I was very sleep-deprived. What if I didn't see it right, or he was telling the truth? An accusation like that would have ruined his career, ruined his life. You have to be sure about something like that."

"Anyone else you've noticed? Float nurses, techs, anyone who doesn't belong in patient rooms?"

"There was a CNA on a recent shift—I don't remember his name. He seemed bitter. Got into a loud argument with one of the residents during rounds. Aggressive body language, sarcasm. It caught everyone off guard. I think it was Dr. Freeman he clashed with, and a couple of nurses saw it too—Lara and Denise from nights."

Tyler made a note. "And the Pyxis incident? Which pharmacist was that?"

"Not sure, but the nurse who told me about it was Jessa. I don't know if she formally reported it, but she mentioned it in passing during sign-out."

"Thanks. You've been more than helpful."

Leilani met his eyes. "Just promise me if something isn't right, you won't let it get swept under. Some of us have worked too hard to protect these patients."

He nodded. "I promise."

As he walked her to the door, Tyler made a mental note to follow up on her observations about the pharmacy, the CNA confrontation, and the unknown drawer activity.

Back in the quiet room, he sat for a moment in the empty chair across from hers.

Leilani was sharp. She paid attention. And she wasn't afraid to speak up.

That made her either an invaluable ally—or a future target.

Chapter 34
Unheard
The Boy

* * *

He despised not being able to talk. Loathed the way his tongue fumbled inside his mouth like it was too big, too heavy, like it belonged to someone else. The words started out normal in his head; he knew what he wanted to say, but by the time they reached his mouth, they were scrambled.

He hated that no one understood. Back when he volunteered at the nursing home, he'd always felt compassion for the stroke patients—helping them dress, eat, and shuffle down the hallway. But now he understood them. The rage. The helplessness. The way every moment felt like shouting into a void that didn't care, that couldn't even hear. How did they ever learn to accept this pitiful existence?

The new nurse—her name was Claire, he thought—was nice. She smiled a lot. She didn't rush. She crouched beside the bed when she talked to him and tilted her head like she really wanted to understand. That helped—a little.

But not enough.

"Try again?" she asked gently, holding the whiteboard closer to him.

He tried to write. His left hand moved slowly, deliberately. The marker squeaked across the board, leaving shapes even he couldn't read.

He grunted in frustration, unable to understand why he could draw detailed portraits but couldn't form basic letters. It made no sense. And it made him feel broken. He dropped the marker. He was feeling increasingly desperate to make her understand.

Claire picked it up and placed her hand over his.

"It's okay. We've got time."

He shook his head. They didn't. They didn't have time.

He pointed to his IV line. Then to the door. He tried to say "woman," but his mouth just kept saying "bowl."

Claire scrunched her brow. "Do you want some ice cream?"

He lost all hope in that moment. This woman thinks he is panicked and desperate to get a small cup of chocolate ice cream. Or at least, that's what the label said. He highly doubted there was any cream in that cup of frozen chemicals.

He started hitting his hand against the bed rail in frustration. With his good hand, he made an injection motion, then pointed out the window.

"If you are trying to get out for a walk, PT will be here soon. They will get you up and walking today. You did great sitting in the chair and pivoting yesterday, so I'm sure you will get there today."

His frustration grew. He draped his IV port over his right hand, made an emphatic injection motion, and pointed out the door.

Claire frowned. "I did hear that someone had done that to you. But," she followed the trajectory of his finger as he pointed, "that cop is keeping you safe. Nothing will happen to you in here."

He shook his head again, now feeling downright panicked. His heart rate was going so fast that it was starting to set off alarms.

Claire glanced at the line, then back at him. "Okay. Okay. Let's just take a breath. You're getting yourself worked up."

He tried to slow his breathing, but it was difficult to overcome the panic he felt. Justified or not, it wouldn't help him get through to her.

He tried again. Lips moving around a word he couldn't say. Then he grabbed the whiteboard again and drew a rough outline of a face. Eyes. Hair. Mask.

"I know. You already gave the detective a great portrait. Try not to think of her."

His whole body was shaking with the effort.

Claire straightened. "I'm going to let your doctor know you're agitated, okay? You need to rest."

He pounded the side rail weakly with his fist. No. No. No.

But Claire just gave him a soft smile and turned to the med cart.

"I know this is hard," she said, drawing up a small dose of Ativan. "But you're safe now."

He wasn't. He knew it.

She pushed the med into his IV, and the room tilted, blurring at the edges. Claire's voice dissolved into a whisper. He tried to blink it away. Tried to stay.

The last thing he saw before the blackness claimed him was a figure standing just outside the glass doors of his room.

The same woman. The one from before. The eyes that had watched him through the haze. She had on some eye makeup and false lashes, but he couldn't forget those eyes. The shape, the color, the crow's feet. She couldn't hide from him.

She raised two fingers to her lips and blew him a kiss, slow and deliberate—like she knew he couldn’t scream.

Then the world went dark.

Chapter 35

The Rush

Tyler

* * *

The storage room behind radiology still smelled faintly of bleach and dust. Jeanette Okoro sat with her arms crossed, posture straight, expression unreadable. Her badge was clean, clipped exactly square to her scrub pocket.

Tyler offered a small smile as he sat down across from her. "Thanks for coming, Jeanette. Everyone I've talked to says the same thing—you're sharp, calm under pressure, and you don't miss much."

She didn't smile back. "I try to stay aware."

"That's exactly what we need right now," Tyler said. "We've been looking into a handful of unusual codes. Some patterns. I was hoping you'd share anything you've noticed—big or small."

A long pause.

Jeanette narrowed her eyes, her voice dropped to a low suspicious pitch, "I notice a lot of things. Are you looking for anything in particular?"

"Anything unusual about the codes. Or other adverse events. Or really anything that stands out as an unusual."

Then, carefully: "I've had concerns."

That was it. No elaboration. Her tone was flat, noncommittal.

Tyler waited, giving her room.

Finally, she asked, "Are you looking at staff?"

"Right now, we're looking at everything," Tyler said. "Including medication access, MAR anomalies, room access, and chart inconsistencies. But yes—if staff patterns overlap with those, we want to know."

Jeanette nodded once, slowly. "Then I'll start with Madison."

Tyler blinked. "Go on."

"I was doing the review of the code sheets for this month, and she was at three codes she didn't belong at—one in Stepdown, two on Med-Surg. The timing of some actions and charting didn't quite line up. In one of those cases, she claimed she went into the room to help before anyone else arrived, but there was no indication she had a reason to be there. She said the charge nurse was already at another rapid, so she was helping out."

"Did any of them survive?"

"No. One died during the code, one made it to the ICU but coded and died within the hour, and the third survived but never woke up. The family had to withdraw care the following week."

"Did anything stand out about her behavior or reactions during those codes?"

"That's all I could gather from the code sheets. You should talk to Danika. I'm pretty sure she was charge for at least two of them."

Perfect, Tyler thought, we can discuss this at the next team debrief.

"Anything else I should know?"

"She said once that she'd gone into the room to help with a new IV. But there were no IV supplies in there. And no order. She claimed it was a verbal order."

Tyler was scribbling now. "You reported it?"

"No. It's not a crime to be flaky. But that wasn't the only time. She's also the nurse who found three central lines pulled out, a chest tube pulled out, and another one disconnected—four separate patients, four separate shifts. And those are just the ones I'm aware of. Said she just walked in and found them that way."

"And you don't believe her?"

"That might happen once, but three times? A chest tube might be easy to pull out by accident, but those central lines are sutured in. It happens once in a while, but three times? That defies the odds. And to disconnect a chest tube without pulling it out would require significant pressure pulling on both sides of the connector. If you only pulled on one side, the chest tube would come out. It is an unlikely accident."

"The chest tubes aren't sutured in? Those seem kind of important."

"They are, but it's more like a drawstring around a slippery pipe. If you pull with a little force, you can slide the tube right out. It's not secure the way most people think it is."

Jeanette's hands stayed folded in her lap. Her tone hadn't changed.

"And Avery?" Tyler asked.

"Avery's trickier. She floats a lot. But she always seems to appear right before things go wrong. She shows up fast—too fast—sometimes before the code pager even goes off. Says she was just 'in the area.'"

Tyler tilted his head. "Does she offer to help during codes?"

Jeanette nodded. "Usually. Respiratory is often needed, so it doesn't raise eyebrows. But it's always her. Even when there were two RTs scheduled, she was the one at the bedside."

"Anything else stand out?"

"There was a patient last week who arrested right after a neb treatment. Avery had just left the room. No one questioned it—ARDS patient, already unstable."

"You report it?"

Jeanette shook her head. "Not much to report. No evidence of error. Just instinct. And timing."

"And meds?" Tyler prompted.

Jeanette's gaze sharpened. "We had a missing amp of epi last week. And a 10-unit insulin syringe the week before that. In both cases, the staff assumed it got tossed in the sharps or biohazard bin by mistake."

"But they weren't documented as given?"

"Correct. No entry. No waste. No witness. But no investigation either. They're not controlled substances. No abuse potential. Not worth the paperwork."

"And no one's digging through biohazard bags," Tyler murmured.

"Exactly."

He leaned back in his chair, impressed despite the chill running down his spine. "You've got a hell of a memory."

"I don't forget things," she said plainly.

Tyler nodded. "You've just validated a lot of what we were seeing. Thank you."

Jeanette stood. "I didn't say it was intentional. But if it is—I hope you're fast."

She walked out without waiting for a reply.

Tyler exhaled and looked down at his notes. Elise's name lit up on his phone. He answered on the first ring.

Without waiting for a greeting, Tyler said, "We're interviewing Madison this afternoon. I'll follow up with Danika after that."

He paused, eyes still on the notepad.

"Jeanette's sharp," Elise said. "Really sharp."

"Jeanette's only still on our radar because there's absolutely nothing pointing to her," Tyler said. "And if there's one thing we've learned about this killer—it's that invisibility might be their signature."

"If Madison's being set up," he added, "it's not sloppy. It's strategic. Someone's making the obvious look guilty so we overlook the invisible."

Chapter 36
The Hero
Tyler

* * *

Tyler sat back in the same creaky metal chair, notebook open on his lap, pen poised. The storage room behind radiology felt smaller with each interview. The stale air was thick with everything unsaid.

Jamie Lin sat across from him, clearly nervous. She kept fidgeting with her badge reel, twisting it until the retractable cord snapped back against her chest. Her scrubs were clean but wrinkled, her ponytail slightly off-center. She had dark rings under her eyes like she hadn't slept in a while.

"Thanks for making time," Tyler said gently. "I know it's been a rough week."

Jamie nodded, not meeting his eyes.

"I want to start with your observations. Not accusations. Just what you've seen. Anything that felt off."

A pause. Then, quietly: "A lot has felt off."

"Tell me."

She glanced at the door, then back at him. "You already know about the codes, right? The ones that didn't make sense?"

"We're reviewing all of them."

Jamie took a breath. "Okay. Well… there were times I walked into a room and the patient was just… crashing. No warning. No alarms. It happens around here sometimes, but the number of times it has happened to me is statistically unlikely."

Tyler waited. Jamie's fingers curled around the edge of the table.

As the silence between them grew, Jamie started to squirm in her seat, then started rambling to fill the silence. "I thought it was a black cloud following me around. For the record, I don't believe in hospital superstitions, but that doesn't mean they aren't real."

Tyler nodded in understanding, but didn't speak, letting the silence grow again.

"And a few times, I noticed things weren't where they should be. An IV line that was freshly primed, but the tubing hadn't been labeled and the nurse hadn't been in. Or meds that were drawn up but not documented. Once I found insulin sitting on the counter with no label and no MAR entry. Just… there."

"Did you report it?"

"No. Not officially. It seemed like routine human error. If you report every little incident, this hospital will drown in paperwork, and you will make enemies of the nursing staff. You can't take care of patients when you make enemies of your entire support team."

"Did you tell anyone else?"

"I told the primary nurse. The expectation is that people learn from their mistakes without punitive action. She said maybe it got tossed out by accident. And honestly, I didn't push. At the time, I thought it was an isolated incident. I thought I was seeing problems that weren't really there."

"You weren't."

Jamie finally looked at him. "Then you've seen it too."

He nodded. "What else?"

She swallowed. "There's someone—I don't know who. I keep seeing this float nurse. Same face, different units. She's always there when things go wrong. But no one can tell me her name."

Tyler nodded again. "You're not the first person to say that."

Jamie let out a shaky breath. "That actually makes me feel worse."

He let that sit. Then, gently, "Tell me about the night in 516."

Jamie's face went pale. "I've taken care of a lot of patients in 516. Are you referring to this most recent code?" she clarified, while vividly remembering the patient she and Ravi had taken care of last year.

"That's the one. Do you have another memorable incident in mind in that room?"

"Not at all. I—I already talked to the code team."

"I'm not asking for the paperwork. Just what you remember."

She stared at the floor. "It was a code. I ran from the ICU. Got there a second before Ravi. Someone was already doing compressions. I did what I was supposed to do—grabbed a line, pushed meds, followed orders. Nothing about it stood out at the time. It felt like just another code."

She paused. "But afterward, when I found out she'd been hypoglycemic—like really hypoglycemic—I started thinking about the insulin I'd seen on the counter that time. And then I started wondering if I might have missed something. Or maybe someone wanted me to."

Tyler leaned forward slightly. "What about Ravi? Anything unusual that morning?"

Jamie's eyes darted away. "Ravi?" she echoed, too quickly.

"You were with him. You arrived together."

"I mean… yeah. He was there. Same as me. Doing his job."

"Did anything strike you? Anything about his response, his timing?"

She looked down at her hands. "No."

Tyler was sure she was hiding something. He didn't press, he just let the silence hang."

Jamie hesitated, then shook her head. "No. I don't know. Perhaps I'm reading too much into things now because everyone else is. He's not—he wouldn't—"

"Wouldn't what?"
A quiet beat.
"It's okay, Jamie. You can say what you're thinking."

Jamie finally added, "Nothing sinister. Just some common burnout." She finally replied without meeting his eyes. "You're going to talk to him, right?"

Tyler jotted it down. "Thank you."

She looked up again, her eyes full of guilt. "Am I in trouble?"

"No," he said firmly. "You're helping."

Jamie nodded slowly. "Then I want to help more."

"Good," Tyler said, flipping to a fresh page in his notebook. "I've got more questions."

He kept her there for nearly an hour, reviewing patient names, unusual moments, and staff behaviors. She remembered everything, though her answers grew more hesitant as the questions circled back to Ravi.

When she finally left the room, Tyler waited until the door clicked shut before answering the phone.

"She's jumpy," Elise said without preamble.

"Especially around Ravi," Logan added.

Tyler nodded at them through the camera. "I noticed."

"You think they're working together?" Elise asked.

"I don't know," Tyler said. "But if someone wanted to build an alibi, having a partner helps."

Tyler stared at the empty chair across from him, Jamie's tension still lingering in the air.
If she was lying, she wasn't good at it.

Chapter 37

The Scapegoat

Tyler

* * *

The storage room behind radiology hadn't gotten any less suffocating. The air was stale with nervous sweat, and the walls were too close. Tyler leaned back in the folding chair, watching the nurse across from him try not to come apart.

Madison couldn't have been more than twenty-three. Wire-rimmed glasses slid down her nose, fogged slightly from her breath. Her round face still carried traces of acne scarring, and a single blonde streak had escaped from her bun to stick to her damp temple. Her gray scrubs were darkening under the arms, her deodorant having long since surrendered. She sat stiffly, knees locked, hands gripping the edge of the metal chair. Her smile was tight. Polite. Strained.

"Thanks for meeting with me," Tyler said, voice gentle. "I know this isn't easy."

She nodded once. "Of course."

"I just want to talk about some patterns we've noticed. Things that came up in incident reviews. It's not about blame—just getting some clarity."

Madison nodded again, a bit slower this time.

"There've been a few events we need to understand better. Three pulled central lines. Two dislodged chest tubes. A patient injured after restraints were loosened. And a few undocumented med administrations—errors with no clear cause."

Madison's hands trembled slightly, then clamped together to hide it. Her fingers twitched at the hem of her scrub top, kneading it without realizing she was doing it. Her eyes were wide, but not surprised. Like she'd been bracing for this conversation all week.

"I always double-check my lines," she said quickly. "Chest tubes, too. I chart in real time when I can."

Tyler nodded. "I'm sure you do. We're not saying you don't. But I also know this place can get chaotic. And if something is going wrong, we need to figure out how."

Her composure cracked. "I don't know how this keeps happening. I'm so careful. I've always been careful. But after the first incident, I have been downright vigilant."

"I believe you," Tyler said.

Madison looked down at her lap. "Lately it feels like… I don't know. Like I do something one minute and come back five minutes later, and it's undone. Supplies missing. Lines that were secured suddenly hanging loose. It doesn't make sense."

"You think someone's interfering?"

"I don't know. I thought I was going crazy. But now… I think maybe someone's trying to make me look incompetent."

"Have you had any conflicts with other staff?"

She shook her head. "Not really. Nothing serious. Everyone gets tense sometimes. But I've never had an issue that would explain this."

"What about Ravi Patel?" Tyler asked. "Anything about his behavior stand out to you?"

Madison hesitated. "He's… confident. Smart. He moves fast. Sometimes too fast. But he's always nice to me. Respectful."

"Have you ever seen him access meds or equipment on your patients?"

"Not directly," she said. "But he's around a lot. Sometimes I'd come back from a break and find things slightly moved. He's one of those people who seems to always be in the right place… or the wrong one."

"And Jamie Lin?"

Madison sighed. "She's sweet. I think she tries really hard. I've never had a problem with her. But she always seems on edge. Like she knows something she doesn't want to say."

Tyler watched her for a long moment. "You seem almost relieved we're asking."

Madison gave a small, wet laugh. "I've been waiting for someone to notice. Everyone just kept looking at me like I was either cursed or an incompetent moron—I'm not sure which is worse."

"We're looking closely now. At everything."

She nodded, then sniffled and wiped the corner of her eye with the back of her hand. Her scrubs were darker now, sweat clinging to her spine.

Tyler wrapped up the interview with a promise to follow up and thanked her for her honesty. She looked broken. But he'd seen better actors in residency interviews. She left quickly, eyes low, shoulders tight.

Seconds later, Tyler's phone buzzed.

"She's not our killer," Logan said. "She's a scapegoat."

Elise agreed. "Who plans all that and still fumbles with chest tubes and central lines?"

Tyler flipped to a new page in his notebook. "Then we start tracking who was on with her. Every shift. Every unit."

Chapter 38

Necessary Consequences

The Killer

* * *

I watched her come out—eyes puffy, face blotchy, scrubs clinging to her back in a shameful bloom of sweat. She looked wrecked.

Good.

A flicker of satisfaction passed through me. Not joy. Not even relief. Just the satisfaction of precision—the way it feels when a needle threads cleanly on the first try. But it didn't last. Because Jamie always made me feel something else, something sour. Contempt.

She reminded me of everything I lost—everything they stole.

Not just back home, where one false, deliberate accusation—made to cover her own mistake—cost me everything. My license. My future. My name. And forced me to flee the country.

But Jamie? What Jamie reminded me of was what happened here. What happened after. When I thought I could rebuild. When I still had hope.

When I still had my daughter.

No one ever says it out loud, but some mistakes come with a face you never forget.

Jamie was the resident that night. I'd seen her before—young, capable enough, but too fast. Rushing through her notes. Relying too much on instinct, not enough on discipline. That night, she didn't double-check the labs. She didn't catch the rhythm change. She didn't call for help until it was too late. I saw it unfold in real time.

The girl in the bed had only just turned eleven.

And afterward? She wept. They all did. They called it a tragedy. An unavoidable loss.

No one questioned it.

No one questioned her.

But she doesn't know tragedy.

And they never would. Because she was one of them. Young, polished, American.

I had to leave my country. Learn a new language. Start over among smug, sloppy Americans who don't understand hierarchy, don't respect precision, who treat medicine like a team sport instead of a discipline.

So I adapted. I watched. I waited.

While they ran their rounds and fake investigations, I pushed carts and blended in. I memorized badge routes, door codes, who forgot to log entries, or left drawers swinging open. I knew their habits better than they did. I made myself invisible. Because invisible people can go anywhere.

Jamie disappeared down the hall now, wilted and small. Breaking. But not broken yet.

That's the thing about control—it only matters if no one sees you hold it. The best power is invisible. Quiet. I don't need credit. I need results.

They think she's just another overwhelmed resident. They don't know she's being sculpted—shaped by consequence, by fear, by truth. If she breaks too soon, it'll ruin everything.

But if she holds it together just long enough—

I'll make sure she learns what it means to pay.

Chapter 39

The Gatekeeper

Tyler

* * *

Ray Delaney was already waiting when Tyler walked into the small interview room tucked beside the security office. He was in his mid-fifties, stocky, with a gut that pushed proudly against his security jacket. The badge clipped to his chest gleamed like a trophy.

" 'Bout time someone brought me in," Ray said as Tyler sat. "I know this place better'n anyone."

Tyler smiled politely. "That's exactly why we're talking."

Tyler's Bluetooth earpiece buzzed with a new text. After a brief pause, a mechanical voice announced Logan as the sender and started reading the text: "Just a heads up—he flunked out of the police academy thirty years ago. Thinks he's Sherlock Holmes. Total overconfidence, minimal follow-through."

Ray leaned back, hands clasped over his belly. "I've walked every hallway in this place. ICU, OR, med rooms, stairwells—hell, I know where the outlets hum different."

Tyler nodded. "So you'd be familiar with the blind spots in the badge system? The doors that don't always log swipes?"

Ray chuckled. "It's an old building. Half the readers are garbage. You want me to map out the broken ones?"

"That would be great. When you can," Tyler already had found the broken ones, but was still interested in how many of them this man knew about.

"What about after-hours?" Tyler asked. "People ever ask you to let them in?"

Ray shrugged. "Sure. Residents forget their badges all the time. Nurses, too. If I know 'em, I let 'em through. They have enough problems."

"And you use your badge for that?"

"No. There is a door release button at the security desk."

Upstairs, Logan swore under his breath. "So the entrance access logs are useless. All of them."

Tyler kept his voice even. "You were on duty the night someone left the fractured catheter kit in Dr. Navarro's office, right?"

Ray blinked. "I was covering ER that night. Didn't see anything."

The same mechanical voice cut into Tyler's ear, this time announcing Navarro as the texter. "That's not true. He was assigned to monitors. He should've been watching that hallway."

Tyler leaned forward. "Ray, help me out here. You're listed as the monitoring officer. So why were you down in the ER instead of watching that hallway?"

Ray shifted. "It was just—look, I had a situation, okay?"

"What kind of situation?"

A long pause. Then a sigh. "Personal. My wife was texting nonstop, and I stepped out to call her. It was stupid. I was trying to calm her down. I didn't think anything would happen in those ten minutes."

Tyler didn’t look away. "But something did happen. A sealed kit was left in Navarro’s office during that window. You understand why this matters?"

Ray looked down. "Yeah. I get it."

Tyler let the silence stretch. "Convenient timing, don't you think?"

He let Ray talk more, let him ramble about stairwell alarms and faulty log data. When Tyler asked about the back stairwell with missing badge swipes, Ray just shrugged.

"Those doors are temperamental. Sometimes the reader logs the entry, sometimes it doesn’t. I’ve reported it."

"If someone wanted quiet access," Tyler said, "no questions asked—would you know?"

Ray shrugged. "It's a big hospital with a lot of employees and a lot of hours to cover. I can't possibly be at every locked door all the time."

Tyler nodded slowly. “Appreciate your time.”

Ray left with the same smirk he’d come in with. Upstairs, Elise peeled off her headset. “He’s cocky as hell.”

Logan was already typing. “And dangerous. He knows the building better than anyone.”

Tyler scratched a note into his pad. “Perfect pawn,” he murmured. “Or the perfect cover.”

Chapter 40

The Tinkerer

Tyler

* * *

The undersized conference room was starting to wear on Tyler—too many hours, too many questions. At least in Kandahar, he thought grimly, you got to interrogate people outside. Tyler sat at the far end of the table, pen resting loosely between his fingers.

Across from him, Evan Krell perched stiffly on the edge of his chair. Early forties, rail-thin, with a sharp nose and pale skin that always looked slightly clammy. His glasses sat high on the bridge of his nose, and the long sleeves of his undershirt were rolled with meticulous symmetry to just below the elbow. He kept adjusting them anyway. One, then the other. Again.

He blinked a lot and always cleared his throat twice before speaking.

"You needed something?" he asked, voice soft but clipped.

"Just wanted to talk about your role in Central Supply," Tyler said calmly. "I understand you've been here a while."

"Seventeen years." He said it without pride, more like he was reporting inventory.

"That's a long time. You must know the place inside out."

"I do."

"You usually work alone?"

Evan nodded. "Mostly nights. I restock the kits. Check for defects. Cycle trays. Clean the bins."

"Ever have to deal with visitors? People wandering through?"

"Not often. Occasionally, an ICU nurse or resident will come down if they can't wait for me to run something up. But usually, if they need it quick, I get it to them quick.

"Family members?" Tyler asked.

Evan shook his head. "Never. They don't even know where the access elevator is."

"Visitors? Patients?"

"No. Not allowed."

"Other staff?"

"Also no. We don't like people wandering through."

Tyler raised an eyebrow. "No one?"

Evan hesitated. "We only tolerate the ICU staff because it's usually life or death. There are no other exceptions."

"Anyone else?"

"Housekeeping," Evan admitted. "They come when they're scheduled. But they don't touch the equipment."

Tyler nodded, made a quick note. "There was an issue with a central line a few months ago. September. Did you hear about that?"

"I read the report. Manufacturer error."

"That's what we thought," Tyler said. "But this morning, a fractured central line was found in a sealed kit. In Dr. Navarro's office."

Evan blinked, froze just a second too long. "That wasn't part of the recall. We sent them all back months ago."

"No," Tyler agreed. "It wasn't."

A long pause.

"Is it possible," Tyler asked, his tone even, "for someone to tamper with a kit down in Central Supply? Swap something out, maybe?"

Evan's lips pressed into a line. "Not easily. But... possible. If you knew the layout. Knew where to hide. It's a big space with rows and rows of equipment. And there is only one of us down here at any given time."

"Would anyone notice if something was missing?"

"Depends on what it was. But most things, probably only at inventory time or if the stock gets really low."

"How often is that?"

"Inventory is once a quarter. Central lines, we are never low on. They are too important."

Tyler studied him. Evan's fingers were tapping the edge of his sleeve now. One, two, three, four.

"You seem nervous, Evan. You know something we don't?"

"No. I—I don't like being pulled into this. I do my job. I keep things clean."

Tyler leaned forward. "You're alone down there most of the time. That kind of isolation—it wears on people. If something were bothering you, who'd even know?"

Evan's eyes flicked to the door. "No one comes down unless something's wrong."

Tyler nodded slowly. "Alright. Thanks for your time."

Evan stood up with too much precision, adjusted his glasses twice, then disappeared into the hallway.

Tyler leaned back and exhaled.

His phone buzzed.

"He has everything the tampering would've required. Plus ample opportunity," Elise said.

"But does he strike you as a killer?" Logan asked.

Tyler stared at the closed door. "He strikes me as unreadable. I don't know. But he definitely has the attention to detail required, unlike some of the other suspects on the list."

There was a beat of silence.

"Why would he do it?" Elise asked finally.

"Maybe boredom," Tyler said. "Maybe pressure. Maybe something darker. People snap for less."

He ended the call and let the silence return. Some motives were invisible until it was too late.

Chapter 41

The Overlooked

Tyler

* * *

The lights in the windowless room never changed, but Tyler's watch ticked relentlessly forward. If it weren't set to military time, he might've thought it was four in the morning. The recycled air, the fluorescent hum, the revolving door of staff—the afternoon's interviews were starting to blur together. Names, faces, voices. Only his notes kept things anchored.

The float pool nurse was next. She was young, jittery, and couldn't stop twisting her badge lanyard between her fingers. Tyler kept his tone gentle.

"You've floated to multiple units recently?"

She nodded quickly. "I'm a float nurse. That's my job. Wherever they need me. ICU. Stepdown. Med-surg."

"Do any of those recent shifts stand out? Any unusual patient events?"

Her eyes darted downward. "I mean… not really. I remember some codes. Crashes that didn't make sense. One guy had just been talking to me five minutes before. But I don't know what happened after."

"Who else was there?"

"I don't remember exactly. I'm sorry. I feel like I should."

"You're not in trouble," Tyler assured her. "We're just collecting threads."

She nodded, but her hands didn't stop moving.

* * *

Then the pharmacy tech. A tall woman in a neatly pressed jacket who folded her arms and answered everything like it was a quiz.

"All narcotics are tracked through Pyxis. We log every dispense, every override. If anything's missing, it's flagged. Period."

Tyler didn't flinch. "Any recent anomalies?"

She hesitated. "Some minor count delays. And a med drawer left open unattended once. I reported it."

"Who had access?"

"Half the unit, honestly. This place is not as tight as it should be."

Tyler made a note.

* * *

The charge nurse arrived with her arms crossed and her expression set to unimpressed. She was older, seasoned, and not interested in speculation.

"I've heard the rumors," she said flatly. "Half the nurses think there's a serial killer. The other half think it's a witch hunt."

Tyler raised a brow. "And you?"

She leaned back. "I think Madison's had a run of bad luck. And that you're chasing patterns in chaos."

"But you've seen the trends?"

"I've seen enough to know we have bigger problems than coincidence. If you're serious about this, look at the people no one watches. Supply staff. Cleaning crews. Anyone with access but no oversight."

* * *

The housekeeping supervisor was next. Neat, calm, clipboard in hand.

"We rotate weekly. Assignments are logged. One employee was recently let go—chronic tardiness. No theft or behavior issues."

She handed Tyler printed shift sheets and badge logs before he could ask. "Let me know if you need more. We take access seriously."

Tyler thanked her. She nodded and left without small talk.

* * *

Last came the EMR tech. Early 30s, with a laptop tucked under one arm and a grin like he enjoyed being the smartest person in the room.

"Chart access is audit-friendly," he said, without being asked. "Every log, every IP, every device ID."

Tyler leaned back. "Any red flags?"

"Couple weird ones. Logins from devices that didn't match the assigned user's workstation. Times that didn't line up with shift records."

"Could someone be using another person's credentials?"

"Easily. Especially if they left themselves logged in. Or left their badge lying around. We installed tap-to-login access a couple years ago." He tapped a few keys. "I'll send you the report."

* * *

Evening came and went without ceremony or a view of the sunset from the windowless interrogation room. Elise and Logan arrived with takeout—

steam rising from cartons, soy sauce packets tucked in napkins. They ate in the security office, monitors glowing.

"Avery's badge was used twice when she was out of town," Logan said, scrolling through the logs.

"Her coat was on a hook in the respiratory department," Elise added. "Badge clipped to the pocket. Easy grab."

They replayed the footage again—the grainy clip of someone limping past Navarro's door.

"That's not Avery," Tyler said. "The limp's exaggerated. Someone's faking it."

Logan nodded. "I'll check badge logs against movement patterns. Maybe we can match the gait."

Outside, the sky was dark. Probably. Inside, the work wasn't done.

The door opened. A tired, jittery ICU nurse stepped in.

Tyler didn't bother to stand.

"Come in," he said. "Let's talk."

Chapter 42

Close to Home

The Killer

* * *

It's not hard to watch them. Not here.

Hospitals are built for quiet surveillance—windows in every door, half-drawn curtains, staff lounges tucked beside conference rooms, patient whiteboards listing everyone's movement in dry-erase ink.

I don't even need to hide—just a pair of scrubs, a borrowed badge, and a clipboard in my hand.

People see what they expect. Someone moving with purpose. Someone who belongs. Someone invisible.

I like the chairs near the vending machines in the basement by the radiology reading rooms. Close enough to the stairwell for an easy exit. One hallway away from the converted storage room where the interviews take place. I've stationed myself there three times this week, nursing the same bottle of ginger ale. No one notices.

No one ever notices.

From that vantage point, I've watched the parade of them—Avery, stiff-backed and defensive. Ravi, sweating through his undershirt, the collar of his white coat limp. Leilani, too calm. Sierra, crumpled and crying. A nervous ICU nurse with too much caffeine in her hand. A charge nurse who talks too much. A supply tech who never looks anyone in the eye.

They all think they're helping. Or that they're suspects. Or maybe both.

Idiots.

None of them have figured it out.

I'm starting to get bored.

The badge swaps worked better than I expected. Residents leave their coats draped over chairs, badges still clipped on. Some leave themselves logged in at shared terminals. They finish looking up a lab or entering an order, and they wander off, like a lost toddler. The masks are a godsend. Nobody looks twice. I can walk in and out of a dozen departments in a day, and no one remembers what I look like.

Still, there are cracks now. Tyler Grayson is asking smarter questions. Not just the who, but the how. The when. The overlap.

I don't like him. But I respect him. A little.

He stepped out of the interview room an hour ago. I noted his path. I followed two minutes later, slipping into the stairwell.

From the corner near the linen alcove, I watched him enter the room.

But who was in that room?

Not a witness.

Definitely not a target.

Still, I waited.

Through a slit in the curtain, I saw enough. The age gap between them was obvious—he, all clean lines and perfect posture, muscles still held with the unconscious ease of someone accustomed to commanding his space, probably mid-thirties; she, all gray now with just a ghost of her former pigment, a woman who looked young when she smiled—but when her face relaxed, the crow's nests and softened smile lines revealed her true age. Still, she was visibly comforted by his presence. A kiss on the cheek. A quiet laugh. The way his hand rested on hers. Her face softened when he spoke. There was an ease between them I hadn't expected—unforced, unguarded, like the kind of comfort you don't fake. It wasn't just tenderness—it was familiarity. Trust. Comfort.

His mother.

At first, I considered it. A potassium bolus, maybe. Or slipping something unnoticed into her IV—just enough to confuse the labs, raise alarms, waste their time. There were ways.

I even workshopped a few—timing, access, escalation. All of it.

But the longer I watched, the more obvious it became: Tyler's a decent investigator, maybe even good. But he's not a threat. Not to me.

Still, if he ever gets close, I'll be ready.

I always have a plan.

He didn't come back out quickly. Twenty minutes passed. Thirty. I shifted my weight against the wall.

I hated how tender he looked. The way he bent toward the bed. The way he touched her shoulder like it meant something.

I don't understand that kind of softness. I don't trust it. People who act like that always have secrets. They think empathy excuses everything.

But it's not the old woman who keeps me up at night.

It's the boy. He saw too much. And he hasn't stopped trying to tell them.

Chapter 43
The Undoing
Madison

* * *

It happened fast.

One moment, she was charting at the nursing station, catching up on notes between med passes. The next, the call light from 310 was flashing red, and a respiratory tech was shouting her name.

"Madison, he's desatting—he's down to 82!"

Her feet moved before her mind caught up. She knew the patient. Mr. Brenner. Late seventies. COPD. Tall, lean frame, always apologizing for needing help. He'd come in last week with a spontaneous pneumothorax—a collapsed lung. They'd placed a chest tube to re-expand it, and everything had been stable since.

Stable until now.

Inside the room, he looked worse than the numbers. His breaths came in fast, shallow gasps—like he was trying to drink air that wasn't there. His mouth gaped with each inhale, eyes wide and darting. His chest barely rose. Sweat beaded across his forehead and soaked the collar of his gown. The pulse oximeter waveform was erratic—uneven peaks, some tall and strong, others barely registering. The spacing between them danced to the same chaotic rhythm as his heart, no two pulses quite the same. The smooth, reliable wave she expected was gone, replaced with a flickering signature of a body in distress. His heart rate bounced between 120 and 140, the monitor lagging a half beat behind each new spike. Afib. Irregularly irregular, the monitor said, as if the chaos could be quantified. The numbers changed every few seconds, taunting her. One-thirty-two. One-twenty-seven. One-forty. Back to one-thirty.

Danika was already checking the monitors. "Tube's in place," she said. "Vitals are live. What the hell—"

Madison's eyes dropped to the chest drainage system beside the bed. The water in the chamber was still—too still. No bubbling, no gentle rise and fall. Just a flat pool of pale blue, undisturbed liquid. The little orange accordion inside the pressure gauge was sucked all the way in to zero, compressed like a vacuumed spring.

The dial was set to water seal.

Before she could move, the respiratory therapist had already thrown a non-rebreather over Mr. Brenner's face and cranked the oxygen to max. He looked at her with wide eyes. "I'm going to grab an intubation tray," he said, already turning.

Madison's heart sank.

No suction.

Her stomach flipped.

The difference mattered. On suction, the chest tube helped draw air out of the pleural space, allowing the lung to fully re-expand. Water seal still allowed air to escape—but passively. Slowly. If the lung couldn't hold itself open yet, it would collapse again.

Which it had.

Madison didn't hesitate. She lunged for the system, fingers finding the dial with practiced precision. She twisted it hard, snapping it from water seal back to suction. The pump kicked in with a low hum that felt too quiet for how urgent everything was.

They both watched the water chamber bubble as the system kicked in—rapid, rhythmic pops like boiling water in a glass kettle, only sharper, more urgent. It was the sound of air escaping the wrong place. She watched Mr. Brenner's chest rise just a little more evenly. He stopped clutching his chest and let his arms fall to the sides. She watched the oxygen saturation crawl back toward ninety. A look of relief settled on his face, although some traces of panic still lingered in his eyes.

He was going to make it.

"Jesus," Danika muttered, barely above a whisper. "He was circling the drain."

Her voice wasn't panicked—it was tight, clipped, the way people sounded when they'd been scared but refused to let it show. She looked at Madison then, really looked at her, just long enough to register the same question in both their eyes:

How the hell did this happen?

It didn't matter that they'd caught it. It didn't matter that he hadn't arrested, hadn't coded.

* * *

An hour later, Madison was pulled into the manager's office. HR was looped in. So was Risk Management. The CNO, too.

Too many incidents. Too many close calls.

The chest tube had been placed correctly. But placing it on water seal—that wasn't something that happened by accident. It would have required multiple rotations of a small dial. It required a reasonable amount of hand strength and dexterity to accomplish. It had to be intentional. And nobody in their right mind would have done that. Not after a week of failed clamping trials. Not with the order for pleurodesis in the morning. But somebody obviously wasn't in their right mind.

Which meant someone had done it on purpose.

She sat there in silence as they told her she was being placed on leave, pending investigation. Effective immediately.

Her badge was deactivated before she even left the unit. Ray Delaney was the one who walked her out—big, self-important strides like he was escorting a criminal. He didn't stop talking the whole way. Something about protocol, about how he'd seen worse, about how HR was just doing their job. He told her not to take it personally. Like it wasn't personal! His voice was too loud, too casual, like he thought filling the silence might make it easier. It didn't.

She walked to the parking garage in a daze. The air smelled like hot asphalt and brake dust. She wasn't crying. Not yet.

She didn't even realize she'd sat down in the driver's seat until she felt the seatbelt dig into her hip.

How many times had she checked that chest tube? How many times had she traced the tubing, confirmed the settings? She knew it had been on suction. She would've sworn it. Would've bet her license on it.

Someone had changed it.

Her patient nearly died.

And now she was the one being punished.

She didn't start crying until she turned the key.

Even then, it wasn't loud.

Just a slow, sad sob.

Chapter 44

The Setup

Elise Navarro

* * *

Conference Room 2C felt brighter than she remembered—high windows pouring in late-afternoon sun, fluorescent ceiling lights competing for attention. It was the perfect room to use as a command center. Heavy mahogany conference tables had been pushed together to form a square around the room, with seats arranged to face inward. It created the feel of a tactical briefing—intimate, focused, present.

Elise had barely slept. Tyler looked worse—coffee in one hand, his pen clicking nervously in the other. Logan leaned over the table, rifling through the badge logs again like one more pass would unlock the answer.

The table was buried in paper: printouts from IT, timestamped badge access records, inventory reports, and medication pull logs. On the whiteboard behind Elise, the names of every staff member interviewed were listed beside columns of scribbled notes. Red asterisks had begun to collect beside a few of them.

Avery. Ravi. Jamie. Madison. Nilesh.

Jen sat with her laptop open, Naomi beside her. Danika leaned in the doorway, arms crossed. Nilesh was perched on the edge of his chair with a Post-it pad in one hand and a multi-color pen poised in the other."

It was time.

Elise didn't bother with pleasantries. "Madison's patient nearly coded this morning. Chest tube sabotage. This wasn't a line pull. This was subtle and intentional. Planned. Whoever did it wanted a close call. They wanted panic."

Tyler leaned forward. "How long could it have been like that? Between switching to water seal and when he crashed?"

Elise shook her head. "It's unpredictable. Could've been two hours, could've been most of a day. Depends on how compromised the lung is, how much air he's leaking, and how strong his compensatory effort is. Too many variables to know for sure."

Danika nodded. "It was water seal. It isn't like you could bump against it and flip a switch. You have to turn that little suction dial several times. He has been failing water seal trials all week. I had personally switched it back to suction after there was a recurrence of the pneumothorax on the chest x-ray in the morning."

"She checked it," Tyler added quietly. "Repeatedly. That's what she told me last night. She doesn't even trust herself anymore."

No one spoke.

Naomi was the first to break the silence. "This makes six events with that same nurse. That's not incompetence."

Jen nodded. "But does that mean she is the killer? Or another victim?"

"Not sure," Tyler replied, but either way, "getting her out of the hospital was the only safe move."

"I agree," added Navarro. "The real killer would never bring that kind of attention to themselves. But her patients aren't safe until the killer is caught."

"Then it's time we stop watching," Logan said. "And start moving."

They reviewed the key suspects.

"One by one," Elise said, motioning to the names marked in red on the board.

Avery's badge had been active during several events—but she'd been out of town for at least two. Her alibi checked out, and her badge had been easily accessible both times. "She's a perfect unknowing accomplice," Naomi said. "Her habits are predictable. So is her grief."

Ravi, on the other hand, was erratic. Sleepless, edgy, and unaccountably present at multiple events. Logan scowled as he listed Ravi's badge swipes across three different med rooms within twenty minutes. "Even if he was trying to help, it's too much."

Jamie's name came next, and Elise hesitated.

"She's dedicated," Elise said. "But obsessed. She's calm during chaos, too calm. And she's always there."

Tyler added, "The hero complex theory fits."

Neither of them has access to med rooms or sterile supply." Nilesh countered.

"That we know of," Logan muttered.

They circled back to the question that had plagued them for weeks.

What does the killer want?

Not money. Not attention. Not revenge—at least not the kind you write about in grievance letters. This was about control. Patterns. Power.

“They’re watching us,” Elise said. “Every move we make. Every interview. Every code.”

“So let’s give them something to watch,” Logan said.

He outlined the start of a plan: a fake staffing schedule, a patient room left apparently unmonitored, an equipment tray stocked with flagged items—a sterile field that could tempt someone to tamper.

But Elise was already shaking her head. "It’s not enough," she said. "There are hundreds of patients in this hospital. The killer’s using multiple strategies. A single bait room won’t draw them out."

Naomi leaned in. "What if we give them more than a patient? What if we give them privacy? Opportunity? A place they think is off the radar."

There was a pause as the weight of it settled. Jen exhaled slowly.

"We’re going to have to do more than just wait for them to slip up," she said. "We need a separate setup for each suspect. A different trap tailored to their habits, their patterns."

Danika frowned. "That’s a huge operation."

Logan rubbed his face. "And what about the suspects we haven’t even spotted yet? The ones still blending in?"

Silence again.

Elise looked around the table. "We do it anyway. As many scenarios as we can set up. We set enough traps, eventually we'll catch something."

No one argued. The plan was ambitious. Overwhelming. But it was the first time any of them had felt like they weren’t just reacting.

They were hunting.

"What about dummy badges?" Jen asked. "I can make a few and we can hang them in accessible areas throughout the hospital. See who uses them?"

"We can put tracer powder on them. So the user's hands glow under blacklight." Nilesh added.

"Great idea," Tyler responded. "That sounds promising."

Elise's eyes narrowed. "The cameras aren't helping us. The ceiling angles are useless—too high, too wide. We need new ones. Discreet. At eye level."

"Hallway alcoves, stairwell doors, empty break rooms," Logan added. "Anywhere someone might loiter."

"Can you get them installed without drawing attention?" Elise asked Jen.

Jen spoke up for the first time. "I've already been strategizing," she said. "We're going to be hiding cameras in the hand sanitizer housings. Eye-level, discreet, hard to spot unless you're really looking."

"That's brilliant," Elise said, nodding. "People ignore hand sanitizer like furniture."

Jen added, "My old college roommate runs a camera shop. She is getting me what we need. We'll have them by tomorrow. Once they're here, we can start assembling the units—test them in low-traffic areas before expanding out. Then I just have to get them hung up without anybody noticing."

"Even if someone notices, it just looks like we're refilling the dispensers," Danika pointed out the obvious. "I can hang them in the ICU. Nobody will think twice about me refilling them. Housekeeping constantly lets them run dry."

"I will get them in the bone marrow unit. Anybody else there will look out of place. I can get the ORs and ER, too." Naomi added.

"I've got the pharmacy and lab covered," Nilesh chimed in.

"Then we catch it on review," Elise said. She let out a slow breath, her voice quieter now. "At least we won't be blind anymore. We will finally have something to work with."

Chapter 45

Diversion

Ravi Patel

* * *

The cursor blinked at him like a metronome for his failure.

Ravi stared at the blank charting screen, his fingers poised over the keyboard but unmoving. His palms were damp. The badge looped around his neck tapped against the desk in a steady rhythm—tap, tap, tap—as if trying to keep time with the rising tempo of his heart.

He hadn't written a word. No vitals. No notes. Nothing to prove he'd even been there.

He was unraveling.

He'd already been interviewed once. That certainly hadn't eased the tension—it only made it worse. The way Logan watched him, the way Elise went quiet. The way Jamie hadn't looked at him since. Tyler's too-casual hallway nod. Elise's unreadable silence. Jamie had barely looked at him in days.

He wiped his hands on his scrubs and tried to steady his breath.

He remembered every detail.

* * *

September

An elderly woman. End-stage COPD. Small cell lung cancer that had metastasized to the bone and brain. Her oxygen needs were through the roof. She was delirious and afraid, clutching at her gown, moaning between ragged breaths. The family was estranged, unwilling to make decisions, unreachable. The attending had written for comfort measures only—DNR, no escalation. It had gone through ethics, with the required two-physician consent. There was no disagreement about the goals of care. No confusion. Just a quiet, clinical consensus that prolonging her suffering was not humane.

Jamie had been quiet at the bedside. Calm. Collected. Her voice was so even when she said, "She's suffering. We can help ease it."

Ravi had hesitated. He remembered that hesitation as if it were tattooed behind his eyes. At the time, he considered it a weakness. Jamie had no hesitation about doing what was needed to do what was best for the patient, but fear gripped his chest like a vice. Not just fear of being caught—but fear of what it meant that this no longer felt wrong. He nodded slowly. He'd drawn the morphine. He pushed more than the chart called for—and faster than comfort dosing ever required. He took her hand in his, hoping human touch would bring her some comfort as he gently stroked her forehead with his other hand.

They'd stayed at the bedside together, watching the pain drain from the woman's face. After one minute, she stopped yelling, and after two minutes, she stopped groaning with each exhalation. After four or five minutes, her breathing slowed to just a few shallow respirations per minute. They stood beside her, still as statues, as minute after minute dragged by. Her oxygen saturation began to drift downward—first to the high 80s, then low 80s.

Jamie moved quickly and quietly, repositioning the pulse oximeter until it hugged her finger side to side instead of front to back—just enough to distort the waveform. A deformed signal would be seen as unreliable at the nursing station; it wouldn't send anyone running. Then, almost casually, she turned to the monitor and changed the alarm thresholds—lowered the heart rate warning to 20 bpm.

She finished just in time. The heart rate, which had hovered in the 120s, was now dropping—90... 80... 60. Ravi held the woman's hand as her chest moved less and less. When her heart rate dipped below 50, the room stayed silent. No alarms. No nurses.

Another thirty seconds passed. Her heart rate was now 30.

Then came the longest thirty seconds of Ravi's life—watching the monitor count down: 29... 25... 22... 20. The familiar blare of the telemetry alarms filled the room. He knew the monitors at the nursing station would be making the same noises, demanding the attention of anyone nearby.

Jamie flipped the heart rate alarm back to 50 just as the nurses at the station burst into the room, but it was already done. The patient was DNR. No code. No panic.

Ravi couldn't place it in the moment, but something about it felt off. They had just killed a woman and nearly got caught doing it. Jamie hadn't flinched. Not at the alarms going off or the thud of the door bursting open. Not even a blink. No startled breath, no reflexive turn of the head. Nothing. He remembered the checklist from his psych rotation: shallow affect, lack of remorse, charm without empathy. Back then, it had seemed like a lecture. Now, it felt like a diagnosis. Maybe not his. But hers.

As the nurses stopped just short of the bed, Ravi couldn't speak. He didn't move.

Jamie met the nurse's gaze as they took a quick mental inventory of the situation. "We were walking by," she said smoothly. "Saw the pulse ox had a bad waveform. We came in to adjust it. Turns out it was her pulse that was bad." Somebody might be suspicious if she didn't throw a morbid joke in there.

Jamie then took out her stethoscope and made a show of performing the death exam. She left her stethoscope balancing on the woman's chest while simultaneously feeling her carotid for a full minute— "no heart tones, no pulse," she announced. She left her hand on the chest for another minute, feeling for any barely perceptible muscle movement— "no respiratory effort." Then, she grabbed the woman's hand from Ravi, who was shocked to find he was still holding her hand. Jamie squeezed the nail bed as hard as she could. "No response to noxious stimuli. Time of death..." she held up her watch, "September 3rd at Twenty-Three-Fifty-Seven." She rattled off in military time, then pulled a pen from her pocket and scribbled 2357 on her forearm so that she did not forget it before writing the death note.

The nurses accepted it without question and began the quiet, practiced process of preparing the body for the morgue.

As Ravi and Jamie walked away from the room, down the silent hallway echoing with footsteps, Jamie broke the silence. "You saw how much she was suffering."

But she hadn't looked sad. She'd looked... relieved. Satisfied.

He hadn't slept since.

* * *

Now, in the present, Ravi felt his body begging for rest. For quiet. He hadn't slept in thirty-six hours. His hands shook when he tried to drink water. His stash was gone. The tight coil behind his ribs was winding tighter with every minute.

He couldn't go into the med room again. Not so soon. Not when he was being watched.

Then the call came.

His patient was getting less stable in the ICU. The nurse needed an order to start norepinephrine. He knew the lady— gram-negative sepsis from an obstructing renal stone. She just came from having a nephrostomy tube placed in interventional radiology. Those procedures were like uncorking a dam, letting a river of bacteria flow into the bloodstream. Ravi was already typing the order in before the call was over. He instructed her to start it peripherally; he would be up to place a line in a minute.

Finally—a chance.

* * *

When Ravi walked into the room, it was already in motion. Kevin, the nurse, was at the bedside, fumbling through IV tubing. He was new. Young. Sweating. The ultrasound was next to the bed on the left, and the familiar central line kit was on the bedside table to the right. The patient was boosted to the top of the bed with the IV and vent tubing pulled mindfully away from the neck, where Ravi would be working. Crap. This guy was on top of things.

Ravi got to work preparing the patient for the procedure, while keeping an eye out for an opportunity to be alone with Mrs. Schneider—or was this Mrs. Jones? Whatever they called her, Ravi thought she was his godsend.

Ravi first headed to the tiny ICU sink. He lathered the soap more vigorously than necessary, scrubbing between each finger and each nail bed, until the skin turned pink. He looked up and met his own sunken eyes in the mirror, bloodshot and rimmed with dark circles.

The shame was immediate. Raw. It twisted his gut.

But then he saw it—just behind his reflection, tucked in the chaos of IV lines and medication bags—the fentanyl bag. His gaze locked on it like prey on a lure. The shame receded just a touch. Replaced by something steadier. Hungrier.

Ravi turned and shook his hands in the air, spraying the general vicinity with small droplets as he turned around. He gingerly unwrapped the sterile blue corners, one at a time, touching only the smallest section of the corner so as not to contaminate his field. Then, he found the sterile caps Keven had placed next to the sink. He carefully peeled the package apart with the opening at the bottom so the cap would land on his field without touching his bare hands. Plop. The first cap landed. Plop...plop. Two more caps. Then the biopatch in the same manner. The piece of foam hit the table without making a sound. Then the sterile probe cover for the ultrasound, wrapped in its own sterile blue towel. Just before it fell from its package, Ravi gave the smallest flick of his wrist...plop-plop. The sound of it hitting the edge of the table and then the floor. There was a drawer full of caps and biopatches on the cart just outside the door. But Ravi knew for a fact he had used the second-to-last probe cover an hour ago. Kevin was going to have to go to the back of the storage closet to get another one.

"Fuck!" Ravi feigned annoyance.

Kevin straightened. "I got it, Doc."

The second the door closed behind him, Ravi moved.

He quickly reached into his coat pocket and pulled out a capped syringe. He pulled the cap off, revealing a needle glistening in the overhead procedure light.

The infusion pump beeped quietly, steady as a metronome. He located the fentanyl bag among the bundle of meds and fluids. He jabbed the needle directly into the bag of fentanyl, before it ever got to that pesky pump that counted fentanyl by the drop. Drew back just enough. Taking it from here, it would be chalked up to being retained in the tubing or the folds of the bag.

He recapped the needle and slid it back into his pocket before anyone saw him. He felt jittery from the pressure. It was a narrow window. His mind briefly went back to how calm Jamie was when the nurses almost caught her as he walked back to the nursing station. He hung his coat over a chair outside the room before returning to scrub...again.

Ravi moved fast, slipping into sterile gloves and taking his position at the top of the bed.

His heart slowed. He had already gotten away with it.

He stared at the large black circle occupying his ultrasound screen. While his mind wandered to his coat and he pictured himself escaping to the call room, his hands worked automatically, guided by muscle memory alone. He plunged a needle directly into the middle of the black hole on the first try, sucking out dark maroon blood. He unscrewed the blood-filled syringe and threw it aside, the needle remaining in position in the neck with blood slowly dripping from the end. Ravi quickly picked up the flimsy guidewire, but his hands were shaking too much to thread it into the small needle hub. He rested his hand on the patient's forehead for support and then put the guidewire through the needle. He fed the wire in until he was holding one end and the other was touching her heart. He quickly pulled the needle out over the guidewire. He took the scalpel and made the tiniest incision where the guidewire was entering the skin. Then, the rigid blue dilator went over the wire before being tossed aside. Then the line itself. He aspirated each port to make sure each drew blood easily before flushing saline through each of the three. He put the special caps on. He tried to hurry when suturing the line in place, but his fingers kept tripping over each other. Finally, he made the last knot. "Would you mind putting on the patch and bandage?" Ravi asked Kevin as he was already grabbing the abdomen of his gown and pulling it firmly forward to break the ties in back.

"Not a problem," Kevin responded, excited to put on his own sterile gloves.

For a moment, everything felt normal.

Until he saw himself in the black reflection in the monitor as he grabbed his coat.

Hollow eyes. Slack mouth. Shadow of who he used to be.

The shame started to creep back in.

Ravi slid his coat back on. Felt the weight of the syringe in his pocket.

Later. When it was quiet.

He'd use it. Just enough. Just to make it stop.

He closed his eyes and leaned back against the elevator wall.

Maybe he was the villain. But he wasn't the only one.

Chapter 46

Stagecraft

The Killer

* * *

The boy was awake.

I made sure to stay out of his line of sight, hovering just beyond the corner where the ICU hallway bent toward the nurse's station. They'd moved him into a glass-fronted room near the back corner of the unit—smart. Easier to monitor. Only one way in or out and in clear view of every nurse in the station, not to mention the uniformed officer still standing outside his door. He wasn't restrained anymore, but there was always someone close.

That would complicate things. But I do love a challenge.

I didn't hate complications. I hated boredom. And this—this was just the sort of puzzle I liked best. If I timed it right, the officer would let me in. I could read the type. He was the kind who'd hold the door open without even glancing up, not wanting to be rude to someone with a badge and a tired look. People like him never really paid attention to our faces. Just our scrubs, our clipboards, our air of authority.

I had time to plan.

Then I saw him—Ravi.

He came down the hall like a man with a hangover and a secret. He didn't even look at the cop. Just waved the clipboard he was carrying and walked past like he belonged there. Which, I suppose, he did. That's what made it perfect.

I followed at a distance, watching him enter the room three doors down.

The line kit was already prepped. A young male nurse buzzed around the bedside, checking drips. Ravi fumbled something, cursed under his breath, then turned.

"Shit. I contaminated the sterile probe cover," I heard him say.

Predictable.

The nurse nodded and headed for the supply cart just outside the door. He pulled open the second drawer and started thumbing through the contents. He quickly found the empty tray of probe covers. His treasure was not in this chest. He turned and walked to the other side of the unit with a pep in his stride and a sense of purpose in his eyes, then disappeared into the store room.

I inched closer. Ravi was alone now, bent over the IV lines, pulling something from the pocket of his wrinkled white coat. A capped syringe. He uncapped it and slipped the needle into the fentanyl bag already running into the patient. Smooth draw. Like he'd done it before.

He quickly looked over his shoulder as he removed the needle from the bag, capped the syringe, and tossed it back into the coat pocket. He emerged from the slit in the curtain, looked me right in the eye without seeing me, hung his coat at the nursing station, and promptly turned back to the room.

I smiled.

He was making this too easy.

I busied myself at the counter next to his coat, looking like I belonged in precisely that spot. With a slight brush of my hip and a sleight of hand honed from years of practice, I slipped Ravi's syringe from the pocket of his coat and replaced it with an identical one—same volume, same clarity of the liquid. A mirror image. But the contents? Entirely different.

That kind of sleight had once kept me alive. A long time ago, in a city that never looked kindly on girls with dirty hands and empty stomachs. I learned early how to take things without being seen. Learned how to smile just enough, vanish just fast enough. I'd clawed my way out of that life with broken fingernails and bloodied pride—only to end up here, in a place where everyone still looked past me.

I stepped back, blending into a huddle of respiratory techs walking by, then slipped into the empty charting room nearby. I waited there five minutes—just long enough for Ravi to finish the procedure, give a few hollow jokes, and wander off with that familiar twitch in his jaw. I knew where he was going. He always went there when he needed to sneak a hit.

The resident call suite was a tomb during daylight hours. Nobody wanted to be caught napping while the attendings were wandering the halls. And like always, Ravi's desperation outpaced his caution. He didn't even bother to close the door to his unit all the way. I could see the light coming from a narrow slit in the doorway of the last room on the left as I passed through the common area. There was a big screen TV that didn't get much use, a couch, a massage recliner, and a dining table with six chairs. There were cafeteria trays with food scraps, crumpled papers scattered everywhere, and a forgotten stethoscope. The couch had one of the cushions half off, with the edge touching the floor, and a pair of scrub pants draped over the arm. These residents were pigs. But seriously, who forgot their pants?

Through the narrow slit, I could see him in the small bedroom. There was just enough room for the twin bed pushed up against the far wall, a small desk occupying the space between the bed and the close wall, and a chair.

Ravi was in the chair with his left foot firmly on the ground next to his right shoe and sock. His naked right foot was propped up on the edge of the chair with his knee pushing into his chest. He had a tourniquet wrapped around his calf as he searched between his toes for a vein big enough to stick a needle in. Beads of sweat were dripping down his forehead.

He uncapped the syringe with shaking fingers and let his eyes focus on his vein. Without breaking his gaze, he pushed the needle just a millimeter or two past his skin until he saw a little flash of red in the hub, and pushed the plunger down.

A beat passed.

Then two.

He blinked.

Then his face changed—not relief. Fear. Then panic.

His hands trembled violently, then stopped. His body tensed, then sagged. He opened his mouth, but no sound came out.

I slipped into the room.

He saw me.

That alone was worth the risk.

I straddled him in the chair, my knees on either side of his thighs. I could feel his legs pressing into mine, twitching slightly at first, then settling into a strange, slack resistance. The heat of his body clung to me—hot, erratic. There was still a trace of something else, too. The faint tension of a recent erection, now ebbing away. I wondered if he'd been that excited to use the fentanyl. Probably. That drug had a way of making people feel invincible—right up until it didn't.

I pressed my face close to his—so close I could see the veins spidering through his sclera. I could see the sweat on his upper lip, the pupils dilating.

"You're still awake," I whispered. "That's the beauty of Rocuronium. Paralysis without unconsciousness. It's all you, Ravi. You get to feel every moment."

His eyes were screaming.

I touched his cheek, then ran one gloved finger over the band of his watch. His pulse was erratic. Spiking.

"You were always a fuck up, weren't you?" I cooed. "Don't worry. You finally did something right."

I leaned in until our foreheads nearly touched.

"You're going to make a very convincing overdose."

He was crying now. Tears streamed from the corners of his eyes.

I watched every single one fall.

No interruptions. No alarms. No heroic saves.

I watched the life fade from his eyes. It was slow at first—pupils losing focus, the shallow rise of his chest faltering. Within a minute, his chest wall had stopped moving entirely. No struggle. No breath. Just the stillness that comes when every muscle gives up at once. I knew what it would feel like—like drowning in open air. Like being held under water while staring up at the sky, surrounded by life-saving oxygen he could no longer draw. His brain would scream for breath even as his body betrayed him. His gaze searched for mercy, for meaning, for someone to stop it.

But there was no one left.

Only me.

I watched him fade from existence.

The needle still hung from between his toes, glinting faintly in the low light. I didn't waste time. I pulled the empty Rocuronium syringe off the hub and replaced it with another—this one full of fentanyl. I had to be quick. He only had a couple of heartbeats left, and I needed it to circulate. No point leaving fentanyl pooled in a dead foot. I pushed the plunger down, smooth and steady. The opioid would wash the Roc out of the needle and spike his blood levels just enough to match the story they'd already decided to believe.

This might be my greatest work of art yet.

Chapter 47

Beneath the Surface

Elise Navarro

* * *

The page came in as she was flipping through code sheets, her eyes half-blinded from staring at the screen for hours. A familiar tone sounded overhead, and her heart immediately dropped. Not another one.

> **"CODE BLUE - RESIDENT LOUNGE.**
> **CODE BLUE - RESIDENT LOUNGE.**
> **CODE BLUE - RESIDENT LOUNGE."**

For a moment, she didn't move. It took until the second time through to understand what the operator was saying, and the third time through before she processed it. The resident lounge wasn't a patient area. Normally, a call like this was a housekeeper hitting the button while dusting. But something in her gut twisted. Does the call suite even have a code button to bump? She wasn't even on service this week, but Elise stood so fast her chair fell backward. She was out the door before it hit the ground.

She ran.

The fluorescent lights buzzed faintly overhead, and her shoes slapped the linoleum with each step. She could hear voices up ahead—panicked, muffled, urgent. The closer she got, the more the air changed—like it always did during a code. Denser. Charged. As if the walls themselves were holding their breath.

The call room suite was in the basement, past a bank of elevators and a quiet stretch of windowless corridor. Elise skidded into the hallway just outside the resident lounge, breath tight in her chest. A cluster of nurses and residents had already gathered, eyes wide, hands clasped over mouths, some crying, others just frozen.

At first, Elise couldn't see who it was. A man was half-dragged into the hallway by his feet, his white coat and shirt crumpled up around his armpits, exposing his brown chest. Jamie was straddling him, knees planted to either side of his torso, compressing hard and fast. There wasn't enough room to work beside him—his shoulders were wedged in the doorframe, and Jamie's body bridged the threshold.

Inside the room, Leilani was lying on her stomach on the floor, legs tucked under the bed. Her eyes were inches from his face, aligned with his mouth, as she struggled to find the right angle for intubation. An intern was drilling into his shin, sweat streaking down his temple. "IO's in," he called.

The pharmacist didn't miss a beat—she handed off the epinephrine. A nurse pushed it straight into the marrow and followed it with a flush in one practiced motion.

Everyone inside the code was focused. Quiet. Efficient. They'd shoved their emotions down where training told them to.

Jamie, too—her movements were sharp, measured, mechanical. The rest of the crowd was cracking at the seams. A few sobbed. Some whispered in disbelief. Most just looked helpless.

As Leilani got the breathing tube in and moved her head out of the way, Elise saw his face.

Ravi.

Elise took one look and knew that no matter how well this team performed, no matter how perfectly the code was executed, it was too late.

His jaw hung slightly open. The pooling in his extremities had already begun—his fingers dusky, lips mottled. The cap refill in his nail beds was absent. And there, just beneath the antiseptic and sweat, was the faint, unmistakable smell of death, just starting to seep in.

But at least—Elise thought with a flicker of grim relief—there was no death poop. One final dignity for a man dying surrounded by his peers.

Livedo reticularis snaked up his exposed back and flank. His skin was waxy. Elise crossed the room in two strides and gently took Jamie by the shoulder.

"He's gone," she said.

Jamie kept compressing. Her eyes wide, unfocused.

"Jamie." Elise's voice was firmer. "He's been gone for a while."

Lelaini hesitated, then let go of the ambu bag and backed toward the bed, as far from the body as possible, her gloved hands shaking. She suddenly looked like a caged animal desperate to get out of this room.

Elise knelt, touched Ravi's arm. Rigor was already settling. It hadn't been minutes. It had been hours.

She stood and dialed. First Logan. Then Tyler.

Minutes later, the room was cordoned off. Logan arrived with gloves already on. Tyler followed with a camera and evidence bags. Jamie sat slumped in a chair, a blanket around her shoulders, whispering to no one. "I knew he was struggling... but I didn't think it would end like this."

Elise wasn't listening.

Ravi's phone was on the desk, upright, plugged in, screen glowing. Notes app open.

Tyler read aloud.

It was a suicide note.

An apology. An admission. Regret and guilt and veiled references to something unforgivable. A final release.

Tyler returned from the hallway and crouched beside Elise. "Leilani just filled me in," he said softly.

She turned to him, her expression grim.

"She and Jamie were looking for Jamie's stethoscope," Tyler continued. "Thought it might've been left in the common area. When it wasn't, they split up to check the call rooms. Leilani took the left side of the hall, Jamie the right. Leilani found him."

Elise's eyes flicked toward the doorway.

"She called Jamie over. He was already down—slumped in his chair before they put him on the ground and dragged him into the hall. She thought maybe he'd collapsed," Tyler said. "But then she saw the syringe."

"Syringe?"

"Between his toes. With a tourniquet lying next to him."

Elise's stomach clenched.

"We missed a drug problem," she muttered under her breath so the amassing crowd wouldn't hear. "That would explain his activities in the med rooms and all of the inappropriate badge swipes."

"Even if he did have a drug problem," Logan frowned, "this looks staged."

"Anything is possible. In fact, when staging a crime, it is common for the perpetrator to craft elaborate ruses to make sure that someone else finds the body."

Tyler paused, eyes fixed on the note. "Or maybe he really did feel guilty. Maybe he knew something—something he couldn't carry anymore." His voice faltered, the words sounding more like a plea to himself than a truth he trusted.

Elise's eyes didn't leave Ravi's face. "Is that what you really believe? Or just wishful thinking?"

Tyler answered her with a heavy silence.

"Maybe someone didn't want him talking."

Logan glanced at her, then at Tyler. "You think he was silenced?"

"Maybe. Maybe he found out something he shouldn't know. Maybe he was on to the killer." Tyler said quietly. "Or maybe he was cracking under pressure and his partner decided he was a liability."

Elise didn't speak. She just looked down at Ravi's face. "Or maybe he was a resident who couldn't cope and developed a drug problem, and we failed him. I failed him."

She had walked past him a hundred times. Read his notes. Signed off on his progress. Had she ever really seen him?

So young. So hollowed out.

The phone screen kept glowing, casting a sickly dim light across the desk, the words still visible.

Chapter 48

The Fall

Tyler Grayson

* * *

Tyler stepped through the hospital's side entrance and felt it immediately—the electric tension in the air, brittle and buzzing like static. Phones were out on every counter. Heads were close together, whispering. No one was talking above a murmur, but with everyone talking at a murmur, it sounded like a dull roar.

A waiting room TV flickered with the headline he'd been dreading: **"Resident's Suicide Note Reveals Fatal Mistakes in ICU Deaths."**

His stomach dropped.

He crossed to the nearest monitor and read the bullet points beneath the banner. They weren't quoting the entire note—just pieces. Enough to control the narrative. Enough to convict a dead man.

"Missed murmurs… failure to report chest pain… critical documentation gaps… fatal air embolism…"

One line stuck with him: "If only I'd caught that murmur… the stroke never would have happened."

It was written like a confession, but it wasn't one. Not really. It was self-deprecating. Judgmental. It read more like a formal reprimand, the kind of letter you'd write to get a subordinate suspended, or the closing argument of a prosecutor. Now that he thought about it, he could recall a judge using the same phrasing while justifying the delivery of a harsh sentence. Not the murmur part, but the taking responsibility part.

The letter went on, "There were signs. I should have spoken up. If I had, the catheter wouldn't have fractured. The epi wouldn't have entered her chest cavity. She'd still be alive."

Tyler's skin crawled. It was too… crafted. Not the disjointed rambling of someone in despair. This had structure. Momentum. A timeline that just happened to match hospital rumors.

He'd read real suicide notes—sloppy, frantic, raw. They left you feeling like you had more questions than answers. This felt like it conveniently answered every question they were asking. It clarified timelines. It wrapped up everything in a nice bow. It was just too neatly orchestrated.

But it didn't matter.

The hospital had already latched on.

He passed another TV on the surgical floor. The same segment looping again—Ravi's student ID photo boxed beside the phrase: *"Silent Crisis in Healthcare: Doctor's Death Raises Questions."* But the questions weren't about the hospital's safety. They were about Ravi. Always Ravi. Nobody else.

He passed by a pair of nurses in the hallway. "Poor guy." "Yeah. But those deaths… it explains a lot, doesn't it?"

By the time Tyler reached the main stairwell, three more people had already nodded solemnly at him, as if they shared some unspoken truth.

They didn't.

He climbed to the second floor and settled into the now familiar 2C conference room. He locked the door and pulled out his notebook.

The note was too polished. Too easy. Ravi had barely been dead twelve hours—who had leaked it? And how was it already cementing the narrative they'd all accept as truth?

He flipped to his interview notes from the stroke case. The boy's sketch still chilled him: a woman in scrubs and a blue jacket, masked. Anonymous, but specific. She wasn't a hallucination. She'd been real.

And someone else had swiped into the room before that stroke happened. A 5'7" white woman with a noticeable limp. He was sure it was the same woman.

Maybe Ravi had blamed himself. Maybe he thought he'd missed something. Maybe the guilt had eaten him alive. Maybe that was his partner. But that definitely wasn't Ravi in the drawing.

Ravi didn't cause that stroke.

Someone else had.

He flipped to the interview transcript from Jamie. Her answers had been sharp. But something had felt… off. She hadn't returned his messages since Ravi died.

She was close to him.

Too close?

He checked again. Still no reply. No missed call. No three dots blinking in the message thread. Just silence.

It wasn't like her. Even in crisis, Jamie was punctual. Responsive. Predictable in the way overachievers are—built like clockwork, each gear wound tight with guilt and ambition. But maybe something had snapped.

Or maybe it hadn't.

Maybe this was her recalibrating. Repositioning. Watching to see which way the dust would settle before she stepped back into the light.

Tyler hated the thought. But it clung to him. Her calm under pressure. Her presence at so many codes. Her silence now.

He turned the stroke sketch over and wrote one line on the back: **If Ravi wasn't acting alone, then who let him take the fall?**

Then he stared at the drawing. The woman's eyes. Not Avery's. Definitely not Jamie's. Not familiar in any obvious way.

But still—somewhere, he knew those eyes.

Chapter 49

Ashes and Embers

Dr. Leilani Kealoha

* * *

Leilani clocked out just after seven, her body aching from the shift, her thoughts heavier still. As she passed the elevators, she caught sight of the flier taped crookedly to the wall: In Loving Memory of Dr. Ravi Patel – Candlelight Vigil, 7:30 PM, Courtyard.

She paused, hand hovering near the call button. A dozen excuses came to mind. She needed sleep. She had to follow up on her consults. She had nothing to say. But none of them were quite true. She sighed and turned toward the courtyard.

The hospital corridors buzzed with the unsettled energy of collective grief. Small groups clustered near nurses' stations, hunched in corners, speaking in hushed tones. Leilani turned a corner and slowed as she approached the main staff bulletin board outside the resident lounge.

The board was crowded with photos—some candid, some official—taped beside clippings of Ravi's published case reports and the faded remnants of birthday cards. But it was the scrap of dark blue cotton that drew her eye: a torn panel from a scrub top, cut from the chest pocket where the embroidery rested, pinned like a memorial ribbon. It flapped gently in the draft from the hallway door, the embroidery catching the light with every ripple: Ravi Patel, MD. His actual scrubs. One of the original three issued at the start of intern year.

In the center, an 11x14 studio portrait commanded the board. Ravi, clean-shaven and alert, wore a tailored navy suit and a slate-gray tie. His smile was faint but full of promise. The light kissed his skin, made his eyes shimmer with something between excitement and trepidation—like he was standing on the edge of the future.

Surrounding it were dozens of sticky notes, layered haphazardly in bursts of fluorescent yellow, pink, and blue—like confetti from a joyless parade. Some were messages of love. Others reeked of guilt.

"You were always kind to the night shift," read one in shaky handwriting.

"I'm so sorry I didn't check in that day," another confessed in small, slanted script.

"You carried more than your share. We should have seen it," said a third, its ink smudged from a trembling hand or tears.

Others offered platitudes—

"Gone too soon,"

"Rest easy, friend,"

"Healers need healing too."

—The kind of things said when the weight of emotion outpaces language. They came from people trained to hold others in crisis, but who'd never learned to hold themselves. Doctors, nurses, techs—those who gave strength for a living but crumbled in silence.

Their coping mechanisms—detachment, dark humor, long hours—had failed them. Now all they had were sticky notes and borrowed words. The sticky notes became their outlet, a fragmented, desperate mosaic of sorrow, guilt, and love.

By the time she reached the courtyard, dusk was settling in. Near the entrance, a young Indian resident stood holding a small brass bowl filled with a thick, golden-brown paste. The bowl caught the fading light and glowed faintly, almost reverently. Leilani slowed as she approached, her curiosity piqued. The paste looked smooth and dense, the color of burnt amber, with tiny flecks of red and orange. The smell—warm, woody, and unmistakable—hit her a beat later. Sandalwood. It reminded her of temples, of incense, of calm.

The resident, his forehead already marked with a small, precise tilak, offered her a kind, weary smile. "It's a Hindu custom," he explained gently, dipping his fingers into the paste. "A mark of respect, of mourning. We place it here—" he touched the center of his own brow "—to honor the soul and remember their light."

Before she could answer, he stepped closer and reached up with reverent care, dabbing a small streak of the paste onto her forehead. The sandalwood's scent lingered, comforting and ancient.

"Ravi's family would have wanted this," he added, voice low. "He used to wear it on Diwali. Said it made him feel connected."

As if on command, his parents and brother arrived at the edge of the courtyard. They were flanked by Dr. Golden, the residency program director, who had personally picked them up from the airport and driven them straight to the memorial. Their faces were drawn, stunned by the sight of candles and colleagues, of the gentle music and Ravi's smiling photo. His mother clutched a folded white handkerchief in one hand and his father's elbow in the other, as if both were keeping her upright. The brother—taller, younger—walked with hollow steps, his eyes fixed on the portrait like he was willing it to move.

Leilani nodded, swallowing the lump in her throat. "Thank you," she said quietly.

The resident gave a soft smile and nodded back, then turned quickly and jogged toward the courtyard entrance—bowl still in hand—as Ravi's family stepped into view. He approached them with reverence, offering the tilak to each member of the grieving family.

Flickering tea lights dotted the lawn, each nestled in a paper cup to shield it from the breeze. A folding table held a large photo of Ravi smiling, surrounded by flowers and messages scrawled on index cards. Someone strummed soft chords on a guitar—off-key but sincere.

Clusters of people stood scattered across the grass. Some held candles. Others wore ribbons pinned to their scrubs. A few attending physicians hovered at the edges, solemn and out of place.

Leilani recognized Logan and Elise near the side entrance, talking quietly. Tyler leaned against a tree farther back, hands in his coat pockets, scanning the crowd. But it was Jamie who drew her eye.

She stood close to the photo table, a candle clutched so tightly in her hand it looked like it might snap. Her posture was rigid, her expression composed—but her eyes darted constantly, as if she couldn't decide whether to run or scream. Her shoulders trembled just enough to betray the effort it took to stay upright.

People began to speak. One by one, residents and nurses stepped forward, sharing stories. Some were warm—funny anecdotes from rounds, Ravi's bad handwriting on call notes, his coffee addiction. Others were more formal: He was the glue of our team. He always stayed late to help.

A MICU nurse added, "He was the kind of doctor who would throw on gloves and help with a boost—no hesitation, no complaints. He always kept a pair of gloves in his white coat pocket, just in case someone needed a hand. Said it made him feel useful." Hung her head and smiled a little so that she wouldn't cry.

Leilani listened, but the words slid past her. They painted a picture she half-recognized. Ravi had been kind. But he'd also been unraveling. She remembered finding him alone in the ICU once, just standing at the window, eyes blank, his hands motionless at his sides.

A nurse from the MICU stepped forward and tried to speak about a patient Ravi had stayed late to help extubate. Her voice cracked halfway through. Someone handed her a tissue.

A voice in the crowd filled the silence, "I've got you beat. He once stayed late to help me clean up a code brown!".

A tense chuckle passed through the crowd. Someone muttered, "Only Ravi would turn a code brown into a team-building exercise."

Leilani managed a small smile. For a moment, it was like he was still there—making the worst shifts a little lighter. Someone behind her whispered a quiet explanation for those nearby: "Code brown means... well, poop."

Even in mourning, gallows humor had its place. Especially among healthcare workers who had no other way to release the pressure valve.

Then Jamie stepped forward.

Her voice, at first, was calm. Controlled.

"Ravi was... more than a colleague. He was brilliant. Stubborn. He cared deeply, maybe too deeply sometimes."

She looked at the candle in her hands.

"Sometimes the system fails. Sometimes we fail. But that doesn't make us monsters. It doesn't mean we were wrong to care."

She paused, blinking rapidly. Her voice wavered.

"We're all just trying to survive. To get through the night. To do right by our patients. And sometimes we mess up. Sometimes we lose more than we save. But Ravi deserved better than this."

She stopped abruptly, staring down at the flame. "I hope he's free now."

She stepped back without another word. Someone reached toward her in comfort. She flinched and turned away.

Leilani couldn't stop watching her.

Something was off. She'd seen grief before—raw and honest and messy. But this was... something else. Jamie's grief didn't look lived-in. It looked performed. A mask over something uglier.

She glanced across the lawn. Elise met her eyes for a moment. Then Tyler's gaze followed. Something unspoken passed between them.

The vigil began to wind down. One by one, candles were placed on the table or left flickering on the grass. Leilani waited until the crowd had thinned before walking to the photo. She placed her candle down gently and whispered something she couldn't quite hear herself.

As the last few people drifted away, Leilani spotted Navarro lingering by the side path, near the edge of the garden. Something about her stillness—alert but not rigid—reminded Leilani of a lifeguard watching a crowded pool. Not grieving. Guarding.

Leilani approached quietly, the sandalwood scent still clinging faintly to her skin.

"You don't have to say anything," she said softly. "I know there are things you can't share. I just... I needed to tell someone."

Navarro met her eyes and nodded once, the barest invitation.

"I don't think Ravi killed himself," Leilani whispered. "I know denial is part of grief. I've read the stats—dozens of articles, lectures about recognizing the signs. But I also knew him."

She looked toward the altar, the candles flickering against the night.

"He was unraveling, yeah. He was exhausted. But he still had his rituals. His humor. He was still fighting. And the note? It sounded like a judgment, not a confession."

Elise said nothing, but her posture shifted slightly—less guarded, more engaged.

"And if he did do something wrong... if he had guilt over a mistake? That's still not suicide. It's fear. Or pressure. Or maybe someone made sure he couldn't speak for himself."

Elise's gaze sharpened, but she didn't interrupt.

"And if it was suicide, why did he go through the trouble of injecting between his toes?" Leilani asked rhetorically, now moving away from the conversation and into her internal monologue. "It was a scenario where we were going to find out either way. Wouldn't it have been easier to use his arm?"

She let the question linger.

"I'm not asking for answers," Leilani added, quieter now. "Just... if you ever need someone to talk to. Or if this doesn't end here. I want to help."

Elise gave a slow nod. "That means more than you know."

Leilani stepped back, letting the quiet settle between them.

As she turned to go, she looked back one last time.

Jamie hadn't moved.

She was still there, still clutching the candle, eyes locked on the flame like it held the answers.

Leilani shivered.

He didn't kill those people, she thought. At least... not all of them.

She didn't know what that thought meant.

But it wouldn't let her go.

Chapter 50

Interrogation Light

Tyler Grayson

* * *

Tyler stood just outside the police interview room, coffee in hand, heart hammering. The hallway buzzed with fluorescent lights and the distant murmur of dispatch chatter, but inside that room—just one wall away—everything was still. Elise and Logan hovered behind the two-way mirror, silent. A uniformed officer leaned casually against the wall nearby. Tyler felt anything but casual.

This was a big one.

He wasn't certain Jamie was the killer. But he was no longer convinced she wasn't.

He took a breath and stepped in.

The interview room was cold—deliberately so. It was meant to make people uncomfortable. Meant to remind them they weren't in control. Gray concrete walls. A single table. Four chairs. A mounted camera with a red light blinking steadily in the corner. A faint hum came from the fluorescent lights above—steady, rhythmic, like a tension metronome counting down.

Jamie sat on the far side, hunched forward, hands clasped in her lap. Her hair was limp. Her eyes—rimmed in red—met his, then dropped. Her scrubs were crumbled. Her whole presence was unraveling, thread by thread.

She hadn't slept. That much was clear.

"Morning," he said softly, setting his coffee down but not sitting. "Thanks for coming in."

Jamie gave a small nod. "Didn't think I had a choice."

"You did."

Tyler finally took his seat. He let the silence stretch a moment longer than comfortable. The fluorescent hum filled the space, too loud for such a small room.

He remembered the first time he broke someone in this room. A gang member was caught near the scene of a murder. Denied everything for forty minutes—until Tyler mentioned his sister's name. He had a gut feeling that it was a revenge murder after the victim had attacked his younger sister. The banger's posture shifted, and the whole story unraveled. Tyler used to be good at this. Could still be. But Jamie wasn't some petty criminal.

"How are you holding up?"

"I'm fine. Just tired."

"Last night was... a lot."

She nodded again, this time slower. "He was a good doctor."

Tyler studied her. "Ravi's note... he took responsibility for that stroke patient. Said it was his mistake. But we know someone else accessed that room."

Jamie's shoulders stiffened.

"Do you know who it was?"

No answer. Her knuckles were white.

"Jamie," Tyler said gently, "I know this is hard. But you've been at the center of a lot of codes. You're fast. You're confident. Some would say... addicted to the rush."

Her head snapped up. "I'm just trying to help people."

"Even if it means going too far?"

"You don't know what it's like," she snapped, suddenly standing. She began pacing, one hand gripping her opposite elbow. "What this place does to us. What it takes from us. You all think you know what happened. You don't. None of you were there."

Her voice was rising. Fraying. Tyler let her speak.

Her breath caught. For a split second, the sterile gray walls seemed to melt away. She was back in the ICU—the shrill alarm of a monitor flatlining in her ears. The smell of antiseptic and the sour sting of panic filled her nose. Ravi's voice, calm but urgent—"Jamie, recheck the labs." The sharp flick of her glove as she reached for the chart. The heart tracing already lost. She couldn't stop it.

She jerked herself back to the present.

"We tried everything," she said suddenly, eyes wide. "We thought we could turn it around. I even asked for a second bolus of epi before the—"

She stopped herself.

Tyler blinked. He wasn't even sure which event she was talking about. That detail hadn't been in any report.

He didn't mention it. Just made a mental note. The light hummed louder now—or maybe it just felt that way.

She dropped back into her chair. Her face crumpled. Tears spilled freely now, ragged and raw.

"But Ravi... he wasn't supposed to die. He wasn't supposed to leave me."

Behind the glass, Elise and Chris exchanged a look.

Elise: "That wasn't a denial."

Chris: "But it wasn't a confession either."

Tyler felt the air shift. This wasn't just grief. It was grief tangled with guilt—or something worse.

He leaned forward slightly. "Jamie... did you do something you can't take back?"

She met his gaze, face streaked with tears. "I've made mistakes. But I'm not a monster."

Silence.

Then, almost too quiet to hear: "If you think I killed those people... more people are going to die while you are wasting your time with me..."

He didn't know if he'd just heard a confession—or a warning.

She turned slowly and looked toward the mirror. Her eyes locked on it. "You're watching, right?" she said, her voice flat and cold. "I hope you're watching."

Just then, a knock interrupted the moment. Tyler turned as a plainclothes officer opened the door and slipped in a sealed manila envelope.

"Urgent," the officer said. "Just came in from Grayson's request. New evidence results."

Tyler took the envelope with a nod, flipping it open. Inside was a blank piece of paper—he hoped seeing evidence against her would help convince her that a full confession was in her best interest.

He slid the file beneath his coffee cup and turned back to her.

As he stared at her trembling frame, a flicker of doubt threaded through his mind. What if he was wrong? What if Jamie was just another casualty of a system too broken to catch what was really happening? He had built his career on certainty, on reading people, on cutting through lies to get to the truth. But now? Now he wasn't sure if he was interrogating a killer—or just victimizing another innocent.

Chapter 51

The Tipping Point

Tyler Grayson

* * *

Tyler was hunched over a cluttered desk in a back office tucked behind Security. His interview notes with Jamie lay scattered beside a half-drunk cup of hospital coffee. The early morning hum of the hospital was slowly building outside the door—pager tones, soft-soled shoes against tile, the occasional burst of laughter that didn't belong.

He was circling something, but he didn't know what.

Then a knock—firm, urgent.

The door opened before he could answer. Naomi stepped in first, her expression tight. Behind her was Nilesh Patel, holding a ziplock bag like it contained a live grenade.

Naomi didn't sit. She handed Tyler a slim binder and said, "You're going to want to sit down for this."

Tyler did.

Naomi flipped open the binder and turned it toward him. Lab results. Red flags.

"We found Legionella," she said. "In a nebulizer setup from the ICU."

Tyler blinked. "That's... a water system contaminant, right?"

"Yes. But these solutions are supposed to be sterile. There's no reason we should find any trace of Legionella inside a sealed nebulizer unit."

Nilesh cut in, voice low. "And that's not all."

He placed the ziplock on the desk. Inside were two vials of heparin—identical labels, same lot number, same expiration date. But one had a subtle difference: the fluid inside sloshed too easily.

"One of these is saline," he said. "Someone's been swapping out meds. We've found five more that appear to have the wrong viscosity. I'm running full assays now, but it's happening. Someone is diluting drugs. Or swapping them out entirely."

Tyler stared at the bag. The implications hit hard. This wasn't a mistake. It was deliberate. Cold.

Sabotage.

"Do you think this is connected to the recent post-op clots?"

Nilesh nodded. "It could explain everything from unexplained thrombotic events to prolonged bleeds. And if it's more than just heparin, we're looking at a full-blown breach."

Naomi closed the binder. "We can't prove it wasn't environmental with the Legionella—not yet—we will have to see if any other hospitals have similar contaminations. If it was at the factory before they were sealed, we won't be the only ones. If we are the only ones, the contamination is happening inside the hospital, inside sterile containers."

Tyler exhaled. The walls felt closer.

He pulled out his phone, texting Elise and Chris: Need full whiteboard meeting. Scope just exploded.

Within minutes, he was back in the security hub, cross-referencing badge logs from the med room.

Jamie Lin's badge appeared twice—both times late at night, well outside her normal shifts. Residents have access to the door of the med room, but not the Pyxis containing the medications once they get inside. What was she doing in there?

He queued up the video. The timestamp blinked in the upper corner—2:17 a.m. The angle was poor, but it showed enough. Jamie lingered just outside the door, glancing down both ends of the hallway. She fidgeted with something in her pocket before swiping in.

Once inside, the camera caught just a sliver of her back. She didn't stay long—less than three minutes. But she didn't look like someone responding to an emergency. She looked like someone doing something she didn't want seen. Residents had no reason to access the med room on their own.

His stomach turned.

She said she was just trying to help.

He called her back in. This time it was short, quiet. Off the record.

"What were you doing in the med room at 2:17 AM?"

Jamie's shoulders were drawn tight. Her eyes flicked toward the door, as if weighing whether to bolt. She didn't speak at first.

The silence was deafening.

"You don't understand," she said finally. "He was falling apart. He was trying to stop, but... withdrawal is brutal."

She shifted her weight, folded her arms, unfolded them again. "He begged me not to report it. Said if it got out, he'd lose everything—his license, his residency, his family's respect."

Tyler waited, giving her space.

She looked down, her voice barely audible. "He was shaking. He couldn't focus. He said he just needed to get through the night. That he'd be okay if I could just get him one more dose."

A long silence.

"I didn't know what else to do," she said, finally meeting his eyes. "I didn't want him to crash. I thought I was protecting him. But maybe I just gave him more rope."

Tyler didn't answer right away. Part of him wanted to believe her. The other part—the part trained to listen to tone, to timelines, to omissions—knew something still didn't add up.

Her story explained the entry, maybe. But not the look on her face in that video.

He logged the details in the back of his mind. Her rhythm was off—too rehearsed, then too messy. It could be truth fighting through guilt. Or a lie collapsing under pressure.

Later, back in the security office, Elise joined them. Chris leaned against the table, arms folded, watching the feed of incoming alerts.

"It's like whack-a-mole," Chris muttered. "Every time we get close, something else explodes."

Elise's eyes were locked on the whiteboard now covered in names, times, lab results, and one growing question in the middle: **WHY?**

Tyler looked at Naomi and Nilesh. "Expand testing. Every container in the ICU. I want eyes on everything."

They nodded.

The list was growing. Fast.

Later, Elise caught Jamie outside the ICU, alone in the staff lounge, rinsing out a coffee mug with trembling hands.

"Jamie," Elise said quietly.

Jamie froze. "Am I being pulled in again?"

"No. Just a question."

She turned, jaw clenched. "You think I'm a killer."

"I think someone's making it easier for patients to die."

Jamie's eyes flickered. "That's not the same thing."

Elise stepped closer. "It is to the families."

Jamie didn't answer. She stared into the sink, the water still running as if she needed it to keep her grounded. Her shoulders rose and fell in a slow, deliberate pattern.

Elise waited, letting the silence thicken. She could see Jamie's reflection in the steel backsplash—watching her, calculating.

Something about it felt too controlled. Too… aware.

Then she said, almost absently, "I wasn't the only one with access to the nebulizer drawer."

Elise blinked. "How did you know it was contaminated?"

Jamie went still. Too still.

"I didn't say it was replaced," Elise said, her voice soft and sharp.

Jamie's face tightened. She set the mug down hard and walked out without another word.

Chapter 52

Sealed with a Kiss

Elise Navarro

* * *

Elise sat alone in the medical director's office, surrounded by two stacks of files and the persistent hum of the overhead fluorescent lights. Her white coat hung on the back of her chair. The clock on the wall blinked 12:41 a.m.

She'd told herself she was just finishing up documentation. But the truth was harder to name. She wasn't ready to go home. Not yet.

Her laptop screen glowed with a spreadsheet of badge access logs. Next to it, a binder of rapid response charts lay open, flagged with color-coded tabs. As she scrolled through the timeline, a pattern began to emerge—one that prickled at the back of her neck.

Jamie Lin's name appeared again.

Then again.

And again.

Always close. Always involved. Sometimes listed as the responding resident. Sometimes just noted as being "present at bedside."

Elise leaned back slowly, eyes narrowing. She reached for another folder—

code blue from Room 516, just five days ago. Jamie. ICU transfer. No direct wrongdoing noted, but she was there.

Her mind drifted, uninvited, to Jamie's strange composure at the vigil. The rigidity. The rehearsed grief. The way she hadn't flinched when Elise confronted her in the staff lounge. How she'd slipped—mentioning the nebulizer drawer.

And then… the moment Ravi's body was found.

Jamie and Leilani had been searching for Jamie's stethoscope. They'd split up—checking opposite ends of the resident lounge. It was Leilani who found him. She shouted, and everything changed.

When Elise arrived, Jamie was already straddling Ravi's chest, performing compressions. Her face was blank—utterly expressionless, like her mind had turned off. Leilani, kneeling at the head, was intubating with practiced focus, her brow furrowed but calm.

They were both quiet. Efficient. But Elise remembered a chill running down her arms. Because their calm didn't feel the same.

Jamie looked like she was going through the motions. Detached. Cold. Robotic.

And where had that stethoscope been? It wasn't found in the call suite, but she had noticed Jamie carrying it around since then. Was it ever lost? Or was it all just a rouse to get the body discovered before her shift was over?

Elise dragged the shift schedule into view. Layered it with the incident logs.

The overlap was staggering.

A chill rippled down her spine.

She closed her eyes for a moment, then stood and walked to the security hub.

* * *

Logan and Tyler were still in the office when she arrived. Logan was hunched in front of the monitor wall, eyes scanning through overlapping footage timelines. Tyler sat across from him, flipping through a spiral notebook.

As Elise stepped in, Tyler stood and stretched. "I'm going to step out and check in with the forensics lab—see if there's any updates."

He nodded to Logan, then Elise. "Text me if anything blows up."

He left without waiting for a response.

Logan raised an eyebrow, then motioned her over. He pulled up the logs, keyed in Jamie's ID.

Elise leaned forward. "Just the last two weeks."

Tyler turned to look at her. "You think she's involved?"

Elise didn't answer.

The screen filled with timestamps and door access points. Twice in the med room. Once in the ICU after hours. A cluster of hits near the fourth-floor stairwell, late at night.

"She was never scheduled on those nights," Elise murmured.

"If she was the one swiping her badge." Logan played devil's advocate.

Logan clicked into one of the camera feeds—the new sanitizer-mounted units they'd started deploying hours earlier. The angle was surprisingly good. Elise watched as nurses and staff filtered in and out of a patient room. Each time, the camera caught them pausing briefly at the sanitizer dispenser.

"Start making notes," she said after watching the feed for five minutes at double speed. "Not of who goes in. Of who doesn't sanitize."

Logan shot her a look. "You think this is how they're doing it? Contamination through contact?"

"I think," Elise said carefully, "it's gross. And the kind of JHACO violation that gets hospitals fined millions. There were three of them in ten minutes. I am going to make a compilation video and shame them at noon didactics."

Logan searched her face for signs of humor. Her eyes were amused, but he was pretty sure it was at the thought of her clever lesson and the residents squirming.

There was silence as the video continued.

Elise didn't say anything more about Jamie. Not yet.

But as she turned to go, she paused by the corner whiteboard. A single chart lay on the table nearby, left open. It belonged to one of the earlier victims—a quiet DNR patient whose cardiac arrest had initially raised no flags.

Elise picked it up, scanned the final notes, then just stared at the page.

Her hand trembled. She set the chart down carefully, but not before Logan noticed.

He stepped beside her, silent. Then, without a word, he reached over and gently stilled her hand with his own. Warm. Steady. His touch grounded her like a hand on a tuning fork.

Their eyes met. Neither spoke.

"You're not alone in this," he said softly. "Even if it feels like it."

Something tightened in her chest. Not panic. Not grief. Something gentler. Something she didn't have time for, but didn't want to let go of.

They were too close. Elise knew it. But she didn't step back.

Logan leaned in slightly, not presumptive—just close enough to notice.

Then the overhead speaker chimed—the familiar tone before every emergency alert. Elise stood still, bracing.

"Code Red. Room 728."

Elise flinched. Logan took a half-step back.

"Code Red. Room 728. Code Red. Room 728."

"That'll be another patient sneaking off to smoke," he said with a dry smile.

Elise snorted once, surprised. "Fourth one this week."

Just like that, the moment was gone. Reality pulled them back.

She gave a small nod and walked out, her pace quickening.

The door clicked shut behind her.

Then, a beat later, it opened again.

Logan turned just in time to see Elise step back inside—eyes focused, steps deliberate. She crossed the room without a word, reached him, and pushed her body against his.

Their mouths met hard—urgent, breathless. She kissed him like she meant to forget everything else for one second. Just one.

Then just as quickly, she pulled back. Her breath trembled. She didn't speak.

Elise turned and left again.

This time, she didn't look back.

Logan stood frozen in the space she left behind. He didn't move. He couldn't. Her breath still lingered in the space between them.

And outside, the night kept going.

Chapter 53

The Cracks Deepen

Dr. Jamie Lin

* * *

Jamie felt it before she saw it—the way conversations dipped as she passed, the glances that lingered a second too long. The ICU was always a pressure cooker, but now it felt radioactive. Every whisper in the hallway seemed to have her name nestled inside it.

She told herself it was grief. Ravi's death had shaken everyone. Of course people were tense. Of course they'd look at her—she had been his closest friend. His shadow.

But the prickle on the back of her neck never faded.

She fumbled a set of notes during morning rounds, her hand slipping as she handed a chart to the attending. Later, she forgot to chart vitals on a septic patient, catching the error only because the nurse double-checked. These weren't the kind of mistakes Jamie made. Not before. Not ever.

In quieter moments, memories crept in—Ravi beside her at the bedside of a crashing patient, cracking a dry joke between bagging breaths: "At least Code Blues don't come with patient satisfaction cards."

She remembered the way his hand had trembled as he typed progress notes in the middle of the night, the way he'd take breaks between sentences just to breathe. Once, she'd walked in on him in an empty call room, sitting on the floor with his back to the door, IV tubing coiled loosely in his hand—not hooked to anything. Just holding it.

He hadn't seen her at first. When he did, he smiled—tired, broken—and said, "Just practicing my knots."

She'd laughed. Because that's what you did. Because that was the only way to keep from crying.

But later, in the silence of the on-call room, he'd curled up on the cot with his arms around his head, whispering, "I can't keep doing this." She could hear him through the thin wall.

There had been other moments, too. Jamie remembered a night in November. Ravi had nearly entered the wrong dose of Lasix for a heart failure patient—double the amount. Jamie caught it just in time. She'd fixed the order quietly, without drawing attention.

Afterward, she found him hiding behind a dumpster behind the hospital, hands shaking, trying to light a cigarette with a half-dead Bic.

“Don't cover for me,” he'd said, his voice low and hollow. “You're not doing me any favors.”

But she had.

Because that's what you did when someone was drowning.

Even if it meant going under with them.

She remembered the night they let that patient go. A decision born of pragmatism, they'd said. Futility. The patient had multi-organ failure. Sepsis. No meaningful recovery expected.

But Jamie remembered how Ravi's voice had shaken when he said, "There's no point."

She'd nodded. Agreed. But later, she'd wondered: was it his clinical judgment speaking—or exhaustion? Fear? Desperation?

They'd called time. Written the note. Moved on.

But it haunted her. The way Ravi hadn't looked at the patient when he pulled off the ambu bag. The way he avoided her eyes afterward.

She told herself it had been the right call.

Most days.

Other days, she wasn't so sure.

In the break room, she caught the end of a conversation as two nurses passed behind her.

"...close with Ravi, right?"

"I heard they were inseparable."

Jamie didn't turn. Didn't breathe.

Her pager buzzed. She ignored it.

Minutes later, she found herself in the med room. She didn't remember deciding to go. She just… needed to check something.

She stood in front of the Pyxis, staring at the screen. Her chest felt tight. If anyone pulled logs from that night, her name might not be there—but the nurse's might be. Would she remember Jamie asking to borrow her badge? Would she tell Tyler?

The silence of the room made her thoughts roar.

She imagined herself trying to explain it. How it wasn't theft. How Ravi had begged. How desperate he'd looked. Would they believe her?

A nurse stepped in briefly behind her to grab supplies. Jamie moved aside, pretending to grab an IV start kit. Her palms were sweating. Everyone was watching her every move.

She didn't try to log in. Didn't need to. Just standing there made her heart pound.

What was she doing?

She left the med room without taking anything.

That night, she went home and pulled out her journal—the one she hadn't touched since the night that patient died. Her pen hovered, then flew:

> *We didn't mean to let her die.*
>
> *That isn't true. We did mean to let her die. To help her die, even.*
>
> *But some days, you don't have a choice about whether you live or die. You only get to choose how you die. We chose a more dignified, painless death for her. Ravi said it would be okay. That he'd be OK. That it was the right thing to sacrifice himself for her.*
>
> *I didn't know it would get so dark.*
>
> *I didn't know he'd leave me.*

She stared at the words. Then added:

> *I scrub my hands but can't get clean,*
>
> *The blood is gone, but not unseen.*
>
> *He died with kindness in his chest,*
>
> *While I still breathe—no time to rest.*
>
> *They say it's grief, a normal phase,*
>
> *But mine comes sharp, in static haze.*
>
> *His voice still lingers in my head—*
>
> *Apologies I never said.*

If guilt could code, I'd seize and fall,

But death picks favorites, after all.

He took the blame, then took the hit.

I stayed behind. I live with it.

She tore the newest page out, struck a match, and watched the paper curl and blacken in the bathroom sink.

She stood in front of the mirror. Her face looked pale. Too composed. Her eyes didn't blink for a long time.

She leaned in.

"Are you a killer?"

The whisper escaped her lips before she could stop it.

Her reflection didn't answer.

But she kept staring.

Her hands gripped the sink edge until her knuckles ached. Her pulse throbbed in her ears. Her mouth was dry.

She leaned in farther.

"Do they already know?" she whispered.

The mirror stayed still. But something in her expression shifted—just barely.

Like maybe it did know.

And maybe… it didn't disagree.

Chapter 54

The Rulemaker

The Killer

* * *

The hospital looks different from above—smaller, contained like a dollhouse, arranged just so. From my perch on the quiet visitor balcony above the atrium, I watch the morning rush unfold below. Nurses in pastel scrubs move like ants across the polished floor. Clipboards. Coffee. Calls overhead—the illusion of order.

They're finally playing by my rules—no more flirtatious banter at the nurses' station. No cliques clustered around whiteboards, pretending not to see who's drowning. They whisper now. They watch each other. Trust has rotted. Every shift is a tightrope walk, every decision laced with doubt. They've started double-checking the med drawers, second-guessing their own instincts. They're looking at charts like they hold landmines. This is how medicine should be—sharp, alert, reverent. Because when people start dying, they finally remember the stakes.

I lean against the glass, my eyes following the familiar forms of Elise Navarro and Tyler Grayson striding across the atrium. Elise's knuckles are white around a manila folder. Tyler's jaw is clenched.

They're unraveling. But not fast enough.

Their investigation has gathered steam—gritty, determined, late-night kind of steam. I admire that. I like a good chase.

Jamie Lin, though. Now, that's an amusement. A delightful unraveling, really.

I didn't even touch her. She's destroying herself without any help from me.

The memory of Jamie's confident, overbright introduction when we first crossed paths tugs at me. So eager to belong. So certain of her brilliance. And now? Twitchy. Paranoid. Haunted. Guilt is a better poison than anything injectable.

I smile.

Then came Ravi. His death—I remember it vividly. The way his body fought—uselessly—as the paralytic took hold. How his eyes darted, searching for an anchor as his lungs froze inside him. A symphony of silence.

There's something poetic about watching a doctor lose control of his own body.

They found the fentanyl, of course, just as I planned. But the rocuronium? That's trickier. They'd have to test for it specifically. With the syringe full of fentanyl hanging out of his foot, they'll have no reason to.

They'll call it a suicide. Wrap it with a neat little bow.

I shift my stance and reach into my pocket. The stolen badge feels warm in my palm—this one from a lab tech who only works weekends. No one's noticed the badge is gone yet, and they won't for days. Someone forgettable. Someone invisible. Like me.

I smooth the front of my scrubs. My scrubs aren't surgical blue. I'm not wearing a white coat. Just the pale, utilitarian beige of someone no one bothers to look at twice.

They keep running badge logs. Footage reviews. Forensics. All chasing ghosts.

You think you can catch me with a clipboard and a security feed?

A cart rattles nearby—someone from dietary, wheeling trays past the nurses' station. No one notices me standing there. No one ever does. Not even when they see me on those new eye-level cameras they are stealthily placing all over the hospital.

I spot a nurse I recognize. One who once rolled her eyes and snapped, "Environmental Services isn't allowed in here during procedures." As if I didn't know that already. As if I didn't know how to keep my hands off a sterile area. As if I hadn't done this procedure myself a hundred times back in my country. I wasn't the dirty one in the room.

There's always someone who deserves it.

A flutter of paper catches my eye. A sign was taped to the desk.

NOTICE: Badge security is everyone's responsibility. Please keep your badge on you at all times. Report any suspicious behavior to Security.

I grin and tuck the badge deeper into my pocket.

You'd think they'd learn to hold on tighter to the things that matter.

Behind me, a pair of residents burst out of a supply closet, laughing, nearly bumping into me. One mutters an apology. Neither looks me in the eye.

I walk away without a sound.

Chapter 55

The Final Push

The Killer

* * *

I see her before she sees me.

Jamie Lin steps out of Room 324, rubbing her temple like the headache's been living behind her eyes for days. She mutters something to herself. Her white coat is rumpled, her scrubs wrinkled and stained at the knees. Her stethoscope hangs limp around her neck, like it's gained ten pounds overnight.

She's starting to splinter. Just a little more pressure, and she will break.

I wait until she disappears down the hallway before I move.

My reflection winks at me from the chrome of the maintenance cart—dull tan scrubs, matching tan coat, ID badge swinging from a lanyard, all topped by an expression of weary disinterest. The perfect disguise. Not because it's elaborate. Because it's mundane.

No one looks at a cleaner twice.

I've made just enough changes to pass: a different part in my hair, thinner brows, and thick glasses. My new name dangles from the borrowed badge—Sara something. The photo flipped against my chest.

I nod to the security guard posted outside the door. He barely registers me. As expected.

The door to 324 swings open easily.

Inside, the boy is asleep—half-turned in the bed, face slack, a line of dried drool curling at the limp corner of his mouth. His IV hums quietly. The EKG monitor beeps a steady, sluggish rhythm.

He looks peaceful. Almost holy.

I wipe the counter first—always start with the counter. Muscle memory. I learned that years ago, in the real world. I spray the surface with disinfectant, let the scent of spice and vinegar fill the room. I hum softly under my breath, just loud enough to drown out the monitor's tempo.

I step over to the window to clean the sill, hooking a loop of IV tubing in my pinky as I pass by the pumps. There is plenty of slack to make it the extra two feet to the window. I could feel the eyes of the staff and security on my back as I held the tubing in front of me. Too bad they can't actually see through me.

The propofol goes in first.

Fifty milligrams. Enough to make sure he sleeps through it. Not enough to stop him from breathing—unless something else finishes the job before it wears off.

There's something thrilling in the timing. This is the moment I crave most—the seconds between certainty and chaos. The air thickens. My pulse slows. I feel godlike.

I check the clock. The nurse won't be in to check the vitals again for at least twenty minutes.

But I don't get twenty.

The door creaks open behind me.

Jamie.

She walks in with a tablet in one hand, rubbing her eyes with the other. Her steps slow when she sees me, but she offers a distracted smile. I return it with a nod and busy myself tying off the trash bags.

She moves to the bedside and glances at the monitor. Vitals look good—just low enough to pass for stable. The blood pressure is probably low, but the cuff only cycles once an hour, so it is still reading 124/86 from 15 minutes ago.

"Hey, buddy," she murmurs, shaking his shoulder gently.

Nothing.

She frowns, leans closer, tries again. Still nothing.

Then she uses a knuckle to deliver a firm sternal rub. Still no response.

I pull the full bags from the canisters and place them on my cart one by one. Calm, deliberate. Just a worker doing her job.

Jamie glances up at the whiteboard, scanning for today's nurse. Her mouth tightens.

She bolts from the room.

I have two minutes, tops.

Next is the potassium chloride.

One hundred milliequivalents into the IV push. I'm almost surprised the burn didn't wake him. Even with the propofol, that much potassium should have lit a fire in his veins. But he stays quiet—deep in his nap. His heart still beats, but the future's already bled dry.

A second syringe goes into the magnesium bag. Another hundred. That one will take longer—ten minutes, maybe more. But it will hit. Like an aftershock.

I murmur as I work. "If he needed this much, they'd give it over ten hours. I'll manage in ten minutes."

I silently dispose of the syringes, double-bag them, and slide them deep into the cart's lower compartment. There's a bin of soiled linens above them—no one ever digs past blood-streaked sheets and used chux pads.

I leave without looking back.

The hall is quiet. I park myself at the nurses' station nearby and start wiping down the laminate counter. The spray hisses. Paper charts shift with the breeze. One nurse glances up, sees the badge and uniform, and returns to her notes.

I watch the monitor.

The boy's heart rate drops—70… 65… 58.

No one notices. Jamie is standing in the doorway of a room two doors down, grilling an alarmed-looking young nurse about when he last saw the patient and what his mentation was. She would have been concerned if she saw it, but she couldn't see the telemetry from where she stood.

The nurses at the nursing station can see it, but they don't notice it. They think it's normal. Fit kid. Post-stroke bradycardia. They've seen stranger things in weirder cases.

HR dips to 45. Then 38. Now people are starting to notice. Each electrical beat on the monitor is getting wider.

A nurse frowns. Reaches for the touch screen to cycle the blood pressure cuff without having to get up. I pretend to organize pens in the supply drawer.

The QRS complex widens, the T wave is huge. For a moment, I am worried they will see the distinctive pattern of hyperkalemia and save him.

The alarm shrieks.

Chaos erupts.

“Room 324! Code blue! Grab the crash cart! I need hands in here!”

A blur of scrubs and bodies rush past me. Crash cart wheels squeal. Someone shouts for airway. The bed rails slam down. Voices tangle in panic.

I stop wiping the counter and wheel my cart out of the aisle so the team can get their equipment by, like any normal housekeeper would do.

"Is it the potassium?" Jamie asks, noticing the obvious changes on telemetry.

"Morning labs came back twenty minutes ago. It was a perfect four-point-oh." The nurse replied confidently.

I almost laughed out loud. She wasn't wrong, and yet she had just prevented the appropriate treatment, sealing his fate.

One of the nurses—Maya, I think—cries out, “He was stable ten minutes ago!”

Another yells for epinephrine. The sound of the defibrillator charging sends a shiver down the hall.

I glance at the board behind the nurses' desk. Someone’s written a joke in dry-erase marker:

"Code Brown:
A cry, a curse, a puddle spread,
A hallway marked by shame and dread.
No warning came, no time to flee—
Just filth, and fear, and misery."

I suppress a smile. Fitting.

My fingers itch to add a tally mark to my mental scorecard.

I round the corner, push the cart into the service elevator, and press the button for the basement. My gloves are already off. I drop them into a biohazard bin as the doors close.

There's a hum in my chest, warm and familiar. Satisfaction.

Another perfect play.

Just another act of God in a godless place.

Chapter 56

On the Edge

Tyler Grayson

* * *

Tyler Grayson sat hunched over the monitor bank in the hospital's security office, the glow of surveillance footage casting shadows beneath his eyes. Logan stood beside him, sipping lukewarm coffee, while Elise leaned against the file cabinet, arms crossed tight over her chest. The air was stale with the scent of stress, caffeine, and spent adrenaline.

Three names. Three people.

"Only four individuals entered Room 321 in the hours before the arrest," Logan said, pointing to the time-stamped log on the screen. "Lucas Kim—first-year nurse, shadowing his preceptor, Maya. Jamie Lin. And this housekeeper—'Sara M.', according to the badge scan."

Tyler stared at the video stills on the screen. Lucas was barely out of school—his nervous posture and constant deference screamed inexperience. His preceptor, Maya, could be seen in the background of one shot, stepping out to take a call. The third figure—the housekeeper—pushed in a maintenance cart, nodded politely at the posted security guard, and went about her business. Jamie entered shortly after, tablet in hand.

"Run the housekeeper's background," Tyler said. "Just to be thorough."

Logan raised an eyebrow. "You think she's our ghost?"

"No," Tyler said too quickly. "I don't know. Maybe she is a partner."

He wasn't ready to let go of Jamie. Not yet. But he couldn't dismiss the eyes that were definitely not Jamie's.

Elise frowned, watching the footage on loop. "You notice the timing? Jamie was in there minutes before the cardiac arrest."

Logan nodded. "Telemetry started showing bradycardia about three minutes after she left."

Logan overlays Jamie's badge-in time with the telemetry change and says something like, "She walked out at 6:04. The first HR drop is 6:07. That's not a coincidence."

"She was never alone in there," Tyler pointed out. Do you think she is bold enough to do something in front of a witness?"

"She probably thought a housekeeper wouldn't realize what she is doing," Elise countered. "And she is probably right. What are the chances that the housekeeper did something that Jamie wouldn't notice?"

* * *

"I just got a message from forensics," Tyler added. "The prints on Ravi's tourniquet are Jamie's. She claims he asked for it to place an IV, and she always keeps one in her coat pocket."

Elis's lips thinned. "Convenient."

Logan didn't speak. His gaze drifted from screen to screen, then to the photo of Jamie from her ID badge. "She's been present at… too many events to ignore."

Logan flicked to a different screen. A still from one of the newly installed low-angle hallway cameras. "Here's 'Sara M.' walking away from 324. Look at the eyes."

Tyler leaned in.

The angle was sharp, taken from chest height and slightly off-center. The woman's eyes were large and distorted behind thick, round glasses. Her brows were thin, arched differently than in the sketch Tyler had grown so familiar with. But the eyes—something about them struck him.

"Could be her," Logan said, "it's hard to tell with the distortion from the glasses."

"I can't even find a headshot," he added. "She works weekend float—barely on the radar."

Elise murmured. "There's definitely something… familiar."

Tyler didn't say it aloud, but the thought was already crawling through his mind.

Jamie's fingerprints. Jamie's timing. Jamie's silence in the interviews. Her spiraling behavior. The med room badge log. And now, this.

He pulled back from the desk and rubbed his temples. "I'm going to request a full background check on the owner of the badge. See who it's assigned to. And get me employment rosters—who worked in environmental services over the past two weeks. I'm going to call the DA to see if we have enough for either an arrest warrant for Jamie Lin or a search warrant for her residence."

He looked back at Jamie's name, now circled in red on their investigation board. So many links. Too many to be a coincidence. But his gut itched with something else now. A possibility he hadn't wanted to consider.

Elise moved toward the board, her finger hovering over Jamie's name, then drifting toward the housekeeper's. "You don't think—"

"I don't know what to think," Tyler admitted. "But I'm not ready to bring her in. Not yet."

Logan flipped to another feed—this time from the break room near the ICU. Jamie sat alone, hunched over a cup of coffee, staring at nothing.

"She looks broken," Logan said.

"Looks can be deceiving," Tyler replied.

Chapter 57

Over the Edge

Jamie Lin

* * *

In the break room, Jamie clutched her mug with both hands, her fingers trembling despite the heat. Her thoughts spiraled. She felt watched. Judged. Every whisper in the hallway carried her name. Ravi's name. The word "suspicious."

She closed her eyes and tried to conjure Ravi's laugh. That throaty chuckle that used to echo down the halls during overnight shifts. But all she could hear was his panicked voice in that final week: "Please, Jamie. Just this once. Don't report me."

She hadn't known what to do. So she'd done the wrong thing.

Now, she didn't know how to undo it.

She pulled a note from her pocket—one she'd found slipped beneath her locker that morning.

"Still hiding? Some of us know. Watch your back."

Her breath caught. She tore it into pieces and flushed them down the staff bathroom toilet minutes later. But her heart hadn't stopped racing since.

She blinked rapidly, thinking back to their last night on call together. Ravi had looked pale, with dark circles under his eyes and a slight tremor in his hands. She'd slipped him saline instead of morphine, just to be safe. He'd caught her, stared her down. Accused her of abandoning him when he needed her most. She didn't answer.

Later that night, she'd caught him in the on-call room, a discarded fentanyl patch wrapper on the table beside him. He looked up, dazed, his pupils shrunk to pinpoints, his lips sluggish. In his hand was a fentanyl patch—once frozen, now ruptured and empty. He'd cracked it open and eaten the slurried gel inside, a risky trick to get the full dose in one go. "Three days' worth," he slurred, eyes half-lidded. "All at once. I don't want to feel anymore."

She never reported it. Now, she couldn't stop thinking about it.

She opened a message to Elise: Can we talk? Her thumb hovered. She deleted it. Tried again. Deleted it again. Then she tucked her phone away and took a shuddering breath.

She clutched her badge and coat tighter, knowing the eyes were everywhere.

Chapter 58

The Evidence

* * *

Back in the security office, Elise stepped away from the board and pulled Tyler aside.

"Can we talk?"

He nodded, following her into the adjacent conference room.

"You're pushing too hard on Jamie," she said quietly. "You're treating her like she's guilty. And we don't have proof. Just correlations."

"Too many correlations," Tyler replied.

"She was Ravi's friend. She's grieving. Scared. Maybe even hiding something—but that doesn't mean she's a killer."

Tyler exhaled, gripping the back of a chair. "I'm not saying she is. But we have to follow the data."

"Then follow it without bias. Because if you're wrong... and we put her through hell... we'll never undo that."

Their eyes locked. A beat passed between them.

"You still trust her?" he asked.

Elise hesitated. "I don't know. But I trust what this hospital does to people.

And I've seen how grief can look a lot like guilt."

* * *

Nilesh Patel and Jenn popped in.

"Tyler. We've got an anomaly in the smart pump audit," Jenn started. "A magnesium bag in Room 324 registered 110 milliliters infused—"

"—on a 100 mL bag," Nilesh finished.

"There's no chance it's variability in manufacturing?" Tyler asked.

"Not a chance. They're pre-mixed at the factory," Jenn said. "We checked. The pharmacy scan matches. No reason that bag should've delivered more."

Jenn added, "These pumps are accurate to within half a milliliter. We've seen maybe one deviation in three years. And never ten percent over."

"The bag and tubing have already been sent to forensics. I'll have them test it for...everything."

Tyler turned to Elise. "You wanted hard data. We might have just found some."

She gave a tight nod. "Good. Let's use it to find the truth—not just someone to blame."

The tension in the room thickened. Tyler closed his eyes, then turned to the mirrored window. In his mind, he rehearsed the words:

Jamie Lin, you are under arrest...

He didn't say it aloud. Not yet.

But tomorrow, he would.

Jamie Lin was too close to too many bodies. She was the one in that room with that bag of magnesium. Alone.

Chapter 59

Gone Without a Sound

Dr. Jamie Lin

* * *

Jamie stepped out of the shower, steam still clinging to the mirror. Her ribs showed more than they used to. At 5'6", she was nearing 100 pounds; there hadn't been much to spare to begin with. She tugged on a pair of loose light blue scrubs—clean, but baggy enough to hide what the last few weeks had taken from her.

Her damp hair clung to her neck as she padded barefoot across the kitchen tile. She dropped a scoop of protein powder into a half-empty shaker bottle, added almond milk, and twisted the cap. She shook it absently, already knowing she wouldn't be able to stomach it. Her insides were knotted too tight for food.

A sudden pounding on the door made her freeze.

Three sharp knocks. Authority, not urgency.

She jumped at the noise and the bottle slipped through her fingers, hit the floor with a hollow thunk, and burst open. Viscous liquid splattered across the concrete and oozed beneath the table, forming a spreading mess that mirrored the unraveling chaos in her expression. For a moment, she considered ignoring it. Pretending she wasn't home. But then came the voice: firm, unmistakable.

"Jamie Lin. Open the door. Police."

The shaker bottle slipped from her fingers and hit the floor with a dull thud.

The door swung open moments later. Tyler Grayson stepped into the apartment, flanked by two uniformed officers. He kept his voice measured as he approached, reciting the Miranda warning like it pained him to say the words. Jamie barely registered the sound over the static buzzing in her ears.

"You have the right to remain silent..."

He met her eyes before he turned her around and placed her hands on the wall.

"Anything you say can and will be used against you in a court of law," he continued, his voice low, almost reluctant.

"You have the right to an attorney. If you cannot afford one, one will be provided for you."

A second officer, a woman, stepped forward. "I'll perform the pat down," she said quietly.

"Do you understand these rights as I have read them to you?"

Jamie nodded slowly at both of them. Her heart pounded in her chest as the woman took her wrists and turned them gently, then moved her hands down Jamie's arms, her back, her hips, her inner thighs, and finally—with the back of her hands—under Jamie's breasts. Jamie stiffened at the sensation. It was clinical, practiced, but it still felt like a violation. Her face burned with shame, and her jaw locked to keep from crying out. She focused on the sound of her own breathing, trying not to crumble before they even made it to the squad car.

She was cuffed, led past the half-mixed protein shake still oozing across the tile, a pale sludge pooling around the powder clumps like congealed snowmelt in a gutter. Outside, the sun had begun to rise, brushing the edges of the sky with lavender and gold. It was a beautiful morning. If this was the last time she ever saw the sky, it was a perfect one—softly lavender, streaked with coral, the kind of dawn that made people believe in fresh starts.

* * *

Jamie Lin's wrists ached from the weight of the handcuffs as the police guided her out of her building. It was early morning; the sky was still dark, and dew clung to the pavement. A few neighbors stood at their windows, one holding a phone out at arm's length, recording. She kept her head down, trying not to meet their eyes. For a moment, Jamie felt grateful that they did this before her shift, out of the scrutinizing gaze of her fellow residents.

In the back of the squad car, her mind fractured. Ravi's laugh—sharp and warm—danced alongside the sterile white walls of the holding cell. Every bump in the road sent a jolt of panic through her chest. Were they really doing this? Arresting her? Was this real?

It was.

Maybe this is what she deserved. Maybe she had crossed lines. Maybe she'd broken rules that couldn't be unbroken. But not like this. Not murder.

When they arrived at the station, Tyler opened her door, encircled his hand around her arm, and gently guided her into the station. He filled out some paperwork on a clipboard and dropped her off at intake. The jail was cold and mechanical, a place designed to strip you of identity. Fluorescent lights buzzed overhead, casting a pale, unforgiving glow on everything they touched. A female officer walked her through the motions: remove your shoes, stand on the taped footprints, and answer questions with a simple 'yes' or 'no'. Her fingerprints were digitally scanned, her photograph taken under the same sterile lighting. Every item she owned was cataloged and zipped into a brown envelope. Her hoodie, her phone, her hospital ID—all cataloged, as if her identity could be boxed and stored away. The machinery of the system began its slow grind against her—each step another layer peeled back, each form signed another nail in the coffin of who she used to be.

Then came the orange scrubs—thin and scratchy, stamped with an ID number—4287159. They handed them to her while she stood naked and shivering, the uniform stacked in a neatly folded pile like it had been waiting for her all along. She pulled them on with trembling hands. The fabric rasped against her skin, rough and impersonal. Then came the flimsy white slippers that barely clung to her feet. She suddenly missed her pale blue hospital scrubs, soft from too many washes, with her name and hospital logo embroidered neatly over her heart. She used to be someone. Now she was a number printed in black on prison orange. It felt like wrapping herself in sandpaper—each movement scraping away another piece of who she was.

The holding cell was a metal box pretending to be a room. A thin mat on a steel bench offered no comfort. Other women occupied the space, some pacing like caged animals, others slouched and silent. Jamie tried to shrink herself into a corner, but there was no such thing as invisible in a place like this.

Time warped. Minutes stretched into hours, or maybe it was the other way around. Her stomach cramped with hunger she couldn't recognize as hunger anymore. Her head ached. Her eyes burned. Outside, life kept spinning—cars moved, clocks ticked, and the sun arced across the sky—but in here, Jamie was suspended in a purgatory of flickering fluorescents and the hollow sound of coughs ricocheting off concrete walls.

She got shoved once—hard. A woman with crooked teeth and matted hair told her to move. "Little rich bitch," she spat. Jamie stumbled into the wall, pain blooming across her ribs, but she didn't make a sound. She didn't even lift her head.

Her bladder became unbearable. She waited, praying someone else would go first, but no one did. Eventually, shaking and humiliated, she shuffled to the stainless steel toilet in the open corner and relieved herself under fluorescent lights and a dozen judging eyes. She tried not to make noise. Tried not to exist.

She didn't cry. She didn't sleep. She just endured.

At some point—hours?—she tucked herself into the corner again, knees drawn up, arms around her legs. Her skin felt like it didn't fit right. Her brain echoed with the sound of Ravi laughing, Ravi yelling, Ravi dying. His laugh. His scream. His silence. Her breaths were short and shallow, each one a silent plea for this not to be her life.

When the metal door finally creaked open, Jamie had been in holding for more than twenty-four hours. She hadn't slept. Hadn't eaten. She was numb with exhaustion and bruised in places she hadn't dared to look. Her throat felt raw from the unnatural tension of holding everything in for so long. She hadn't spoken a word since Tyler arrived at her door yesterday morning.

A guard appeared in the doorway. "Court time," he grunted.

They marched her out with two others—one sobbing, the other muttering under her breath. Jamie's legs felt like stilts made of paper. In the courtroom, her knees buckled slightly as they sat her down beside a man in a crisp black suit who smelled faintly of Old Spice. He leaned over and whispered, "I'm Greg Cho. Your parents hired me. Just sit tight and don't speak. I'll take care of everything."

The hearing was short. Greg spoke calmly, efficiently. Bail was granted. Jamie barely processed the words until she was being marched back into holding.

Three hours later, the same guard returned. This time, his voice was flat. "You made bail."

Her parents stood on the other side of the holding room doors. Her mother's eyes, usually unreadable, shimmered with the pink tint of suppressed tears. Her father's jaw was clenched tight, the only outward sign of the storm beneath his skin. They didn't reach for her. They didn't speak. They simply looked at her—taking inventory of the bruises she couldn't hide and the exhaustion she couldn't mask. Chinese to the core, they wore their grief like armor, every emotion folded neatly away for later.

They didn't say anything as they walked her to the car. Only when they were safely in the confines of the vehicle, the doors shut, the highway humming beneath them, did her mother finally cry. And only then did her father reach across the console and hold her hand in silence. Once the engine was humming steadily down the highway, her mother finally asked, quietly, "Did you do anything wrong?"

Jamie couldn't answer. Not truthfully. Not with the tangled mess of secrets in her chest.

"I need to go to the hospital," she said instead.

Her father's knuckles whitened on the steering wheel. "Jamie—"

"I left some things there. I won't be long. Please."

Her mother looked at her father. He exhaled slowly and turned the wheel.

The hospital looked colder and emptier at night. Jamie didn't use the main entrance. She circled to the old back door near central supply—a door everyone knew stayed slightly ajar, thanks to a piece of duct tape someone kept taping over the latch. It was a popular place to sneak a smoke. The same place she had found Ravi smoking after that medication error last year.

The hallway was silent. She moved like a ghost.

When she reached the resident call suite, yellow crime scene tape stretched across the threshold. Two security guards stood nearby, one frowning at her.

She didn't linger. She turned and headed down to the pre-op wing—quiet now, mostly unused. A few rooms had been repurposed as temporary resident rest areas. She hoped someone would be there. Someone she could talk to.

Someone who might still believe her.

The hallway stretched long and dim. Motion sensor lights blinked to life as she passed. Her breath caught in her throat. The scent of antiseptic still lingered, mingled with a faintly sweet aroma.

She peeked into one of the bays. Empty. Another—empty again.

"Leilani?" she called softly. No answer.

Her voice cracked. "Anyone?"

Footsteps behind her. She turned—too late.

Arms encircled her from behind, tight, controlling. A gloved hand holding a wet cloth over her mouth.

She tensed, heart slamming against her ribs. "The police—" she started to think.

Then the scent hit her. Sweet. Like fruit just past its prime. Chemical. Wrong.

This wasn't a cop.

This was something else.

She tried to fight, but her limbs betrayed her, going limp far too fast. The last thing she saw was the darkened pre-op bay, yawning like a mouth.

And then—

Nothing.

Chapter 60

Cut Down

Dr. Jamie Lin

* * *

Jamie drifted awake in stages—first to the weight in her limbs, then to the bite of pressure at her wrists and ankles. She tried to move, but her arms and legs wouldn't obey.

Her mouth was dry, her tongue stuck to cloth. Her ears throbbed with the rhythm of her pulse. For a moment, she thought she was waking from another brutal call shift… until she noticed the silence. No pagers. No monitors. Just her own ragged breath echoing back at her.

Her mouth wasn't dry, she slowly realized; something dry was in her mouth, thick and choking. She gagged against it instinctively, but it didn't budge. Her lips were sealed with silk medical tape, layer upon layer forming a silent muzzle.

Her vision stuttered. Blinding white light overhead. She blinked, squinted. OR panels. Bright. Too bright. It felt like an explosion in her already throbbing head. The table beneath her was narrow and unforgiving. She was strapped down—full five-point hospital restraints: wrists, ankles, chest. A Posey vest wrapped around her torso, cinched tight enough to restrict her breathing.

The room smelled sterile—antiseptic and metal. It was too clean. Too empty. The OR table gleamed, the metal counters scrubbed to a shine. One of the lights overhead flickered, casting shadows that danced like a silent ballet of panic across the expansive white of the walls.

Her heart thundered. She couldn't move. Couldn't scream. The restraints creaked faintly as she thrashed against them, the leather digging into bone.

Her ears rang, the silence broken only by the faint hum of a ventilation fan. Somewhere, metal scraped across metal.

Footsteps. Slow. Measured.

A woman stepped into view.

Jamie froze.

She recognized her—one of the housekeepers. Always there, pushing the cart with its chipped yellow bucket, always quiet, invisible. Jamie had never noticed the color of her eyes until now.

The lady smiled. "Finally awake."

Her voice was unhurried. Calm. Almost warm.

Her accent was faint—Eastern European, maybe. Once it had likely been strong. Now it was barely perceptible, sanded down by years of silence and assimilation.

Jamie strained against the Posey vest again, her muffled scream swallowed by the cloth and tape. Her chest burned.

"You know," the woman said, laying out instruments on a small surgical tray beside the OR table, "I used to be a doctor. In Georgia. Not the one with peaches—the one with tanks."

She selected a pair of forceps, studied them like old friends. "I trained in Tbilisi. Top of my class. When the war came, we did what we had to do. Internal medicine. Surgery too. Pediatrics. Obstetrics. I ran a trauma ward out of a basement clinic. We had no electricity, no heat. I performed amputations by flashlight. Intubated children with tools I boiled on a hot plate. I delivered babies in blackout conditions. Rewired defibrillators with scavenged parts. Now I mop vomit off vinyl floors. I deserve some respect." She almost spat when she said respect.

Jamie blinked, her vision fogging.

"My husband was a cardiologist. My daughter was ten—born with a heart defect. We had to leave. Not just the hospital. The country. It wasn't safe for us anymore. I tried to get out through Turkey." Her voice faltered—just for a second. "He didn't make it."

She snapped on gloves. Her movements were fluid. Mechanical. "They told me America would save her. Best healthcare in the world. I believed them. So I came here. No license. No board exams. Just a mop and a cart and shit-stained sheets. I got a job here in housekeeping so I could be close to her, every day, every hour."

Jamie's chest heaved. Her mind reeled.

"She was here. You remember. You and Ravi were interns on your pediatrics rotation. That bitch Sierra was floated to the floor that month." She continued with venom in her voice. "You don't remember her name. But I do. I remember every note you didn't write. Every vitals check missed. Every time she cried for water and no one came."

She turned and pulled back Jamie's gown. "You think I'm insane. But I see it more clearly than anyone. What you call burnout, I call permission."

Cold antiseptic pooled against Jamie's groin. "Wouldn't want you to get an infection," she started cackling at the irony.

"One error here. A shortcut there. And someone dies." She opened a sterile kit. "You all think you're careful. But you're only careful when you're watched."

“Not anymore,” she added quietly. “Now, you're afraid.”

Jamie thrashed wildly as the scalpel flashed in the light.

She looked down at Jamie. Her face softened. “You strut through the halls like you’re smarter than everyone. Like you matter.”

She leaned in closer. “You don’t see people like me. You never even turned your head when I passed. None of you did.”

She pulled back Jamie’s gown and exposed her right groin. Cold antiseptic soaked the skin. She worked efficiently—confidently—clearly practiced. She kept speaking as she prepped the field.

"Trust me. I know. I was replaced before I even left. They said it was politics. That's what they always say. I made the wrong person look bad, and suddenly, I didn't matter anymore. Not as a doctor. Not even as a human being."

She lifted the scalpel. “I could use a needle,” she mused, “but where’s the fun in that?”

The incision was smooth. Precise. She cut inferior to the inguinal ligament, dissected down through the fascia, and found the femoral artery. She missed every vessel she didn’t intend to hit. Almost no blood spilled. Jamie thrashed, but the killer’s hand clamped just above her knee, squeezing the quadriceps so tightly that Jamie couldn’t bend her leg no matter how hard she tried. Pain bloomed outward, hot and jagged.

Jamie tried again to scream, but her throat was raw, her voice lost beneath the gag.

"But you don't matter," she said flatly. "You are easily replaceable. They are already interviewing candidates to replace your friend. They won't even need to conduct new interviews for your replacement. They will just pick their second favorite from that first batch."

She sank a large, 16-gauge needle into the exposed artery, watching the blood surge into the connected tubing. The crimson line crept upward, inching toward the clamp, bold and steady.

Until she opened the clamp.

Jamie felt the pressure change instantly. A dizzying rush, a hollow pull. Her heart pounded faster to compensate, but it only hastened the flow. Blood surged through the tube in rhythmic pulses, deep red against sterile plastic. The first few pulses sent the tubing twitching like a live wire, a red arc splattering across the sterile floor tiles—violent, visceral, impossible to ignore.

"I didn't choose this," the woman said. "But I was already invisible. Might as well be useful."

Jamie's vision blurred. Panic gave way to ice. Her limbs went numb. Her vision blurred at the edges.

The housekeeper leaned in again. "You're not dying for nothing, Jamie. You're a lesson. A cautionary tale."

Jamie couldn't blink. Couldn't cry.

Just before her vision tunneled completely, a flicker broke through the haze—a single, aching thought.

Her parents.

They were waiting. Right now, in the dark. Parked in that faded gray Camry just outside the hospital's west entrance, hands clenched around a thermos of tea they'd brewed at home. Her father would be gripping the wheel with both hands, staring ahead in silence. Her mother would be pretending to read a devotional pamphlet, but not turning the pages.

They would wait until sunrise.

And Jamie—bound to a table beneath flickering lights—couldn't even say goodbye.

The drain gurgled faintly.

"You couldn't keep my daughter's heart beating long enough to get her on the transplant list. Let's see how long yours can keep up."

"You always wanted to matter. Now you never will."

She stepped back.

Jamie lay still.
The drain gurgled.
The room, once again, was silent.

The bag was already half tied when she heard it—voices, echoing from the stairwell. Laughter. Residents looking to rest their heads for a few minutes, heading her way. Too soon.

* * *

She stood, removed her gloves, and peeled the restraints off one by one, wiping them clean with antiseptic. Everything was placed in the red biohazard bin just outside the OR, along with a small, worn leather notebook. She froze, pulse quickening. There wouldn't be time to slip out unnoticed with the bag in hand. Not if they turned the corner now.

* * *

She knew she shouldn't leave them all of this, but she couldn't, but it wasn't worth the risk.

* * *

She left the OR without a sound, empty-handed. She made it to the other side of the recovery area and slipped through the back stairwell just as the residents rounded the corner.

Let them find it.

Let them wonder.

Let them know how close they had been.

Chapter 61

The Waiting Room

Tyler

* * *

The Camry's engine had long since cooled, but Jamie's parents hadn't turned on the heat. They sat in silence, light spring coats zipped to their chins, hands wrapped around the now-lukewarm thermos of chrysanthemum tea they'd brought from home.

"She said just a few minutes," her mother murmured.

"That was two hours ago," her father replied, his voice tight. He hadn't taken his hands off the steering wheel in nearly forty-five minutes. The devotional pamphlet his wife had tried to read was crumpled in her lap.

They finally stepped out of the car and walked stiffly into the hospital. The security guard at the front desk looked up with surprise as her mother explained, voice shaking, that their daughter had gone in earlier and never came back out. She wasn't answering her phone.

The guard radioed it in.

Tyler was heading down the east stairwell, jacket slung over one shoulder, when the call came through security walkie-talkies: "Security request, main entrance. Dr. Jamie Lin reported on campus, unaccounted for."

He paused mid-step. The words hit like a slap.

He spun around and bolted down the hall, every instinct screaming.

Within minutes, the command center was reactivated. Tyler, Logan, and the house supervisor gathered in the conference room. Elise arrived moments later, hair damp from the drizzle outside, eyes instantly scanning the board for details.

Logan stood before the surveillance console, one hand on the mouse, the other pointing at a paused frame on the screen—Jamie, stepping through the old supply hallway entrance. "That's the last confirmed visual of her entering. The next camera caught her at the call suite elevator bank, turning away after spotting the security guards. From there, she moved toward the old pre-op area. She entered through the curtained-off section where patients once prepped for surgery—an area with no active cameras—and never reappeared. No signs of her leaving the building," he said. "We've checked all recorded exits since 10:00 p.m.—no match."

"Could she be hiding?" Elise asked. "Trying to avoid the press? The board?"

"Maybe," Tyler said. "Or maybe she knew she would be locked up for life, and she was here to make one last move—revenge, maybe. Or one final transgression before lockup."

The search began. Residents, nurses, techs, and security swept every floor. Closets, restrooms, stairwells, supply rooms. Tyler checked the cath lab lounges and the old simulation suite. Logan pulled up every angle of security footage they could access, but there were no security cameras installed in the ORs themselves—these zones were considered secure, closed to the public, and protected for patient privacy.

Just after 2:00 a.m., a strangled scream echoed from the back of the hallway near OR B. A nurse named Camila stumbled backward out of the call room, her face pale.

Tyler ran toward the sound.

He pushed past the curtain, then stopped cold.

Jamie lay on the OR table, skin blanched, eyes open and staring. A line of half-dried blood trailed into a floor drain. A long piece of tubing still hung loosely from her groin. Angry bruises encircled her bare ankles and wrists.

She was still warm. She hadn't been gone long.

He reached for a pulse out of reflex, knowing it was futile.

"Clear the area," he said, voice rasping.

Someone sobbed behind him. Elise pressed her hand to her mouth.

Logan arrived, silent. He didn't ask what happened. He just stood there, still, his eyes scanning the room.

They recovered her phone just inside the doorway, screen locked. Her duffel sat on the chair by the wall. No suicide note. No last message. No clue.

For the next several hours, the OR wing became a crime scene. Jamie's body was carefully removed by the coroner's team as forensic investigators began their sweep. They dusted for fingerprints, photographed every angle, collected fibers, fluids, and impressions. Tiny yellow evidence markers multiplied across the floor like spores. The scent of antiseptic warred with the coppery tang of blood, and the silence was punctuated only by camera shutters and clipped radio chatter.

A few feet from the table, in a red biohazard bucket half-filled with bleach water, they found a peculiar set of round glasses. On closer look, on pulling them out of the bleach water, the lenses were magnifying glasses—worn, thick-lensed, clearly not prescription lenses. That explained the distorted eyes on the new camera feed. There would be no fingerprints or DNA. The bleach had done its job.

No one spoke for a long time. The ticking of the clock intruded loudly into the room. The second ticked by slower than usual.

Finally, Tyler broke the silence. "Let's say," he began, "that Jamie and Ravi were working together."

Logan looked up.

"She wanted to save people. He wanted to end suffering," Tyler continued. "He started taking drugs—fentanyl, morphine. She covered for him at first. But it got worse. People started to die. She tried to rein him in. When he spiraled, she panicked. Maybe she even gave him that final dose. She couldn't live with it."

"That doesn't explain this," Elise said quietly.

Tyler didn't look at her. "No note. No fight. No signs of forced entry. No evidence of anyone else being there. She had access to restricted rooms. She was found with the same precision she admired in the ICU. It was controlled. Intentional."

Logan crouched near the table, careful not to disturb anything, and examined the telltale signs. "She was restrained," he said grimly. "Adhesive residue on the face, bruises on the wrists and ankles in distinct patterns consistent with hospital restraints, including Posey chest straps." He paused, then added, "That's not suicide."

"But she could've faked it," Tyler argued. "Or set it up. A cry for help that went too far."

"No one strips naked to kill themselves," Elise snapped. Then softer, "And not Jamie. She wouldn't have wanted to be found that way."

Tyler rubbed his eyes. "I'm just saying—we've been wrong before. And if this is staged… if it's some act of remorse—"

"—then she would have left a message," Elise finished.

Silence again.

"Ravi was the mercy killer," he said with dwindling conviction. "Jamie was the hero. They fed each other."

Logan stared at the floor. "Or someone else used that story to cover their tracks."

No one answered.

They startled a bit as the door suddenly banged open behind them.

Jamie's mother stumbled in, sobbing, her footsteps uneven on the slick OR floor. A security officer called after her, too late. Her husband followed at a distance, his face slack with shock, lips drawn in a pale, silent line. His eye fixed on the body on the table.

The smell of iron filled the air—raw, metallic, unmistakable. The overhead lights were blinding.

"Jamie," her mother cried, voice cracking into syllables that no longer formed words. She surged forward.

Elise caught her just in time, wrapping her arms around the older woman, holding her upright as her knees gave out. Jamie's mother collapsed into Elise's shoulder, wailing, while Elise blinked back tears of her own, bracing both of them. She could feel the woman's sobs rack through both of their bodies. For a moment, there was no doctor, no friend—just two women grieving the same impossible truth.

Her father stopped at the edge of the threshold. He didn't move. Didn't speak. He simply looked at the pale form of his daughter on the table, then slowly turned away, staring at a smudge on the wall as if trying to hold himself together one breath at a time.

Tyler stood frozen, shame churning in his gut.

The hallway outside the OR was eerily quiet. Somewhere, down in the ED, a trauma was being called. Life was still moving.

Inside this room, though, they were frozen.

Jamie Lin was gone.

And the real killer was still out there.

Chapter 62

Invisible Hands

The Killer

* * *

They called me in to clean up the mess. Fitting, really.

I arrived just after dawn, wearing the wig with the sharp bangs and the too-dark roots. My hair was pinned tight beneath it, every strand controlled. My foundation was several shades too warm, paired with heavy eyeliner, brown lip pencil, and the thick slash of mascara. My features were entirely unrecognizable.

I wore my usual tan hospital scrubs beneath a housekeeping apron and sensible shoes. My laminated badge read "Gloria S." and had a bar code that still scanned—lifted from last night's shift supervisor. She wouldn't notice it was missing until she tried to get in tonight.

I stood at the periphery of the flimsy yellow tape, holding a mop and a gray caddy of supplies.

The security guard at the door looked up, confused. "Sorry, ma'am, this area's closed. Still under investigation."

I held up my badge. "¿Limpieza?" I said gently.

The man looked over his shoulder, then back at her. "I thought they were sending a team... whatever. They want this place sanitized by noon. Go ahead."

I nodded, smiled, and slipped on my gloves as I stepped inside. The restraints were gone—bagged as evidence, probably—but the rest was mine. Mine to clean. Mine to remember.

The door shut behind me with a soft click. Silence returned.

There was more fingerprint powder than blood—black, dusty clouds that settled into the grooves of the floor tiles and clung to the metal edges of the tray tables. It smelled faintly chemical, dry and acidic, like burnt plastic and rubber gloves. Beneath my shoes, the gritty residue whispered with each step, a quiet, abrasive shuffle that reminded me of walking through ashes. The powder coated everything it touched, more stubborn than blood, more revealing in its cling. A forensic snowfall—and yet, it revealed nothing at all. Black smudges across the glass, across the old tray tables, across the edge of the bed where they'd dusted for handprints. None of them would be mine.

There were spatter marks on the ceiling. An arterial arc across the underside of the lamp. How overzealousness. It had been a beautiful cut, but I had been surprised by the force that the tubing jerked with. Her blood pressure must have been very high, I mused, relishing the memory as it replayed in my mind.

I set the mop bucket down and clicked the lid open. Inside: something of my own making. A bottle of cleanser I'd prepared at home, the scent subtle but distinct—vinegar infused with crushed mint and bay leaves. The smell of old kitchens and cold stone corridors.

Leaning against the bucket, wrapped in plastic, was the final piece of a design I was genuinely proud of. I pulled out the extension rod and began taping it to the mop handle using a roll of medical tape I'd lifted from the trauma bay near the OR entrance. The last foot came from a telescoping splint, swiped from the ortho OR just next door. Everything scavenged, nothing suspicious. Just trash, repurposed with purpose. A thing of beauty, really.

"They think it's over," I mumbled under my mask.

I could hear the mop as it sloshed into the bucket. I wrung it out, lifted it high, and began to scrub the overhead lamp.

"They think the girl broke."

Swish. Circle. Swish.

"That the boy gave up."

I dipped the mop again, then dragged it across the streaked tile floor.

"They think they can sleep again. That the hospital is safe."

She was still warm when they found her. Her head tilted just slightly to the side, mouth agape beneath a crusted ring of dried tape residue, like she had been mid-scream. Her eyes—wide, vacant—seemed to search the ceiling even in death. There was no more noise in the room. Not the whine of machines, not the shuffle of carts or nurses. Only silence thick enough to smother, broken by the low swish of bleachwater and the hush of my breath behind the mask. I'd timed it just right. The restraints left bruises, the tape left residue. They might not buy the suicide story with evidence like that—but I don't care. Let them investigate. Let them speculate. They still won't find me. I'm too careful. Too ordinary. Too beneath their notice.

She paused at the floor drain. The blood was almost gone now. What little remained turned the rinse water pink, swirling down into darkness.

As I worked, I couldn't help smiling beneath my mask. "They pay me to clean up after myself."

The thought made me laugh, soft and low. The mop swished in gentle rhythm. A lullaby.

She stepped back and surveyed the room. The tray table. The empty restraints bagged and gone. The coiled tubing. The subtle indentations in the mattress.

She cleaned it all.

They'd watched footage for days. I remember one night in particular—weeks ago now—when a patient had coded in the ICU. The hallway was chaos, lights flashing, people yelling. I slipped past the nurses' station with a vial tucked in my glove. I even paused right by the trauma board, pretending to wipe a spill. Security footage would've caught the entire scene. I was certain of it. The angle was good. My timing, not so much. I saw a guard glance at the monitor, frown, and then look away. A flicker of recognition, then dismissal. Just housekeeping, after all. Just me. And so I moved on. Cleaned the spill. Watched them miss everything.

How many times have I walked through these halls, caught on camera? How many times did they watch me in the footage—rewind, fast-forward, pause—without seeing me at all? Rewound and rewatched. Analyzed angles. Compared timestamps. But they hadn't once noticed the woman with the mop. The one who walked the halls with quiet purpose. Who passed through doors without a glance. Who stood in corners just beyond the edge of sight.

I'm not hiding.

They're just blind.

I hum as I work, a gentle rhythm meant for no one. Not a melody—just sound to fill the silence, to hear my own echo sing to me. The lullaby of the invisible.

Chapter 63
Unmasked
The Killer

* * *

I was almost done. The bag was packed. My badge—the original one—was in pieces. The rest I kept, each tucked into a cloth-lined box at the back of my closet. Ravi's, Jamie's, even Madison's. All my little trophies. The uniform I'd worn was stripped and burned. The mop handle had been left in the stairwell trash chute, split in half. I had no more errands to run, no more names on my list. And yet.

A good exit deserves punctuation.

Not another resident. Not some housekeeper's revenge.

No. This one had to mean something. Tyler Grayson—obsessive, tenacious, righteous Tyler—had played his part beautifully. Picking apart theories. Pulling threads. Doing exactly what I hoped he would. So I chose her. His mother. One last amusement to remember this town by. A final twist to keep him too distracted to follow me. Or notice me. The perfect final cut.

Security was tighter now. Too many eyes. Too much tape. But I knew these halls better than anyone. I waited outside the locked unit, mop in hand, watching staff come and go. I bided my time until a nurse exited with a stack of linens. I fell into step behind her, silent as breath. When the door swung wide, I passed through unnoticed.

The oncology wing smelled like ammonia and old coffee. I obviously hadn't been cleaning this wing. The typical fluorescent lights buzzed overhead. The hallway was mostly empty. I moved with purpose, pushing a small cleaning cart I'd built myself. No barcodes. No ID. The faint scent of vinegar and mint, with a hint of bay leaf, clung to the cart—my special cleanser reminded me of home.

Room 543.

I turned the handle slowly and eased the door open.

She was there. Pale and small beneath a fleece blanket. The oxygen cannula snaked around her ears. Her mouth was slack in sleep. But I wasn't looking at her.

He was in the chair.

Tyler.

Slumped to one side, chin resting on his chest. A paperback spread open across his thigh. His hand gently covered hers, fingers curled like he was afraid to let go.

I stood there for a moment. Listening.

His breathing was soft. Slow. The kind of sleep that only comes from complete exhaustion. The coffee cup beside him was still warm. I could smell the faint bitterness of it. There would be no injection here. No quiet, clinical farewell. No poetic symmetry.

I cleared my throat softly and called out, "Housekeeping," letting the word echo in the room like a dare. He didn't stir. I wheeled the cart up beside him and brazenly emptied the trash can, my movements methodical, deliberate, the rustling bag the only sound. Then I turned and walked out.

I didn't leave because of mercy.

I left because I didn't have to kill her.

I could. I could have walked forward, placed the syringe into the IV port, and emptied it. She wouldn't even stir. He wouldn't wake up. They'd come in hours later and find a still, silent room.

But the point wasn't the death.

It was the choice.

If you only kill, you're just another animal. But if you choose—truly choose—who lives and who dies, you are something more. You are balance. You are correction. You are what others pretend to be.

I backed out of the room. And pulled the door shut with a soft click.

Let him keep her.

As I exited the room, I passed two familiar figures heading toward me from the far end of the hallway—Logan and Dr. Navarro, deep in conversation. I didn't flinch. Didn't pause. Just lowered my gaze and kept rolling the cart, shoulders relaxed, posture unremarkable.

Logan glanced my way. A flicker of hesitation crossed his face. Recognition? Suspicion? But then Navarro said something, and he turned back toward her. I disappeared around the corner.

I wheeled my cart back down the corridor, away from the fluorescents and the false hope. No one looked at me. No one stopped me. I tossed the gloves into the trash outside the stairwell and removed the badge that bore my newest name. It fluttered down into the bin, landing facedown.

At the end of the hallway, I stepped into the staff elevator. The doors slid closed. When they opened again, I was met with two figures standing just outside—an older couple, hunched with grief. The mother's face was drawn, eyes red. The father's jaw was clenched, unmoving.

They stepped in. A cardboard box was cradled in the mother's arms. 'Jamie Lin' was scrawled in black marker across the lid.

I held the door for them.

The elevator hummed. None of us spoke.

When we reached the first floor, I offered a small, apologetic smile and let them step out first. The mother paused, blinked, and stared straight at me. Could she know? Was it mother's intuition? But then the father touched her shoulder, and she kept walking.

My shoes clicked softly against the concrete as I crossed the loading dock. Behind me, the hospital glowed in the pre-dawn dark, full of noise and blood and stories no one would ever hear. Ahead of me: nothing. Freedom.

At the corner, beneath a flickering streetlamp, I stopped. My fingers hovered at my throat.

It had been so long since I said it. Since I heard it aloud. The name on my degree. The one I signed at the bottom of medical charts in Tbilisi. The one they erased when they took my license.

I closed my eyes.

"Natia Gelashvili," I whispered. My voice cracked with it.

I opened my eyes and smiled.

They'll never see me coming.

I started driving East. No destination, just distance. The headlights slice through early fog, white lines unspooling like thread. Outside, another hospital glows in the dark — a box of light and promises. I don't bother turning to look at it. I'm past need, past mourning. What was soft in me hardened into certainty a long time ago. In my rearview, the city shrank to a shimmer. I took a deep breath and exhaled. There are other hospitals.

Other cracks. Other chances.

Chapter 64

Embers and Echoes

Logan Dean

* * *

The car was still. The world outside was quieter still.

Elise sat with her fingers curled around a coffee cup gone cold. In the passenger seat, Logan mirrored her posture. His gaze tracked the slow sweep of sunrise over the parking structure, the warm amber light slanting through the windshield and gilding the dashboard in gold.

They'd arrived together, as they had nearly every morning for the past two weeks. She still hadn't named whatever this was between them. But it felt solid. Quietly necessary.

"Two new interns start today," Elise said, her voice soft.

Logan nodded. "Time marches on."

She looked down at her cup. "I never thought I'd be giving the tour again so soon."

He didn't answer. He didn't need to. The silence between them had grown comfortable—dense with things unsaid but understood.

After a beat, he said, "It's been a month."

Elise didn't have to ask what he meant.

"No new codes. No new sudden arrests. No patients bleeding out in the middle of the night." He stared out the window, then added, "Maybe it really is over."

"Because the killer is dead?" she asked. "Or because they've moved on?"

Logan didn't answer right away.

"There's only one way those gloves could have ended up in that biohazard bag," she said. "And they all know it. They were all emptied at eighteen hundred, just like they are every night. There was one item inside. Gloves soaked with Jamie's blood—on the outside. Fingerprints on the inside, not matching hers. Not Ravi's either."

"They're still analyzing," Logan said. "There are no hits in CODIS. None in the local database, either. Tyler is trying to locate the manager of the background check vendor the hospital used for fingerprinting her during the hiring process."

Elise turned her face toward the sun. "So it wasn't suicide."

Logan's voice was careful. "You didn't see what she went through. Jail. Accusation. Shame. Grief. Sometimes... it's enough. I don't think it was suicide, either. I just can't rule it out."

"She didn't set herself up like that, Logan. Naked. Restrained. There was tape residue on her face. The autopsy report said there wasn't even any lidocaine in the tissue. Why would she do that to herself?"

"I don't know. To punish herself. Or because she wasn't rational."

"Right. And she taped her own mouth so she didn't hear herself screaming from the pain."

Logan took a breath. "In Afghanistan, we had this guy in our unit. Medic. Sweetest person I knew. Saved more lives than anyone else on base. But one day he just... snapped. Shot a teenager in the street. Said he couldn't tell if the kid had a bomb. He didn't. But after that, he never came back from it. He wasn't a bad person. Just... broken."

He looked at her now. "It's easier to believe it wasn't someone you loved."

She didn't argue. But she didn't agree.

"And Ravi?" she asked quietly. "You think he really killed himself?"

Logan's lips thinned. "The autopsy showed a massive overdose."

"Yeah."

"They said he was using."

"I know. But there is a long way from using drugs to committing suicide."

The silence returned. But this time it was heavy.

"His phone didn't have any fingerprints." Logan finally broke the silence.

"Not even his own." Elise countered.

Finally, Logan changed the subject. "They're re-interviewing me next week."

Elise turned to him.

"The FBI," he said. "I interviewed before I took the job here. Right after I was shipped back, I was burnt out. I needed something slower. But this—" Logan gestured toward the hospital, toward everything that had happened. "—this reminded me I've still got something to offer."

"They're taking you back?"

"Not officially. But they were understanding. Said they'd consider me again."

Elise smiled faintly. "You deserve it."

She reached for his hand and gave it a soft squeeze.

Then she opened the car door and let the breeze hit her skin.

"Time to meet the new interns," she said, stretching her shoulders.

Logan gave a half-smile. "Try not to scare them off."

"No promises."

She stepped out into the morning light. Logan watched her go—watched the way her silhouette softened in the haze, how she paused at the doors to straighten her badge, take a breath, and disappear inside.

He sat a while longer, finishing his cold coffee.

In the distance, the first helicopter of the day descended onto the roof. A city waking up. A hospital returning to rhythm.

As Elise passed the call suite, she saw Jamie's old locker—now scrubbed clean, the nameplate missing, a small memorial in its place. As she made her way upstairs, she saw a young patient Ravi once championed, limping slowly on crutches beside a PT aide, each step a small miracle. She remembered he almost fell in his first session and was too scared to participate. Ravi stayed with him the whole session that day, helping him sit at the side of the bed, helping him to stand.

Logan opened the glove box, brushing his fingers over the folder labeled with the FBI seal. Then, quietly, he placed his hand on the passenger seat where Elise had been moments ago.

Somewhere below, the world churned on. But beneath it all, he felt a dull, persistent nag—like a warning half-whispered, a thread left hanging in the quiet between storms.

And somewhere, he knew Elise did too.

Epilogue

The Killer

* * *

The hum of the floor polisher purred beneath me like a well-fed cat. I drifted down the corridor at dawn, a Zamboni for suffering, stripping away the footprints of the night shift. Above me, the fluorescents buzzed faintly. Below me, the floor gleamed. A fresh coat of wax on a blank canvas. There was something almost holy about it.

The hospital here smelled different. Saline and sunscreen. I'd traded frigid winters for sunshine and salt air. I looked out the window at the purple flowers of the jacaranda trees and the fuchsia of the bougainvillea blooming over white stucco. Palm trees swayed behind them. The uniform was lighter—seafoam green with gray trim. And no one looked at me twice.

Perfect.

They didn't know me here. No one called out when I passed. No one squinted as if trying to place my face. I was invisible again, anonymous beneath a visor and scrubs. A blur in the periphery. Just another tired woman pushing a mop.

Just the way I like it.

Back west, they were still chasing ghosts. Revisiting autopsy slides. Running DNA on gloves that shouldn't exist. Arguing theories over rehydrated coffee and grief. Let them. I left them breadcrumbs and watched them follow each one into a different dead end.

Here, I wipe the slate clean.

I passed a patient's room. A teenage boy twisted against soft restraints, sweat slicking his forehead. "Please," he said, voice hoarse. "I don't want to be here. I'm not crazy."

I didn't slow down. But I looked. Just long enough.

At the nurses' station, someone laughed too loudly. A nurse tossed her head back, flirted with a resident. Another grumbled about a mother who kept asking for the on-call doctor. "She acts like she knows better than us."

I let the loathing bloom in my throat. Familiar. Comfortable.

In the lounge, someone had left a protein bar wrapper on the counter. I picked it up with gloved fingers and dropped it into the trash. Order. Cleanliness. Discipline. They think those are hospital values. They're mine.

They don't know what it means to serve. To sacrifice. To allocate resources when there aren't enough. To make peace with death in the name of the living.

But I do.

They say if you only kill, you're a monster. But if you choose who lives and who dies, well...

That makes you something else entirely.

It makes you a god.

I smiled as I turned the corner, fluorescent lights catching the gleam of the polished floor like morning sun on still water.

The badge on my chest read Catalina Ionescu, Environmental Services.

It wasn't my name.

But it would do for now.

Acknowledgments

To everyone who put up with me on my long, winding journey through medicine—the sleepless nights, the missed birthdays, the years of "just one more shift"—thank you. Without your patience, encouragement, and understanding, I never would have made it to this moment, penning a story that grew out of that world.

And to you, dear reader: I am humbled that you not only picked up this book but carried it with me to the last page. Time is precious, and you gave me yours. I hope this story was worth it. Thank you for letting me live in your mind for a little while—it's the greatest gift a writer could ever receive.

Author's Note

I wish I could tell you this book was a grueling labor of love, full of writer's block, tortured drafts, and long nights staring at a blinking cursor. Truth is, *White Coat, Black Heart* practically wrote itself. I've lived in this world for years—the chaos, the triumphs, the heartbreaks—and once I finally sat down to tell the story, the words poured out like a case of verbal diarrhea.

What surprised me wasn't how easy it was to write, but how much fun I had doing it. The hospital in this book is fictional, but the pulse of it—the long shifts, the quiet moments of humanity, the impossible choices—is absolutely real. If anything, this book is my way of showing you the view from the inside, with all its mess and madness intact.

Thank you for picking it up, for reading it, and especially for finishing it. There are a thousand books you could have spent your time on, and I'm humbled—and honestly a little giddy—that you chose mine.

With gratitude (and maybe just a touch of sleep deprivation),
Sierra Maze

P.S. No patients were harmed in the making of this book… probably.

Sneak Peek – *Juno Rising*

If you enjoyed reading this book and couldn't put it down, you won't want to miss my next novel, **Juno Rising**—a gripping, emotional journey that begins in childhood innocence and spirals into a fight for survival, following a girl forced to grow up too fast and the woman she becomes when the world refuses to stop testing her strength

Prologue: Third One's a Charm

There's blood in my mouth, and it isn't mine. I didn't swallow it on purpose. But here it is—metallic and unfamiliar, sharp against my tongue, tickling as it slides down my chin. I wipe it with the back of my sleeve and stare at the mess I made.

He's sprawled on the floor like a discarded marionette, one leg twisted under him, arms frozen in a limp, half-hearted surrender. His belt buckle hangs loose, pants tugged just low enough to expose the top of his ass and his soft, lifeless dick. There's a dark patch spreading across his jeans, sharp and sour, the stink of piss filling the air. "Nice going," I mutter, voice flat. "Even dead, you're pathetic."

The knife is jammed point-down into the linoleum next to his twitching foot, where I dropped it once I was safe again.

The rage in me isn't fading.

I can still smell him—sweat and aftershave and something rotten underneath. His trachea is gaping open, cartilage yawning like a second mouth, pink and obscene. It looks like his throat is still trying to scream. For one stupid second, I almost laugh. It looks like his neck has its own facial expression. First shock. Then disgust.

My stomach flips. I look at my hands. They're steady. I'm pretty sure a normal person would be shaking. But I'm obviously not normal.

I crouch low, arms on my knees, and stare into his eyes, glassy and blank, the blue already leaking away. He's not seeing anything, not even me, which is probably a mercy.

He made me do this. Just like the others. And yet, for half a second, I wonder—did I have to? Could I have walked away? *Should* I have walked away? The thought flashes and fizzles before I can answer.

I see his face, but it flickers—morphs into the last one, and the one before that. Their voices blur. Their hands. Their breath. They blur until I can't tell which memory belongs to which man, only that they all end the same. With me, shaking. With blood.

Why the fuck do they keep making me do this?

I didn't slit his throat like they do in movies. I pulled. I jammed the blade into the side of that smug, hairy neck and dragged forward until it unzipped like a stuffed animal—guts instead of fluff. His mouth hung open, trembling, but no sound came—just a wet hiss bubbling from the wound in his neck. The air turned thick with blood mist, acrid and stinging, like tear gas choking the room. It burned my nose, coated my tongue with metal, made every breath taste like what dying feels like.

He didn't even have time to bleed out. I stood there, panting. Numb and electric all at once.

A part of me is horrified. Another part is eerily calm. I stare, chest heaving, boots sticky on the floor.

"Why the fuck do they keep making me do this?" This time the thoughts escape my mouth.

The words echo in the empty room. They sound stupid, like I'm blaming a corpse. But goddamn it—he started it. They *always* start it.

I pace. Step over his fingers. Press my palms to my temples like I can hold the scream in.

I didn't want this. I didn't *want* this.

Seven years. *Seven fucking years* since the last one. I walked the line. I meditated. I went to therapy and college and laughed in rooms full of people who didn't know I had *a body count before I could drive.* Before prom. Before my first kiss. Before anyone ever thought to ask why I flinched when touched.

I was good. I was trying.

And now I'm not.

I kick him in the ribs. Hard.

A scream tears out of me—raw, guttural, animal. It bounces off the walls, scaring even me. It aches my throat. Locks my ribs.

I stop pacing. Sit. Back rigid, legs crossed. Inhale. Exhale until it hurts. Inhale again, grateful like it's my first breath.

I will not let the actions of others affect my emotions.

I will not let the actions of others affect my behavior.

I will not let my emotions control my actions.

Only I can control my behavior.

The mantra lands soft. The static muffles. My heart slows. My breath evens. My vision narrows.

I look at him. No name. Just *him.*

He started it. But I finished it. That part was mine. That's the part I carry.

My sleeves are soaked. I wipe my face again. These clothes are ruined. I'll have to burn them.

Think, Juno. Think like the girl who read forensics textbooks and memorized crime scene protocol. There—a smear of blood trailing off the wrench. Almost missed it. I snatch a rag and wipe it clean, fingers trembling. My eyes dart to the floor, scanning for another trace. A single bloody footprint by the door. Fuck. I scrub harder, heart pounding, replaying every forensic file I've ever studied. I can't miss a thing.

No cameras. No windows. Tools scattered like props on a murder stage. My fingerprints are everywhere. That's bad. They're in every goddamn system that matters. Another murder, and I'm done. No more second chances. Just a straight shot back to hell.

So I wipe. Everything. Door handles. Light switches. Tools. The misty red bloom from his final breath. I scrub like my life depends on it—because it fucking does.

There's a streak on the floor I almost miss. Then a small dot by the baseboard. I double back. My breathing is ragged, but I focus. Rag. Spray. Wipe. Repeat.

I look back at his body. The third one.

"So I guess that makes me a serial killer now." The word hangs. Heavy. Foreign. I test it again. "Serial." My throat closes around it. Like it's not mine. Like I'm stealing someone else's story.

I never set out to kill anyone. I'm not hunting. I'm surviving. Still, three makes a pattern. That's what they'll say. That's what they'll use to define me.

My spine tingles, and a shiver crawls over my arms. Part of me wants to scream, deny it, to kick.

The other part? The one that keeps winning? She just nods, slow and steady, like she knew this was always where we'd land.

I tried so hard not to get here.

But the world doesn't let girls like me retire. We're either dead or dangerous.

Today, I choose dangerous.

I chew my cheek. Don't cry. The mirror—shattered, naturally—shows my face smeared in blood. Not his. Not mine. Ours.

“Dexter wouldn’t have done it like this.”

I laugh.

“Dexter would’ve planned. He would’ve worn gloves.”

So I wrap his fingers one by one in a rag, each knuckle bending like a puppet's joint, each nail chipped and dirty. It's slow work—deliberate. My hands should shake, but they don't. Then the wrench. Then the floor.

I glance down at the blade again—still buried like a flag—and whisper: “Third one’s a charm.”

White Coat, Black Minds

Coming Summer 2026

Some killers can't stop. They only learn to hide better.

After disappearing without a trace, a nameless predator finds a new home under bright tropical skies, where medicine isn't just used to heal—but to manipulate, control, and destroy.

Now, Dr. Leilani Kealoha is stepping into her fellowship at one of the nation's top hospitals, unaware that a dark force is already at work. Patients are dying in ways that make no sense. Trust is fraying. And every white coat might hide a black mind.

Coming **Summer 2026**, *White Coats, Black Minds* takes you deeper into the heart of medical power—and into the twisted thoughts of someone who will never stop killing.

About the Author

Sierra Maze is a critical care physician turned thriller writer who has spent years standing at the thin line between life and death. After countless sleepless nights in the ICU, witnessing humanity at its most fragile and most resilient, she began weaving those truths into fiction that lingers long after the final page.

When she's not writing, Sierra can usually be found snowboarding, surfing, or throwing herself into an obstacle race—often followed by generous amounts of time spent recovering from said adventures. She's happiest outdoors, surrounded by nature, with a good story in her hands and a new one brewing in her head.

White Coat, Black Heart is her debut novel, the first in a series of medical thrillers exploring the darker corners of medicine and morality. Learn more about upcoming releases, exclusive previews, and bonus content at www.SierraMaze.com.

The story doesn't end here...

If you liked this book, come hang out with me online. I send out occasional updates, behind-the-scenes hospital stories that are too wild to print, and maybe even a few bonus chapters.

Sign up at SierraMaze.com—no spam, no weird pop-ups, just more dark medical thrills delivered straight to your inbox.

Glossary

Acinetobacter – A genus of bacteria that can cause infections in healthcare settings, particularly in ICU patients. Known for being resistant to antibiotics and associated with outbreaks in hospitals.

Adrenal crisis – A life-threatening condition that occurs when the body does not have enough cortisol, typically due to adrenal insufficiency. Symptoms include low blood pressure, severe fatigue, confusion, abdominal pain, and may lead to shock if untreated. Requires immediate treatment with IV steroids and fluids.

Air embolism – A rare but dangerous condition where air enters the bloodstream and obstructs blood vessels. Can lead to stroke, cardiac arrest, or death depending on the location of the embolism.

Amio (Amiodarone) – An antiarrhythmic medication used to treat and prevent certain types of serious, life-threatening ventricular arrhythmias (irregular heartbeats).

Ambu bag – A manual resuscitator used to provide positive pressure ventilation to patients who are not breathing or not breathing adequately.

Art line (Arterial line) – A thin catheter inserted into an artery (usually in the wrist) to monitor blood pressure continuously and obtain blood samples.

Asystole – A cardiac arrest rhythm characterized by a flatline on the ECG, indicating no electrical activity in the heart. Not shockable and has a very poor prognosis.

Attending – A fully licensed physician who has completed residency and is responsible for supervising medical students, residents, and patient care.

Ataxia – A neurological sign consisting of lack of voluntary coordination of muscle movements, leading to gait abnormalities and imbalance.

Capnography – The monitoring of the concentration or partial pressure of carbon dioxide in respiratory gases. Often used to verify placement of an endotracheal tube.

Cath (Catheterization) – Common shorthand for a urinary catheter or the act of inserting a catheter into the bladder to drain urine. May also refer to cardiac catheterization in certain contexts.

Celestial discharge – A dark-humor slang term used among hospital staff to refer to a patient's death, particularly when it results in one fewer task or discharge to document.

Central lines – Central venous catheters placed into a large vein (usually in the neck, chest, or groin) to deliver medications, fluids, nutrition, or to monitor central venous pressure. Dislodgement or inadvertent removal is considered a significant complication due to the risk of bleeding, air embolism, or loss of vascular access.

Chest tube – A flexible plastic tube inserted into the pleural space of the chest to remove air, fluid, or pus and help re-expand a collapsed lung.

Code Blue – A hospital emergency code indicating that a patient is in cardiopulmonary arrest and requires immediate resuscitation.

Crash cart – A mobile unit stocked with emergency medications and equipment used during a Code Blue or other critical situations.

Cross-cover – When a healthcare provider, typically a resident, is covering patients outside of their usual team, especially overnight.

CTA (CT Angiography) – A diagnostic imaging test that combines CT scanning and contrast dye injection to visualize blood vessels.

COW (Computer on Wheels) – A mobile computer station used by medical staff for bedside charting and order entry.

CT surgeon (Cardiothoracic surgeon) – A physician specializing in surgical procedures of the heart, lungs, esophagus, and other organs in the chest.

D5 (Dextrose 5%) – A common intravenous (IV) fluid composed of 5% dextrose (a form of glucose) in water. Used for hydration and as a vehicle for medication delivery. Can increase blood sugar levels.

Dextrose – A form of glucose (sugar) administered intravenously to raise blood glucose levels, especially in cases of hypoglycemia.

DKA (Diabetic Ketoacidosis) – A serious complication of diabetes that occurs when the body produces high levels of blood acids called ketones, often due to insulin deficiency. Symptoms include nausea, vomiting, abdominal pain, and altered mental status.

DNR (Do Not Resuscitate) – A medical order indicating that a patient does not wish to receive CPR or advanced cardiac life support if their heart stops or they stop breathing.

DVT (Deep Vein Thrombosis) – A blood clot that forms in a deep vein, typically in the legs. Can lead to pulmonary embolism if the clot travels to the lungs.

DVT prophylaxis – Preventative measures used to reduce the risk of deep vein thrombosis, including anticoagulants, compression stockings, and mechanical devices.

Dysarthria – Difficulty in articulating words due to problems with the muscles that control speech, often caused by neurological injury or stroke.

ED (Emergency Department) – The hospital unit where patients are initially assessed and treated for acute and urgent conditions.

EMR (Electronic Medical Record) – A digital version of a patient's paper chart, containing comprehensive health information, clinical notes, medication lists, lab results, imaging reports, and documentation of all interactions with the healthcare system.

Epinephrine (Epi) – A medication used during resuscitation to increase heart rate, blood pressure, and cardiac output. Commonly administered during cardiac arrest.

FAST criteria – A mnemonic for recognizing stroke: Facial droop, Arm weakness, Speech difficulty, Time to call emergency services. Intended for use by non-medical individuals.

Flaccid – A term used to describe muscles that are soft, limp, and lacking normal muscle tone, often as a result of neurological injury.

Float nurse / Float pool – A nurse or group of nurses who are assigned to different units based on staffing needs, often working in unfamiliar settings.

Floor patient – A patient who is stable enough to be managed outside of the ICU or step-down unit.

Foley – A catheter inserted into the bladder to drain urine, commonly used in hospitalized patients.

Full code – A medical order indicating that all resuscitative efforts should be made in the event of cardiac or respiratory arrest.

H&P (History and Physical) – A standard clinical document that summarizes a patient's history and findings on physical examination.

Handoff – The process of transferring patient care responsibility from one healthcare provider to another.

Heparin – A blood thinner (anticoagulant) used to prevent or treat blood clots. Administered via injection or IV. May be found in low doses in flushes to prevent clotting in IV lines.

ICU (Intensive Care Unit) – A specialized department in a hospital where critically ill patients receive care from a team of healthcare providers using advanced monitoring and life-support equipment.

ICP (Intracranial Pressure) – Pressure inside the skull that can affect brain function; closely monitored in patients with brain injury.

Intern – A physician in their first year of residency training after graduating from medical school.

Lactate (Lactic acid) – A marker of cellular oxygen deprivation, often used to assess the severity of sepsis or shock.

Laryngoscope – A tool used to visualize the vocal cords and facilitate placement of an endotracheal tube during intubation.

MAR (Medication Administration Record) – A legal document in the patient's chart that records all medications administered, including dosage, time, route, and by whom.

MCA infarct – A stroke occurring in the territory of the middle cerebral artery, typically resulting in weakness, sensory deficits, and speech/language impairment on one side of the body.

MD, RN, PA, NP – Common abbreviations for healthcare roles: Medical Doctor, Registered Nurse, Physician Assistant, and Nurse Practitioner.

MICU, SICU – Medical and Surgical Intensive Care Units, where critically ill patients receive specialty care based on their primary condition.

Midline catheter – A long peripheral IV catheter placed in a large arm vein, used for medium-term medication or fluid delivery. Not the same as a central line.

Necrotic – Refers to tissue that has died due to lack of blood flow, infection, or injury.

Necrotizing – Describes a rapidly spreading condition, often an infection, that causes death of tissue, such as necrotizing fasciitis.

Neglect (neurological) – A condition in which a person does not attend to or acknowledge one side of their body or environment, often due to stroke affecting the parietal lobe.

Neuro check – A brief neurological assessment performed regularly to monitor brain function.

NPO – A Latin abbreviation for "nil per os," meaning "nothing by mouth." Used to indicate that a patient should not consume any food or drink, often prior to surgery or certain medical tests.

NIH (NIH Stroke Scale) – A standardized tool used by healthcare professionals to measure the severity of a stroke and assess neurological deficits.

NP – Nurse Practitioner, a provider with advanced clinical training who can diagnose and manage medical conditions.

On-call / Night float / Cap / Sign out – Terms relating to physician scheduling and the transfer of clinical responsibility.

Orthostasis / Orthostatic hypotension / Orthostatic blood pressure – A form of low blood pressure that happens when standing up from sitting or lying down, often causing dizziness or fainting.

PACU – Post-Anesthesia Care Unit, where patients recover immediately following surgery.

Pager – A small wireless device carried by medical staff to receive alerts and communications, particularly for emergency codes and consults.

Palliative care – A medical approach focused on improving quality of life for patients with serious illness, emphasizing symptom management and support rather than curative treatment.

Patient-controlled analgesia (PCA) – A method of pain control that allows patients to self-administer preset doses of pain medication, usually through an IV pump.

PEG (Percutaneous Endoscopic Gastrostomy) – A procedure to place a feeding tube into the stomach through the abdominal wall.

Pericardium – The thin, double-walled sac that surrounds the heart and contains a small amount of fluid to reduce friction during heartbeats.

Pericardiocentesis – A procedure in which a needle and catheter are used to remove fluid from the pericardial sac surrounding the heart, typically to relieve pressure.

Perc chole tube (Percutaneous cholecystostomy tube) – A drain inserted through the skin into the gallbladder to relieve obstruction, typically in cases of cholecystitis when surgery is not immediately feasible.

Phlebotomist – A healthcare professional trained to draw blood from patients for laboratory testing.

PFO (Patent Foramen Ovale) – A small, usually harmless hole between the left and right atria of the heart. Can allow emboli to bypass the lungs and reach the brain.

Post-op / Pre-op – Terms referring to the periods after or before surgery, respectively.

PRN – A Latin abbreviation meaning "as needed," commonly used for medications.

Pressors / Vasopressors – Medications used to raise blood pressure in critically ill patients by constricting blood vessels. Examples include norepinephrine and dopamine.

Pulse Doppler – A type of ultrasound used to measure the velocity and direction of blood flow, often used in emergencies to detect a pulse.

Radiologist – A physician specializing in interpreting medical images such as X-rays, CT scans, MRIs, and ultrasounds.

Rapid Response / RRT (Rapid Response Team) – A group of healthcare providers who respond quickly to hospital patients showing signs of clinical deterioration.

Resident – A medical school graduate undergoing specialty training in a hospital setting. Residents typically rotate through various departments as part of their training.

RN handoff / Rounds list / Charting – Key nursing documentation and communication tools used in daily patient care.

RN – Registered Nurse, a licensed healthcare professional responsible for administering medications, monitoring patients, and coordinating care.

Rounds – Regularly scheduled visits by physicians and their teams to evaluate and plan care for hospitalized patients.

RT (Respiratory Therapist) – A healthcare professional who specializes in airway management, mechanical ventilation, and respiratory treatments.

SBAR – A communication framework for healthcare providers: Situation, Background, Assessment, Recommendation.

Scrubs / Badge / Whiteboard – Standard components of hospital culture and workflow: attire, identification, and patient communication boards.

Sitter – A person assigned to observe a patient continuously, often due to safety concerns like fall risk, confusion, or suicidal ideation.

SOAP note – A structured format for clinical documentation: Subjective, Objective, Assessment, Plan.

SpO2 (Oxygen saturation) – A measure of the percentage of hemoglobin in the blood that is saturated with oxygen, typically monitored via pulse oximeter.

STAT – A term used in medicine to indicate that something should be done immediately.

Step-down unit – A hospital unit that provides an intermediate level of care between the ICU and regular inpatient wards.

SVC (Superior Vena Cava) – A large vein that returns deoxygenated blood from the upper body to the heart.

Syncope – Temporary loss of consciousness due to a sudden drop in blood flow to the brain, often referred to as fainting.

Tamponade (Cardiac tamponade) – A medical emergency where fluid accumulates in the pericardium, compressing the heart and impairing its ability to pump effectively.

Telemetry – Continuous monitoring of a patient's heart rhythm, often used for patients at risk of cardiac events.

Typhoid Mary – A reference to a historical figure (Mary Mallon) who was an asymptomatic carrier of typhoid fever; used colloquially in medicine to describe someone unknowingly spreading infection.

VQ scan (Ventilation-Perfusion scan) – A nuclear medicine test that evaluates airflow (ventilation) and blood flow (perfusion) in the lungs to diagnose or rule out pulmonary embolism.

www.ingramcontent.com/pod-product-compliance
Lightning Source LLC
LaVergne TN
LVHW100510110826
845146LV00002B/584

* 9 7 9 8 9 9 9 6 2 0 9 1 0 *